DISCO FOR THE DEPARTED

Colin Cotterill

Quercus

First published in Great Britain in 2008 by Quercus

This paperback edition published in 2008 by

Quercus
21 Bloomsbury Square
London
WC1A 2NS

A CIP catalogue record for this book is available
from the British Library

ISBN 978 1 84724 585 4

10 9 8 7 6 5 4 3 2

Printed and bound in Great Britain by Clays Ltd, St Ives plc

To Siri and Soun, who, despite all the tragedies, have survived and grown and now have two beautiful daughters. To Poki and Panoy from Loong C.

FORM A223-79Q

ATTENTION: Judge Haeng Somboun
C/O: Department of Justice,
People's Democratic Republic of Laos

FROM: Dr Siri Paiboun

RE: National Coroner

DATE: 13/6/1976

RESUME:

1904 Plus or minus a year - years didn't have such clear boundaries in those days. Born in Khamuan Province, purportedly to Hmong parents. I don't recall it myself.

1908 Whisked off to live with a wicked aunt.

1914 Dumped in a temple in Savanaketh and left to the will of the Lord Buddha.

1920 Graduate from the temple high school. No great feat.

1921 Buddha investment pays off: shipped to Paris by kindly French sponsor intent on making something of me. The French make me start high school all over again just to prove it wasn't a fluke the first time.

1928 Enroll at Ancienne Medical School.

1931 Meet and marry Bouasawan in Paris and join the Communist Party for a lark.

1934 Begin internship at Hotel Dieu Hospital. Decide I might want to become a doctor after all.

1939 Return to Laos.

1940 Frolic in the jungles of Laos and Vietnam. Reassemble broken soldiers and avoid bombs.

1975 Come to Vientiane hoping for a peaceful retirement.

1976 Kidnapped by the Party and appointed national coroner. (I often weep at the thought of the great honour bestowed upon me.)

Sincerely,

Dr Siri Paiboun

CONTENTS

1

GUESTHOUSE NUMBER ONE

Dr Siri lay beneath the grimy mesh of the mosquito net watching the lizard's third attempt. Twice, the small grey creature had scurried up the wall and ventured out across the ceiling. On both occasions the unthinkable had happened. The animal had lost its grip and come plummeting down with a splat onto the bare concrete of the guesthouse floor. For a house lizard this is the equivalent of a man coming unstuck from the ground and falling up with a crash onto the ceiling. Siri could see the stunned confusion on its little puckered face. It looked around to get its bearings then headed once more for the wall.

For over a month, Dr Siri Paiboun, the national coroner, had started to wonder whether his new incarnation might be disruptive to the natural laws of animal behaviour. The peculiarities could have started before, but it wasn't until the mongrel from the ice works began to build a nest in his front yard that he took any notice. She somehow managed to drag old car seats and cement sacks through his front gate and mould them into a very uncomfortable-looking roost. And there she sat patiently, day after day, as if waiting for an unlikely egg. A week later, the paddy mice at the back of the compound formed what could only be described as a gang and started terrorising his neighbour's cat. This morning, as he was leaving his house in Vientiane for the trip up country, he'd looked back to see a hen on his roof. As there was no sign of a ladder, he had to assume the thing had flown up there. And now the lizard. Even if these were coincidences, it was still very odd.

Ever since Siri had discovered his shaman ancestry a lot of strange things had happened in his life. He worked the nail of his pinky finger around the inside of his mouth, counting off his teeth. It was a habit he'd started a few months earlier when he found out he was different. All there – all thirty-three of them. The same number of teeth as old Prince Phetsarat the magician; the same number as some of the most respected shamans in the region; the same number as the Lord Buddha himself. Siri was in hallowed company. But even though he had the right number of teeth, he hadn't yet taken control of his abilities.

It was little more than a year ago that Siri had learned he hosted the spirit of an ancient Hmong shaman – Yeh Ming. Until then, he'd always thought his contact with departed souls in his dreams was some kind of mental illness. He hadn't bothered to try to interpret messages, hadn't even realised the spirits in his dreams were leaving clues to the manner of their deaths. But, all that had changed the previous year. Yeh Ming had become more active, woken up you could say, and had drawn the attention of the malevolent spirits of the forest. These evil spirits, these *phibob*, were gunning for Siri's ancestor, and, as Siri was the host, he was suddenly in the line of fire. All those supernatural fireworks were spilling over into Siri's life.

Very little could really shock the old surgeon any more, but he never ceased to be amused by the mysterious events happening around him. His own life seemed to grow more fascinating every day. While others his age began to wind down the clock into a frail twilight, Siri had become reborn to a period where fantasy and reality were interchangeable. Every day was a kick. He felt more alive than ever. If this were truly some kind of senile insanity, it was one he was secretly enjoying: one he was in no hurry to recover from.

That May, Siri had arrived at his seventy-third birthday and was still as sturdy as a jungle boar. His lungs let him down from time to time but his muscles and his mind were as taut as they'd been in his thirties. His head boasted a shock of thick white hair and his likeable face still drew flirtatious smiles from women half his age. None of his friends could imagine Dr Siri Paiboun running out of steam, not for a long while yet.

Now here he was in Party Guesthouse Number One in the cool north-east of the People's Democratic Republic of Laos and the year was 1977. 'Guesthouse' was hardly an appropriate name for the two-storey building designed by Vietnamese rectangulists a few years earlier. It looked nothing like a house and its inmates were certainly not guests. It was mostly inhabited by those who had sinned, ideologically, against Party lines. Here, the village heads, government officials and army officers of the old royalist regime were lulled into believing they had come for a holiday in the mountains of Huaphan province. Invited to visit the revolutionary headquarters, they were soon moved along to the work camps around Sop Hao on the Vietnamese border. Despite its lack of facilities, the guesthouse was as good as life would get for them for quite some time.

Earlier that evening, Siri and Nurse Dtui had sat

drinking coffee with a group of men from the south who had once held senior ranks in the royalist police force. They still assumed they were merely attending a seminar and would soon return to Vientiane with a new enlightened understanding of the Marxist-Leninist system. The mood had been jolly as they sat on the ground-floor veranda on uncomfortable red vinyl chairs. The men had spent their first afternoon doing 'getting to know you' activities and still wore their paper name tags stapled to their top shirt pockets. Each man's name was followed by the word 'officer' then a number. As if unwilling to break rank, they sat in numerical order around their small circle of chairs.

Siri listened to them tell of their good fortune to be seeing a part of the country that was as alien to the urbanites as any foreign land. They talked of the locals as a tourist would of Africans or peculiar Europeans. Little did they know their brief excursion to the provinces would likely extend to months, in some cases, years. Little did they know they were to be trucked from the comparative luxury of the guesthouse to a site some eighty kilometres away. There they would be assigned to work gangs to rebuild roads, repair bombed bridges and help the local peasants till a booby-trapped land littered with unexploded ordnance. In the evenings they would sit around blackboards in study groups beneath the yellow light of beeswax lamps. They would learn the dates of the most famous battles, the numbers of casualties, and the names of the great leaders of the revolution. This, and often much much worse, was Lao re-education.

Eventually, either by sincere personal choice or through desperation, they would swear undying devotion to the cause. If they were convincing enough, they might one day be returned to their families. If not, the families would be invited to travel north to join them. Only the women who truly loved their husbands and were prepared to forgo the luxuries of city life would accept such an offer. The majority fled across the Mekhong to take their chances on the Thai side.

But these jolly men on the guesthouse patio knew nothing of this. They still saw the trip as a simple conversion, like switching a motor's consumption from petrol to diesel. They imagined they'd learn a little about communism, have a guided tour of the caves, and go home with snapshots to put in an album. They'd said as much during their chat with Siri and Dtui.

'So, what's a pretty thing like you doing so far from home?' Officer Three had asked of the solidly built young nurse. He was a portly red-faced man who'd learned how to talk to women in dark nightclubs. He'd been staring at her chest since they arrived.

'I'm with my boss,' she said, nodding in Siri's direction.

'Dirty weekend by the looks of it,' said Officer Four, nudging his neighbour in the ribs. Dtui and Siri blushed in unison bringing great howls from the men.

'That would be nice,' Dtui countered with a typical Lao Band-Aid smile that covered no end of emotional cuts and bruises. 'But it's work, I'm afraid.'

'Work, eh? That's what I always told my missus when I was going off for a little weekend R and R,' Officer One confessed proudly. 'What *work* is it you do exactly?' Dtui frowned but didn't snap. Siri was impressed by her composure.

'I'm a nurse. My boss is a surgeon.' She decided nothing

would be gained by telling them she was Siri's trainee at the morgue.

'So they're here playing doctors and nurses,' said Officer Two, producing even more exaggerated laughter from his mates.

It occurred to Siri these men were trying too hard, being too blokey, and the reason was obvious to him. They were afraid. Despite their bravado and their unreasonable expectations, they were in enemy territory and all they had as a weapon was this false camaraderie.

Siri was concerned about their families. He wondered how their wives and children might survive with their breadwinners breaking rocks on a charity road gang. 'Is the Justice Department taking care of your kin while you're up here?' he asked.

Officer Two thought that was a very funny question. 'They haven't paid us a brass *kip* since they took over.' There were no coins in Laos so a brass *kip* would have been worth even less than a paper one. That, in turn, presently stood at six to the US cent. On the occasions there was money available, a policeman under the new system would have received seven thousand *kip* a month plus a small rice ration.

'Then how do you live?'

'Oh, we have resources. Some of us managed to put small nest-eggs together under the old regime. We sent money out of the country. We anticipated the damned Reds coming in and messing things up.'

'Look, I don't want to throw you gentlemen into some hysterical panic here but I'm one of those nasty Reds who spoiled your party,' Siri said.

Officer Two blushed. 'Really? Sorry. You didn't look like ... Then, what are you doing here? I mean ...'

6

To undo the damage, Officer One hurriedly asked Dtui where she and the doctor were based.

'Mahosot hospital.'

'Then you're a long way from home, too.'

'You aren't kidding,' Dtui said. 'I haven't been outside Vientiane for twenty years. It's so exotic up here.' She cast a sideways glance at Siri. 'I'm looking forward to seeing my first pog.'

'Your first what?'

'Pog. My ma used to tell me about them when I was little.'

Siri looked away so the policemen wouldn't notice his smile.

'Can't say I've ever heard of them,' the officer confessed. 'What are they?'

'You can't be serious. You haven't heard of a pog? I admit they're rare, but up here in the north-east the animals are never penned up. They all roam around together, the chickens, the dogs, the goats, the pigs. With animals being the way they are, there's a fair amount of experimentation that goes on, if you know what I mean.'

Siri could control his face no longer. He got to his feet and walked over to the front steps to look at the full moon reflected hazily on the surface of the pond. It was a beautiful setting for such a dishonest political racket. He chuckled under his breath but made it sound like a cough. Dtui continued at her most convincing best.

'... and here in Huaphan, probably due to the altitude, or, some say, the sulphur in the water, on occasions, the union of a randy male dog and a sow, produces ...'

'You cannot be serious.'

'I swear on my brother's life. I've seen the photos. They

7

have the face of a pig and the paws and tail of a dog. I can't believe you don't know about them.'

'Yeah, I've heard of 'em,' said Officer Four.

'You haven't,' said Officer Two.

'Now you mention it, I might have seen one on a farm just outside Tha Reua. Didn't know what it was, though. Odd-looking thing,' recalled Officer One.

'That's right,' said Dtui, 'and up here they're everywhere. If you see one around perhaps you could grab it for me. I'd love to take one back for my ma.'

'No problem,' said Officer Four, 'I imagine they're really easy to catch.'

'Well, I'm afraid we have to get up early,' said Officer Two, who obviously knew his curly tail was being tweaked. He stood and stretched painfully like a first-time jogger. The others stood also. 'We have an hour of tilling to do from six in the morning.'

He still sounded like a tourist on an adventure holiday. Siri walked back to the group. 'You be careful where you dig. There are unexploded bombs all over this area.'

The officer chuckled. 'I very much doubt they'd send us into a minefield, Doctor.'

'You just be careful. I don't want to spend tomorrow sewing legs back onto foolhardy policemen.' Although he said nothing more, Siri could think of few more effective mine-clearance techniques than sending a chorus line of corrupt royalist policemen with shovels across a field.

'Have a good night's sleep, you two,' said Officer One with a wink. The others laughed and walked off to their dorm room leaving Siri and Dtui alone on the patio. Dtui poked out her tongue when they were out of sight.

'Creeps,' she said.

'Just victims of the money culture,' Siri said. 'They'll change. Taking away a man's comfort strips him down to basics – lets him see what he really is. Suddenly finding himself with nothing can add a dimension. If they survive the cold and the hunger and diseases up here they'll be more real than they are now, more humble.'

'Ah, you'd find primroses in a pile of poop, Dr Siri. I'm sure you would. But they won't change.'

'Have a little faith, Dtui.'

'Once a pig, always a pig.'

Siri raised his bushy eyebrows. 'Unless it's a pog.'

Once their laughter had died down, they sat looking up at the crags that blended into the night sky.

'Do you think we'll get a chance to do some sightseeing?' Dtui asked.

'Who knows? We don't even know why we're here. They might have us bumbling around all over the north-east. Why, where do you want to go?'

'Mum says there's a temple up near Xieng Khaw with a relic of the Lord Buddha.' Siri gave a wry smile. 'What?'

'Which particular relic is it this time, Nurse Dtui? A tooth? A severed toe? An eyeball?'

'You're an old cynic,' she huffed. 'I'm not telling you.'

'Cynicism has nothing to do with it, dear. It all comes down to mathematics and physiology. Just count the temples around Asia that claim to have an actual bit of the Lord Buddha or his footprint. If all their boasts were true, his holiness would indeed have been a sight to behold. There he'd be plodding around the countryside with feet the size of water urn covers, a couple of thousand teeth crammed into his mouth, and toe and fingernails shedding like the hair on a rabid dog. It doesn't bear thinking about. No wonder people followed him.'

Dtui shifted to the far side of the table. 'Where are you off to?' he asked.

'Nowhere. Just don't want to be sitting beside you when the lightning hits you.'

Siri laughed. 'You obviously haven't been paying attention at your political briefings, comrade. Unless you count the politburo there are no gods. Even if a real one were able to sneak under the Party barbed wire, he'd be a grounded god. They've decommissioned fire and brimstone.'

'No God? I bet your old Karl Marx didn't make this scenery.'

'Heretic.'

'It is lovely up here though, Doc.'

'It certainly is, when you have time to enjoy it.'

'When you aren't dodging bombs, you mean?'

'That's all I did for ten years. That and put back together people who hadn't been so lucky.'

'When do you think they'll tell us why we're here?'

As always they'd been given short notice to get to Wattay Airport with their equipment. Judge Haeng had told them nothing of the mission, just the name of the person who'd contact them the next day.

'Comrade Lit should be here by nine tomorrow.'

'And who's he again?'

'Regional commander – security division.'

'Right. Did you know him when you were based here?'

'I don't recall the name. But when all the senior comrades and the ranking army officers moved down to Vientiane, a lot of young bucks were promoted at a rate of knots up here. Cadres were flying up through the ranks at such young ages I heard the regional quartermaster was still in diapers when he arrived at his office. They had to confiscate his rattle before they could get any work out of him.' Dtui chuckled. 'I don't know. I might have seen this Lit fellow around.'

'Does he know you've brought your cuddly and gorgeous assistant?'

'I'm sure he'll be delighted. Who wouldn't be, after all?'

Again, the calm around them lulled the two into a peaceful silence. An amateur fisherman cast his mushroom-shaped net out into the inky black pond. The squirrels chirped like sparrows with sore throats. Dtui looked towards the staircase behind Siri.

'Doc.'

'Yes?'

'At the top of the stairs ...'

'I don't know.'

'How do you know what I'm going to ask?'

'You're going to ask why there's a partition up there with an armed guard sitting in front of it.'

'Ooh, you're good. Did your spirits tell you what I was thinking?'

'No need. I read your mind myself. You're insatiably curious, so it was only a matter of time before you asked. I also heard you flirting with the guard.'

'He wasn't very sociable.'

'You mean he wouldn't tell you what's behind the partition?'

'Not a word. I hate mysteries.'

'No doubt we'll work it out before we go.'

*

But now, in his lumpy kapok bunk, drowsily watching the moths fly clockwise around the bulb, Siri too was contemplating the mystery behind the plywood partition. Access to a small upper wing of the building was blocked. From the grounds he was able to estimate there were three or four rooms up there. He wondered what was so special about them. He clawed his fingers through his thick white hair and sighed. It was some time after 11PM and he feared he'd be unable to find any sleep at all. There was too much on his mind. If he didn't think himself awake all night, *they* would certainly keep him up. He reached for the ancient white amulet that hung on a tightly woven white plait of woman's hair around his neck. As his fingers made contact, a surge of energy ran in a current the length of his body. He could suddenly hear them even more clearly chattering in the distance. His feelings and instincts of a few months hence had begun to take on tangible forms. Spirits he once encountered only in his sleep had become bold. Some even appeared in daylight, often at the most inopportune moments. Even before the old Russian Mi-14 helicopter had come in to land that afternoon, he could feel the souls of the thousands killed during the war. They passed through him like sightseers at an historical palace, deciding whether he was a shaman they could trust.

All around Guesthouse Number One, their voices could be heard: mothers calling their children in from the open fields, old women crying for the old men they'd left behind, toddlers giggling – too innocent to realise they'd been dead for many years. How could Siri sleep to such an accompaniment? Then, as if things weren't already bad enough, at about midnight the awful disco music started up. It destroyed any hope of sleep. He wondered what type of people would start dancing in the middle of the night, how anyone could enjoy such an ugly Western din. Or, perhaps this was one of the Party's torture techniques to punish the officials from Vientiane. He could think of few things more cruel.

2

THE RED-TAG BAG ROOM

Geung Watajak was born in October 1952 in a village on
the outskirts of Vientiane called Thangon. There was a
temple and a tiny collection of wooden huts that
constantly blew down in the wet season monsoons. Its only
reason for appearing on maps at all was its ferry which
laboured back and forth across the Nam Ngum River
taking people to and from the great reservoir. Few travellers stopped in Thangon for any other reason, but a
village had grown there nevertheless. Despite its proximity
to the capital, and its constant stream of passing gentry, it
was very much a hick town.

Beliefs were simple there. According to the locals, there
were only two categories of mental infirmity: slow as a tree
growing, and fruity as a bad batch of plum cider. Thangon
had itself one of each. Auntie Soun had briefly been the
shaman for the region before she completely forgot how to
release the evil spirits back to the forest. They became
bottled up inside her like soda gas until one day she flipped
her lid. She became renowned for wild solo rantings and
spontaneous acts of flashing.

Geung, on the other hand, had been a very quiet baby,
one of seven children. He displayed the physical characteristics of Down's syndrome so just one look at his face and

everyone knew there was no point in sending the boy to school. It's true he was a slow learner but that may have been because nobody ever tried to teach him anything. Only his mother called him by his name. His father, brothers and sisters all called him 'Moron'. It wasn't said in a nasty way and Geung reached eighteen years of age still thinking it was his mother who'd got it wrong.

As the Watajaks were a farming family, their routines were repetitive and uncomplicated and that suited the happy boy. Hard work built up his slowly developing muscles and being around his family all day gave him a feeling of loyalty and belonging. But that security came to a sudden end on the day his father took him and two of his siblings to Vientiane to find them work. They were big enough to work and cost too much to feed. It was time for them to give a little something back to the lazy man who had gone to all the trouble of fertilising them. Their mother had no say in the matter.

The sister got work in a bamboo and corrugated-tin nightclub out on Hanoi Road by the market. It was a sad fact she'd make most of her money with her feet in the air, but for a fourteen-year-old farm girl with no schooling, she had to think herself lucky to have any kind of paying work at all. Geung's younger brother got work at the bus terminal touting for passengers, collecting tickets and hanging out of the door of the speeding bus yelling where it was headed at the top of his voice.

But his father knew that finding work for Geung was going to be the biggest challenge of all. Who in their right mind would want to take on a moron? But not only was the old man a layabout, he also possessed the nerve of the devil. He took his eighteen-year-old son to Mahosot hospital where he offered the boy's services free of charge in exchange for food scraps and a floor to sleep on. Hospitals, after all, were supposed to look after sick people. He reminded the hospital employment section of this fact and the clerk on duty made the mistake of displaying a moment's hesitation before saying 'no'. So, when she left the office at the end of the day, she saw young Geung sitting alone on the wooden bench at the front. He had a newspaper-wrapped parcel on his lap.

'Where's your dad?'

'Home,' he answered in a matter-of-fact way.

'Well, you can't stay here. You know that, don't you?'

He smiled a line of teeth that looked as if they'd all been borrowed from different people's mouths. When she arrived for work the next morning, Mr Geung was sitting in the same position, and the next day, and the next. Each day he smiled with his unmatching teeth and wished her good health, and his newspaper parcel got smaller and smaller till all his dried fish was eaten. So it was that Geung Watajak became an unpaid member of staff at Vientiane's newest hospital.

As it turned out, there was a job that *normal* people were unable to do for any period of time. It was in the clearing room behind the hospital laundry and had seen off four applicants in two months. It was the place where red-tagged bags arrived from the wards and operating theatres. The tag denoted 'soiled items'. This generally meant blood and excrement but there were often other little surprises wrapped hurriedly in the sheets and blankets. Over the five years he worked there, Geung could probably have put together several complete human beings from all the spare parts.

His task was to rinse through the red-tag linens and surgeons' rubber aprons and take out the bits and pieces before sending the laundry off to be boiled in the industrial washers. He was given a small room to sleep in and coupons to use in the staff canteen. He never complained about his gruesome job or his lack of income. This was his destiny. Every now and then, his father would make a very brief appearance on one of his 'salary collection runs'. Although Geung had no money to give him to take back to the farm, the old man would bring a little fruit and a baton of sticky rice in bamboo with news of people who only barely registered in Geung's memory. The young man never asked to return home.

Geung's uncomplicated honesty endeared him to the nurses and other medical staff. He became so popular that one of the doctors, Pongruk, decided it was time to rescue him from the red-tag bag room. Since Geung had first come to Mahosot, the Americans had rented Laos and most of the people in it. The colonisers' money was paying government salaries, bankrolling the military and setting up selected pockets of infrastructure in an attempt to hold back the advancing Reds. USAID funding had sent Dr Pongruk to Bangkok and Washington to learn the trade of forensic medicine. Upon his return he was to set up a new morgue in the hospital grounds.

As well as Dr Pongruk's wage, there was a 'half salary' available that the Lao authorities envisaged would pay for the services of a part-time nurse. When the doctor told them he'd found someone very competent to work full-time for the small salary, they were delighted – until they found out whom the doctor had in mind. Like most other people, Dr Pongruk had been appalled when he found out

Geung had worked for all those years without payment. He understood that with his condition, and without written qualifications, the hospital couldn't officially hire Geung in any capacity. But the use of slaves in Laos had died out by the end of the Lan Xang kingdom and he wanted to pay Geung back somehow.

The interim American administration agreed that this would certainly be the right thing to do so the doctor set about training Mr Geung as his morgue assistant. He showed infinite patience and put in many extra night hours to get Geung to a point where he was proficient at morgue duties. And the young man took to the job with great enthusiasm. He could take off the cap of a skull without grazing the brain and snip through ribs as if they were chalk with his long-handled cutters. He carried bodies and their errant parts around the lab like a caring member of the deceased's family would.

The doctor told his wife one night, 'It's a bit like using *kee see* sap to seal the planks of a boat. You have to be patient till the resin takes hold but once it sets you couldn't prise it apart with a mallet and chisel.' So when Dr Pongruk and his wife floated across the Mekhong river one night to escape whatever the communists might have had in mind for academics, they left behind a morgue assistant with a knowledge of the procedures of autopsies second to none in Laos. But there was no longer a coroner to work with, and the morgue was shut. For six months Geung was returned to the red-tag bag room. He didn't complain or see it as a demotion. It was his destiny.

Then one day, Dr Siri arrived, Nurse Dtui was pulled from the wards, and the morgue was alive again. They needed Geung's expertise, and very soon the three became a team. It couldn't, however, be called a team of forensic professionals. Siri had been a surgeon all his life but had never conducted an autopsy and didn't particularly want to. He sought the retirement he thought he deserved and was very reluctant to begin a new career. The amateur forensic team spent that first year learning and guessing. If it hadn't been for Siri's gift – his ability to communicate with the spirits of the dead – there would likely have been some very serious mistakes made. Even now, with no lab, no modern equipment, and no textbooks outlining up-to-date techniques, the Mahosot morgue was often a scene of rampant experimentation.

But the experience had brought the three colleagues very close together. To Geung, Dtui was a sister, and Siri a grandfather. Although he couldn't explain his feeling, Geung loved them like no other people in his life. Even when he wasn't sure what was going on, he suffered along with them. He felt their victories and cried their tears. He was sensitive to their emotions like a barometer in an airship that soared to the highs and dived to the depths. They trusted him, and his honest vein prevented him from making promises he wouldn't be able to keep. That, in turn, increased the value of the ones he did make. Honouring promises took precedence over everything else in his slow-grinding mind. Before they'd left on this latest trip, comrade Dr Siri had made him promise to look after the morgue until they came back. The chains that held this promise in place would be crucial to what would happen over the next few weeks.

His duties were simple when the doctor was away. The hospital could accept no more than two bodies. Geung would be responsible for storing them, bunk-bed style, in the single freezer. There was unlikely to be a sudden intake of corpses demanding autopsies. The dengue outbreak in the Vientiane basin was spreading fast but there were no mysteries as to how it did its deadly deed: fever, lethargy, bleeding and death. The morgue only handled unexplained fatalities at the state hospitals and the odd murder referred by the police.

When they took on cases, Geung was indispensable. He knew the ins and outs of the morgue even better than his colleagues. But he was not a mortician and could only perform his tasks in the presence of the doctor. All he was allowed to do while Siri and Dtui were away was dust, sweep, chase away cockroaches, and stand guard over the office. He took his role so seriously he'd even brought a blanket and pillow from his room and was preparing to spend the nights in the cutting room.

He was an unlikely sentry. He was the angel of peace. Anger and aggression had never been a part of his make-up, and he could feign neither. He was no scarier than a Chinese dumpling. So, when the two surly-looking men in uniform marched in through the morgue entrance and called out his name, he came to greet them with a smile. But it dropped from his face when he saw their weapons.

'Wha ... wha ... what can I do for you, c ... comrades?' he asked.

They pointed their pistols at him and pulled their triggers. After a split second of astonishment, Mr Geung fell to the floor like a ripe jackfruit from a tree.

3

A RESTAURANT WITH NO FOOD

Siri was disturbed from his early morning thoughts by the
rousing refrain of Patriotic Work Song Number Seventeen –
We Shall Hoe For the Republic – written by the President
himself.

'Oh, my lord. Now what?'

Bones cracked as the doctor eased himself to a sitting
position half in and half out of the mosquito netting. If he'd
slept, he certainly had no recollection of it. At seventy-three
years of age, time had acquired a value, and he'd just given
away six hours of the stuff without getting anything in
return. He got to his feet and staggered, dull as a stack of
pillows, over to the window.

Through the gap in the green nylon curtains he could see
the singing policemen with their farming implements over
their shoulders climbing onto the back of an army truck.
Although their warders stood well back and held their
weapons down at their sides, they appeared no less threat-
ening. Each movement was directed by the shriek of a
whistle. The inmates all stood eyes front and the truck
headed off along the dirt track. The song vanished into the
mist along with its choir. All around, the crags melted into
the fog like some grey Chinese watercolour. The sun wouldn't
break through for another two hours.

Siri showered under a cold spout in the communal bathroom. Stale water that smelt of carbolic and dirt squirted up between loose tiles under his feet. He got dressed and walked to breakfast. He passed the solitary guard who nodded in half sleep on a fold-up chair in front of the plywood partition.

'Good health,' Siri said, but got no response.

The dining room contained twelve wonky tables without cloths, several framed black and white photos of the heroes of the revolution, and Dtui.

'Morning, Doc.'

'Good morning. How long have you been down here?'

'About an hour. Couldn't sleep.'

'Me, neither.' He sat opposite her in the silent room. 'I feel we may be expected to sing for our breakfasts.'

'This is a creepy place, isn't it.'

'You feel it as well?'

'Probably not the way you do. I don't get ghosties creeping into my bed in the middle of the night. But this building makes me feel strange. Plus, I've never ...' She scrunched up her nose.

'Never what?'

'Never, you know, slept by myself before.'

'Dtui, I feel this is another pog.'

'No. I'm dead serious. I've always been with Ma – or in the nurses' dorm. Can't say I feel very safe up here by myself.'

'You're going to have to get used to it. I dread to imagine you in Moscow announcing that you're unable to sleep alone, although you'd certainly be a popular import. You won't have your ma or the nurses with you in the Eastern Bloc, you know?'

'If I get there.'

'I have no doubt.'

Siri looked back over his shoulder to see whether there was any chance of service. He was also a little embarrassed for raising Dtui's hopes again. Of course there was doubt. She'd taken the exams for students applying to study in one of the communist countries in Europe. For several years she'd studied secretly, not wanting to give the hospital administrators the idea she was smarter than they thought she was. Initiative could be interpreted entirely the wrong way in times such as these. She'd taken politics, medicine, and Russian. She stood an excellent chance of beating the medical students. They'd suffered since their teachers floated away across the river. The only fear Siri had was that she'd be elbowed off the list by relatives of the faithful cadres.

She had to play the game. Siri taught her what to say to fool the interviewers. He was an expert. He'd been playing communist charades for most of his life. His faith in the system had long since evaporated as he watched a perfectly good doctrine destroyed by personalities. What should have been a tool was being used as a weapon and he felt little pride in his forty-eight-year membership of the Party. Dtui needed these three years in Moscow more than most. With all the student grant money and the possibility of part-time nursing work, it was a rich harvest for the impoverished Lao. Most of the scholarships went to those with connections and the only person Dtui knew with influence was Siri. Unfortunately, he had refused to be sucked down into the same corrupt bog that had claimed most of his comrades in recent years. He hadn't called in favours from the politburo or used his position with the Department of

Health. He had, however, insisted his way onto the board that vetted the applications. He was certain if things were decided on merit, Dtui would be on her way to the Soviet Union in the New Year. His presence on the committee increased the odds of fair play. But nothing could be taken for granted in the People's Democratic Republic of Laos.

Siri looked around the stark shadowy dining room but saw no signs of life. With the seminar attendees off blowing themselves up, it appeared the staff weren't expecting other guests. The evening before, there had been nothing available in the kitchen so the empty stomachs of Dtui and her boss were grumbling back and forth across the breakfast table. It was probably the rumbling that caught the ear of a large lady who appeared in the doorway. She was wearing an apron over camouflage fatigues.

'What are you doing here?' she asked.

'Waiting for food,' Dtui told her.

The woman's sandals flapped against the loosely tiled floor as she walked to the unexpected guests. She was sturdily built with an impressive scar across her left cheek. 'Why aren't you out with the others?'

'We aren't on that tour,' Siri told her. 'We're on the three-day, two-night padlocked-historical-temple package.'

She dropped her eyebrows and stared at him, her expression as empty as the National Bank.

'Sorry,' he conceded. 'We're here at the invitation of the Security Division. We'll be here for a few days.'

'Hm. Nobody told me.' She folded her arms as if challenging them to suggest otherwise.

'Sorry! That's my fault.' The voice came from behind the woman and they had to lean back in their chairs to see its owner. He was a tall lean young man in glasses. He wore the green uniform of a Lao People's Revolutionary Party policeman, but there were no badges or epaulettes attached to it. He smiled and rounded the obstruction. 'Dr Siri?'

Siri smiled and held out his hand. 'Comrade Lit?'

'Sorry to have kept you waiting.' As he shook the doctor's hand, both the visitors noticed the withered index finger on Lit's right hand. It seemed to curl up like an unwatered plant.

'Not at all. We weren't expecting you till nine.'

The large woman interrupted their greetings. 'This isn't good enough, comrade. You know I need a P8.8 at least three days before I can accept new guests. The night staff should never have taken them in without it.'

'You're quite right, comrade Sompet. I have the requisite form right here. This was something of an emergency. I apologise.' He handed her the form and she marched out of the room still grumbling under her breath.

Comrade Lit remained standing. 'Well,' he said, looking across the table at Dtui.

'This,' Siri said, 'is my assistant, Nurse Chundee Vongheuan.'

She smiled. 'You can call me Dtui, comrade.'

'We were just about to start eating the flower arrangements,' Siri said. 'Would you care to join us?'

Lit laughed. 'Not very nutritious I'm afraid. They're all plastic. Let me take you both somewhere else to eat.'

As they drove in his Chinese jeep through Vieng Xai, Lit pointed out the towering cliffs, locally known as karsts, that housed famous caves. 'That's where General Khamtay lived and where the military strategies were all put together,' he said. 'Over yonder is the home of the Prime Minister.'

The tour was for Dtui's benefit. Siri had visited all the caves during his stay in the north-east and knew exactly what elaborate chambers and tunnels these turrets of limestone contained. But to Dtui there was nothing to distinguish one tower from the next. The American planes flying low back and forth through this valley for years had been confronted with the same problem. Even the crags that were bombed late in the war had held up to the random seeding of five-hundred-kilogram shells. It seemed incredible to Dtui that two million tons of bombs could be dropped in the communist-held territories without leaving so much as a bruise on any of the leaders.

The town of Vieng Xai was an odd place conceived as a capital for the new regime. It was set out in a grid of wide streets and bordered by the crags where the old soldiers had spent ten years of their lives. This was the view they saw every day from their caves and it represented freedom. Until four years earlier it had been a vast empty expanse of rice fields. Under fear of daylight raids, the locals all hid until the sun went down and came out to tend the fields at night. But with the ceasefire, the comrades emerged from their mountains and began to build their dream. They'd imagined a grand city as a fitting monument to the years of struggle.

But Laos was more than Huaphan province. It was a country of some three-and-a-half-million people. There were no available figures and as many as five hundred thousand might have fled to Thailand, but the bulk of the population remained in and around the capital. Once the Pathet Lao had marched triumphantly into Vientiane to claim the country for communism, Vieng Xai suddenly seemed remote and inaccessible. To run a country you had to be where the people were. They weren't in Huaphan, and they didn't appear to be in Vieng Xai. Two more guest-houses and a market were under construction here but the bamboo scaffold was green with moss. There was a feeling that this was a project on hold: a dream that had been half forgotten at sunrise.

Beside the market site stood a single shop that sold *feu* rice noodles in bowls deep enough to bath a small baby. Siri and Dtui ate heartily with their left hands and fought off flies the size of coat buttons with their right. Lit had already eaten so he watched the guests conducting their breakfasts and told them why they were there.

'We probably wouldn't have found it at all,' he began. 'Every now and then rocks at the top of the karsts come loose. Some that got hit by rockets take their time to fall. We think that's what happened in this case. A big hunk of rock came crashing down onto the concrete path we'd laid from the cave to the new house. You'll notice, Doctor, most of the senior comrades have built houses in front of their old caves.'

'Hm. Not wanting to leave the warmth of the womb. It's common in primates,' Siri said. 'And whose cave are we talking about here?'

'The President's. He's due back here in a little over a week so the Party really needs to work out what happened before he gets here.'

'Right,' Siri said. 'So the rock broke the concrete path …?'

'… and there it was, sticking out of the broken section.'

'What was?'

'The arm.'

'And is there a body attached to it?' Dtui asked. She

wiped her mouth with a napkin and abandoned the last of the broth to the flies.

'We don't know.'

'Why not?' asked Siri.

'Well, the arm's sticking out of the concrete so if there's a body in there, we'd have to break up the rest of the path to get to it.'

'And you can't do that because … ?'

'Because there are very strict regulations about making alterations to government-initiated structures. We had to submit the request forms to Vientiane to ask for permission. They said we have to wait for you.'

'I see. I hope you've covered the arm. The flies up here have quite an appetite.'

'We tied a plastic bag over it. I'll take you up there when you're ready. We can stop off and pick up a couple of labourers and tools on the way.'

'Then, let us not keep our concrete person waiting. Finished, Nurse Dtui?'

'Ready when you are, Dr Siri.'

You didn't have to travel very far out of Vientiane before the road turned to pebbles and potholes. Travelling in a truck was like falling down an endless flight of uneven stairs in a coffin. They'd passed the turn-off at Kilometre 6 where the old US compound had been reinvented as a resort for communist politicians. They'd just reached the intersection that led to the National Pedagogical Institute at Dong Dok when Mr Geung came round. He was thumped out of his stupor when the front wheel dropped into a deep rut. Although his mind was still back looking after the morgue, he found his body lying on a blanket on the wooden boards of an old truck. Above him were the open sky, a vicious June sun, and two rows of knees. He lay in an aisle of black boots that stank of polish. The toecaps penned him in so tightly he could do nothing but lie stiff and wonder where he was, whose were these legs that ended at the knees? He lifted one arm and waved, which produced an immediate response.

'Sergeant, the mongoloid's awake.'

There was a loud cheer and laughter and a gruff voice yelled above the sound of the motor, 'Get him up.' Bodies leaned over him and hands reached down to pull him into a sitting position. From there he found himself staring at two rows of smiling soldiers. He smiled back. The sergeant was at the end of one row.

'Your name's Geung, right?'

Geung had little contact with the military but he'd been to parades and played soldiers when he was little, so he knew what he should do. He saluted. There was another loud cheer and half the men saluted back. Two of them shifted sideways to make him a space on the bench, then pulled him up. He could see unfamiliar fields bouncing past the truck, buffalo with no mud to wallow in, and shades of brown everywhere.

'Damn, boy. I thought you were dead,' the sergeant shouted to him. 'Never seen a man shot with an empty gun before.'

'You f … frightened me.'

'Just messing with you, son. Just a little joke.'

'I fainted.'

'You sure did.'

'Wh … wh … where are we going?'

'Nam Bak.'

The name meant nothing to Geung. 'Why?'

'Top secret mission.' The sergeant put his finger to his lips to show there was a need to keep quiet about it. Geung felt very important to be going on a top secret mission, but he'd made a promise. He got clumsily to his feet and walked to the tailgate using the chests and knees of the soldiers to keep him up. The sergeant caught hold of him before he vanished off the end of the truck. 'Now what do you think you're up to?' the old soldier asked.

'I ... I ... I ... I have to g ... guard the morgue.'

'No you don't, son.'

'Yes. Yes I d ... do. I promised comrade Dr Siri a ... a ... and comrade Nurse Dtui.'

'You don't work at the morgue any more.'

It was a serious revelation to Geung. 'No?'

'No.'

'Where d ... d ... do I work?'

'You'll find out.'

'B ... B ... but I ... I pr ... pro ...' The words began to collide again and Geung's head spun.

'Geung, young brother, I don't want any trouble from you. You understand?'

'I ... I ...'

'Just go back to your seat and enjoy the journey. You'll like ...' but before the sergeant could say another word, Geung passed out again, this time across the laps of the Third Division of Lao People's Liberation Army Infantry on its way to the north to hunt out insurgents.

4

CONCRETE MAN

The jeep pulled up in front of the President's compound and Siri looked up the slope to the pretty pink and green villa that nestled in among the towering cliffs. Carved out of the rock opposite was a one-and-a-half-car garage and where the steps began to wind upward, an ornamental heart-shaped pool had been lovingly fashioned from a bomb crater. It was all so creepily quaint.

'You know, Doc?' Dtui said as they started up the concrete steps. 'All this time I had visions of you lot living up here like cavemen, wrapped in bearskins. I didn't dream it would be so – civilised.'

'Surely you didn't expect the president of the republic to be catching his breakfast with a bow and arrow?'

'It wouldn't surprise me, given how hard it is to find breakfast up here.'

Lit took them to the walkway that wound up to the cave entrance. Up the incline a little way, a boulder the size of a bloated buffalo lay on a bed of flattened itchy fruit blossoms and poinsettias. It would have given the concrete one heck of a thump when it landed, then bounced into the garden. The force of the falling rock had tilted up a long straight section of the three-metre-wide path causing it to snap at various points. Now it lay in sections like carriages after a train crash.

Ahead, a small canvas tent had been erected over the path between two of the sections. Lit lifted the canvas from its frame to reveal the bizarre sight of a mummified arm protruding from one side of the wide gap in the concrete. It was covered in a transparent plastic bag tied to the wrist. Its palm was up and its fingers were bent into a claw. From its position, Siri estimated that its body, assuming it had one, would be on its back inside the unbroken slab of concrete.

'Well, I suppose we should get cracking,' Siri said to the two workmen who'd followed them up. Both had stone-mason's chisels and metal mallets.

'How would you like it, Doctor?' one asked.

The section that lay before them was over a metre and a half long and one metre deep. Siri pondered for a moment. 'I think we should attack it from the sides. Here, I'll give you some marks to guide you.' He used a block of white limestone to score a line on either side of the broken section of pathway.

'Uhm, Dr Siri,' Lit asked. 'Wouldn't it be easier to go in from the end where the hand's sticking out, or from the top?'

'Easier, yes, comrade Lit. But not as beneficial.'

'I don't think I understand.'

'Nurse Dtui will explain it to you.'

Dtui was shocked out of her daydream. 'Will I?'

'Certainly.' This was Siri's way. He often threw her in to see if she'd float. He wouldn't come to her rescue until he was absolutely certain she couldn't bob to the surface on her own.

'Okay.' She looked at the peculiar scene and quickly ran through the possibilities in her mind. 'Right!' she said. 'If there's a body it'll be face up. Judging from the state of the arm, it's mummified, ergo, it would have shrunk.'

Siri smiled and she knew she was on the right track. She continued with more confidence.

'As he probably didn't get inside the concrete after it was set, we have to assume he was deliberately buried in wet concrete – or fell in. That means the concrete hardened around him. As the body shrank, a mould would have been left of the original person. That mould could tell us as much as the body itself. So, we don't want to damage the concrete too much. Dah Dah,' she sang. 'I don't hear clapping.'

Lit and one of the workmen did indeed applaud. The security chief looked at her with undisguised admiration. 'Very well done,' he said. 'Yes, excellent.'

Siri, still smiling, was looking more closely at the hand. He removed the plastic bag and took a closer look at the clawed fingers. The skin was the colour of dark chocolate, not so unusual in mummified bodies. But the palm seemed several tones lighter than the back of the hand. He knew a body at this stage of mummification wouldn't be giving away many secrets.

The workmen began to chisel along the dotted line as carefully as archaeologists at an ancient dig.

'Gentlemen,' Siri urged. 'It's concrete. At the rate you're going, you won't get through it until the year 2006. Smash the hell out of it for goodness sake.'

And smash they did. They worked from either side while Lit, Dtui and Siri sat at the foot of the karst. A feeble sun had finally burned a hole through the north-eastern mist but hadn't yet warmed the land. Dtui and Lit filled the following hour with their friendly chatter while Siri dozed.

The young couple seemed to have a great deal in common. Both had spent the later years of their lives caring for a sick parent. Dtui told him how her mother, Monoluk, had cirrhosis and that they were presently living at Siri's house. She explained that the doctor didn't like to live alone and he'd managed to gather a peculiar collection of waifs and strays to share his large Party bungalow. Lit's father, on the other hand, had lost both his legs and a length of intestine to a bomb that exploded beneath his feet. A few months ago he'd succumbed to his injuries.

Both Lit and Dtui had taken every opportunity to study. Lit got to his position, despite his relative youth, by working his way through the public service texts. Dtui had memorised numerous medical books in self-taught English. Then, when the American aid vanished, she'd gone through the same subjects in self-taught Russian. Her dream was to join the 2,500 Lao presently studying in the Eastern Bloc and send home whatever she could save to aid her mother's recovery.

Their conversation was terminated by the sound of a loud crack. Siri looked up from his slumber. The workmen had reached air from either side of the slab and had succeeded in prising the top layer loose with crowbars. The concrete lid broke in two as they lifted it off the base. Everyone stood around looking at the result. The mummy, as if in frozen horror, lay in a trough that had once been its shape. One arm was by its side. The other was held high above its head. Its knees were bent slightly and it seemed to be dressed in nothing more than a pair of nylon football shorts that were now several sizes too large for it. Their brilliant red contrasted sharply with the almost-black chocolate of the corpse.

But, what shocked the onlookers most, even Siri who

had seen death in many forms, was the agony on its face and the huge gaping hole that had taken the place of its mouth. They had no doubt this had been a torturous death – and no accident.

'What ... what happened to its face?' Lit asked in horror.

Siri went to the concrete lid of the accidental tomb and heaved it back to study its interior. The mould was complete there, an almost perfect concave mask of the head. And, where the mouth had attempted its muffled cry for the last time, a trunk of concrete curled downward. Embedded at its base were the missing teeth.

'I think this explains the hole,' Siri said, not looking up. The others came over to take a look. 'It would appear the final breaths of our friend here were of liquid concrete. When it hardened and the body began to shrink, the teeth remained in their original position, stuck here against the roof of the tomb. I wouldn't be surprised if we found more concrete in the lungs.'

'My God,' Lit said. 'You mean he was alive when he went into the concrete?'

'It looks that way,' Dtui confirmed.

'What a terrible way to die. Who would have done such a thing?'

'I'd have to suppose, judging from the size of the original body, that it was somebody of enormous strength,' Siri replied.

'Or several people,' Dtui added.

'Yes, indeed. Good point. Comrade Lit, do you think the President would object if we used the meeting room in his house as a makeshift morgue?'

'I have the key,' Lit told him. 'But he'll be here next week for the concert.'

'I imagine if we haven't worked this out by then, we never will, son. It doesn't take me that long to concede defeat.'

Judge Haeng came back from another half day of fussy domestic disputes in the courtroom. A city whose criminals and potential criminals had all been incarcerated, in which crime had been abolished, was a dull place for a magistrate. He walked past the simple desks of the Justice Department clerks who sat sweating into their clunky typewriters. They nodded with little enthusiasm as their young boss went by. In the year since he'd taken up his position, fresh from Moscow, he hadn't spoken to any of them civilly. Usually he addressed them through Mrs Manivone, the senior clerk. When he approached her desk she stood politely and smiled her meaningless smile. She wore a neatly ironed khaki blouse and a black *pasin* ankle-length skirt. Usually, she was equally unruffled.

'Good health, Judge Haeng.'

'Has he gone?'

'Who?'

'The freak at the morgue.'

She sighed. 'If you mean Mr Geung, they collected him last night. He should be there on Wednesday.'

'Good. Excellent.' He set off for his office.

'It's just ...'

He turned back. 'What?'

'Well, I'm not sure I understand, Judge. Everybody's very fond of Mr Geung.'

'Fond? Fond? Are we running a government department or a home for social outcasts? I'm very fond of my grandmother (Mrs Manivone didn't believe that) but I wouldn't give her a responsible job in the national morgue. What image would foreign visitors take home if they came and saw a moron working for the State?'

Mrs Manivone had a number of possible responses to that but under her breath all she managed was, 'One of compassion?'

'What was that?'

'I don't think Dr Siri's going to be very pleased about it when he returns.'

The judge sauntered back to her. 'Oh, you don't?'

'No.'

He leaned on her desk and raised his voice so the others could hear. 'And remind me – does Dr Siri work for the Justice Department?'

'Yes, Judge Haeng.'

'And, am I the head of the Justice Department, Missy?'

Mrs Manivone once again reminded herself she had three children to feed. 'Yes, Judge Haeng.'

'So, does he do what I tell him, or do I do what he tells me?'

'Well, neither, in fact, as I've seen, comrade.' It was a rash comment, albeit true. She knew there was a Party slogan on its way.

'Now, don't get fresh, comrade Manivone. Every bee in the socialist hive is as important as the next. But if the worker doesn't show respect to the queen, the honey does not flow as sweetly. Remember that.'

'Yes, Judge Haeng.'

He looked around at the clerks, whose heads snapped back to their work. He smiled and walked smugly to his office. It would have been a spectacular exit had his door handle not stuck again. He swore at it and finally fought his way into the room before slamming the door.

'God save the Queen,' mumbled one clerk to the muffled laughter of his colleagues.

As the truck drove further and further from Vientiane, Geung's anxiety level increased. Some of the soldiers were concerned that something might burst inside him. To them he seemed like an animal caught in a trap, the type that might bite off its own foot in order to escape. Even the sergeant felt a pang of guilt as he watched Geung shuddering on the bench. But he had his directive. 'Delivery to a work team in the north.' The order was direct from the Justice Department so he was in no position to argue. Once the sun had gone down, their prisoner stopped responding to the soldiers' questions, and any attempt to cheer him up was no more productive than sowing seeds on concrete. They couldn't imagine the guilt Geung was feeling for letting his friends down, or how terribly alone and sad he was.

The unit was to spend the night at the 8th Battalion camp just outside Van Khi. The truck pulled into the fenced compound and Geung looked up to see the gate close behind him. There was no escape.

5

THE MISSING MORON

An autopsy has one purpose: to solve mysteries that surround a death. If, after three hours, the original mysteries remain and have been supplemented by even deeper mysteries, one should begin to consider the operation a failure. Siri and Dtui looked at each other with every new unanswerable question and shook their heads. Admittedly, the condition of the corpse made their task a good deal more difficult. The concrete had been laid in late January so the body had slowly mummified over the subsequent five months. Everything had contracted to the point that wounds or any traces of disease would have become hidden in the tight ripples of the skin or the tangle of knots beneath.

Three small peculiarities had presented themselves right away. First, clenched tightly in the fist of the right hand was a key. It was a long, thin type with a circular top and an uncomplicated shape at the bottom. Second, of no surprise to either of them, the corpse's teeth were pink, indicating the man had probably died a violent death. Third, sticking from the concrete where the victim's chest had lain, they found a peculiarly long broken fingernail, although the corpse's own nails were trimmed short. It was coated in some type of varnish that had kept it in good

condition. They could only conclude that the nail had originally been embedded in the victim's skin.

These peculiarities had been comparatively easy to spot.
The others took longer. For example, they didn't discover
the bullet hole in the chest until much later, and only after
a meticulous inch by inch fingertip examination of the skin.
Siri was able to insert a French crochet needle deep into the
minute aperture but didn't hit a bullet. They decided that
would have to wait for the internal examination.

There were a number of characteristics that suggested
the man wasn't Asian. The bone structure of the face and
the fullness of the lips made him look negroid. Siri agreed
this could have been accounted for by post-mortem distor-
tion but the skin itself was darker than he'd ever seen in a
mummification. The confirmation was in the teeth. Dtui
had been able to carefully chip them away from the
concrete to reveal the shape of the palate. The upper inci-
sors formed a deep U, and that strongly suggested the
mummy was indeed that of a negroid.

The dissection of the body didn't produce a great deal
more information. Dtui and Siri were mystified as to how
there could have been such a neat bullet hole but no trace
of a bullet. The channel didn't pass completely through the
body, but no end of searching was able to turn one up. This
they added to their list of questions.

Lit came to hear of their findings. He sat with the visitors
around a thermos of tea and three tin cups on the veranda
of the guesthouse. It was four in the afternoon and surprisingly quiet. They hadn't yet got around to discussing the
victim.

'Looks like the policemen got lost,' Dtui said, noting that the trucks hadn't returned. Siri hadn't thought to tell her of his suspicions as to their fate. Comrade Lit was more forthcoming.

'The American lackeys won't be back here tonight,' he told her quite casually. Siri was used to the labels the Party attached to the officials of the old regime, but he saw Dtui's eyebrows rise. She looked as if she were seeing a different version of the chief. She shouldn't have been surprised. A cadre didn't rise to the position of security head at such a young age without knowing how to tightrope walk along the Party line. It was an ever-swaying line and it was easy to fall off.

'Why not?' Dtui asked.

'They've been transferred to a camp,' Lit told her.

'Really? I didn't see them loading their suitcases on the truck this morning.'

'No.'

It was a 'no' that Lit anticipated would mark the end of this line of enquiries, but he didn't know Dtui.

'How can they be transferred without their belongings?'

Siri could see her stepping very close to the edge. Lit had been most polite all day, but staunch Party members didn't expect to be questioned – weren't used to it.

'I think we should talk about our concrete man,' the doctor said.

But Lit wished to continue. 'They won't be needing belongings where they're going, Nurse Dtui.'

'No belongings?' Dtui stood over the crumbling precipice. 'No clothes? No toiletries? No mementos of home?'

'No.'

'Why on earth not?' There was suddenly a vacuum between them.

'Because they have to learn to live without them.'

'Live without clothes? It's cold up here at night. They'll catch their deaths.'

'That may be the case. Those unable to adapt to new conditions naturally become their victims.'

Siri tried again. 'I think we should ...'

'Adapt? What? Do you expect them to grow thick body hair overnight?' She had plummeted down into the chasm and was beyond saving.

Lit straightened in his seat and spoke loudly. 'We're not animals, comrade Dtui. Of course we provide them with a blanket each and basic supplies. But we expect the early days at Seminar to be hard for the corrupt American lackeys who have lived fat lives bleeding the masses. Their own excesses have softened them. We're giving them an opportunity to become valuable members of society.'

'Through hard labour and cruelty?'

'Dtui!' Siri raised his voice. He was becoming annoyed, not by the questions, which he considered valid, but because she'd failed to recognise it was time to keep her mouth shut.

Lit was on the attack now. 'Your type never take the trouble to understand.'

'My type? And what exactly is ...'

'Shut up!' Siri smashed his tin cup down hard onto the table. Tea bounced out of it and splashed across the varnished wooden surface. 'Both of you. I didn't travel four hundred kilometres to argue ideology. We're here to discuss a crime, and a horrible crime at that. Would you both mind showing a little professional discipline?'

It was the closest Dtui had ever seen her boss to a tantrum. She suspected he was bluffing but she knew she'd pushed too far. 'Sorry, Doc. You're right.'

Lit still glared at her but spoke to Siri. 'You're right, of course, Dr Siri. What information do you have for me from today's inspection?'

With a sigh of relief, Siri described the condition of the corpse and its peculiarities. Dtui kept silent.

'In conclusion,' Siri said, 'it appears that the gentleman was shot, then, still alive, was held under the wet concrete until he drowned. It was certainly the concrete that killed him, although I imagine the gunshot wound would have weakened him considerably. It certainly punctured a lung.'

'And you believe he was black,' Lit added, now nothing more or less than a sober investigator of crime.

'I wouldn't bet my life on it but I strongly suspect so. And, that would have to make him Cuban.'

'Why?' Dtui asked, breaking her silence.

'The only dark-skinned foreigners you're likely to find up here are Cubans,' Siri said. 'Mr Castro has been very generous with aid and personnel. There used to be a joint Cuban–Vietnamese hospital project not far from here.'

'They're still here,' Lit told him.

'Really? Is Dr Santiago still in charge?'

'He's managing the hospital aid money, I believe. I wouldn't say he's in charge of anything.'

'Ah, good. We know each other well, or, at least, as well as two men who don't share a common language can. It might be a good idea to pay a social call on the good doctor and see if any Cubans were lost around the time they laid the path.'

'Then, ehrr, I can leave that line of enquiry up to you, Doctor?'

Siri thought it odd the security man would relinquish his role in the investigation to a mere coroner but didn't bother to ask why. He enjoyed a bit of detective work. 'Certainly.'

'Good,' Lit said. 'Then I should get back to my office. I'll check in with you the same time tomorrow. I've arranged for the kitchen here to have food for you three times a day. The staff won't have much else to do for another week.' He stood and nodded.

'Until the next batch of lackeys gets in,' Dtui told Siri. If Lit heard her, he ignored the comment and walked away. Once his jeep was off on the dirt road, Siri glared at Dtui and shook his head.

'What?' she asked.

'You haven't spent very much time around communists, have you?'

'You're a communist.'

'There's a vast difference between being a paid-up member of the Party and *being* a communist. Real communists take life quite seriously. If you don't agree with their doctrine then you're the enemy.'

'Their doctrine? Dr Siri, you're one of them. It's your doctrine too.'

'And there were long periods when I truly believed. In fact, I still think a well-run socialist system could rescue the world from its lethargy and selfishness. But it's something people should come to of their own accord, through common sense ...'

'Not torture.'

'Correct. But it isn't a situation you're going to change by attempting to shout down people like comrade Lit. Nobody shouts louder than a Red.'

'So how's it going to change?'

'It'll burn itself out.'

'But before then a lot of people are going to suffer.'

'And I don't want one of them to be you. So, keep that pretty mouth buttoned. And that's an order. You aren't going to make a dribble of a difference. You know what they say about loose tongues.'

'They fall out?'

Siri laughed and slapped her in slow motion. He never had been able to maintain an effective flow of earnest gravity for any sustained period. Dtui sulked, but she understood. She knew Siri's views had come as a result of years of trying to make changes from the inside, and failing. His relationship with the woman he loved, and was faithful to for almost forty years, had brought him into the Communist Party and kept him there. He'd been distant enough from it to see the Pathet Lao become lapdogs to the Vietnamese, just as the royalists had slobbered around the heels of the French and the Americans. He was resigned to the fact that his Lao brethren were destined to always be the fool to some bigger fool. He wasn't a terrific example of a man who knew when to keep his mouth shut, but Dtui knew he didn't offer advice lightly.

That night, exhausted though he was, Siri still rolled from side to side on the lumpy mattress. So many ghosts were calling to him from the fields. Impressionable young cadres were among them. He'd put many back together in field hospitals after their encounters with the Hmong resistance. They were telling him, 'Look at us. What good did it do? All you did was fix us up so we could go and be killed in the next battle.' They were right. He didn't want to listen to them. He wanted sleep, but in sleep he'd have to face the malevolent spirits who lurked in the dark alleyways of his nightmares.

The room was unimpressed by the starless blackness of the chilly night. Even with his eyes wide open he could see none of the ill-matching furniture – not even see the hand he held out before him. An invisible beetle was fluttering against the mosquito netting and he hooked his attention onto the buzzing of its wings. By imagining he could see it, by hearing only the buzz, he believed he could hypnotise himself asleep. And he was almost right. The voices had stopped, he was dipping out of consciousness, and at exactly the moment he was about to fall, the infernal discotheque started up again. Even though it was far away, the tremor of the base worked its way across the ground like an earthquake, even to the second floor of the guest-house. It vibrated through the bedposts – through Siri.

What had happened to his country's youth, he wondered, that they should develop such awful taste in music? This wailing of tortured Americans. He lost count of the number of grating tunes he had to endure before he finally found the sleep he craved. In the sleep world it was quiet, a rare quiet for his dreams. A crow sat high on a wire beside a sparrow. They were a long way above the ground. This was a wire that could only have existed in a dream, because a T28 fighter passed beneath it, strafing the fields with its guns. Bombs plunged into the paddies and sank into the mud, none exploding. In fact it was a silent dream without even the accompaniment of music. The crow preened the sparrow as if both were unaware of their positions in the caste of birds or their proximity to a battle. They were engrossed in one another. Nothing else seemed to matter. It was a peaceful scene: the birds preening, the T28 strafing, the non-exploding bombs tumbling.

Siri was suddenly shocked to find himself outside his mosquito net. He was standing shuddering in only his undershorts: a slightly chewy smorgasbord for carnivorous insects. He had no idea how he'd left the sanctity of the mesh or why he was standing there. But there was now light from a full moon oozing through the curtains, and in the vacant bed on the far side of his room, a child lay. She was about four and malnourished. When Siri walked to her she looked up at him.

'When did you get here, darling?' he asked. 'Why don't you have a net?'

She smiled. When she spoke, her voice seemed older than she was. 'I don't have much time, Uncle.'

'What can I do?'

'Take notice of what you see,' she said. There was a rumbling sound and the ceiling came crashing down on their heads. The floor beneath them gave way and they tumbled slowly downwards like leaves falling from a tree. A cockerel joined them in their descent. It looked into Siri's eyes and crowed hoarsely.

A pale light was seeping in through the nylon curtain. Above his head, the corpses of a dozen flying beetles lay bottom up on the roof of the netting. Although the spirits had been known to spring trick endings on him, this second awakening had a feel of reality about it. The falling chicken crowed again and was joined by a howling dog. From somewhere close, a *klooee*, a green bamboo flute, began to play. It was a simple tune, executed with technical accuracy but with little heart. As he listened, he squirmed around under the quilt to discover what bones and muscles would ache that day. He had no say in this. He tended to extend himself in his dreams and suffer for it the next morning. But today, even as he stood, everything seemed to work fine.

He walked over to the spare bed and looked at the unruffled quilt that covered it. For no logical reason he could think of he pulled it back. There was nothing there. Of course. This was real life. What did he expect? He was in the process of putting it back when he squashed something beneath his bare foot. He heard the squelch and wondered whether he might have put the non-stick lizard out of its misery, but it was just a berry. It had fallen from the dish of fruit on the table. It was a small red currant. He'd seen its kind before but couldn't put a name to it. A few years earlier he would have thrown it out. But everything that happened these days seemed to have relevance to some other thing. There were no coincidences. 'Take notice of what you see.' He wrapped the berry in a sheet of tissue from the table roll and put it into his bag.

Mr Geung had heard of Luang Prabang from Dr Siri and his adventures there. It was a place, like Paris, like Mrs Kit's Broom and Brush factory, like the moon. These were all words to Geung. Visiting them was unthinkable and unnecessary. He had his own world and had no need to visit any other. So, when the convoy arrived in Luang Prabang province, he was neither impressed nor glad to be there. The journey had been a bone-jarring ordeal for all of them, but especially for Geung. Hopelessness sat heavily in his mind. As he was unable to cope with all this new information, he sat where he'd been put on the wooden bench and stared bemused at the passing scenery, a mountainous vista like nothing he'd ever seen in his limited life.

Whenever the truck stopped and the soldiers all climbed down to stretch their aching muscles, Geung followed them off into the forest to relieve himself. He'd become so docile and uncommunicative that the soldiers had begun to treat him more like a kitbag than a prisoner. He'd offload himself from the truck and they'd stand him in a corner. They'd lead him to the mess tent or to the bunks. Wherever they put him, they knew that's where he'd be if they needed him. There was so little thought invested in him that by the time they reached the barracks at Xieng Ngeun, he'd been totally forgotten.

The sergeant ran up the wooden steps and knocked on the frame of the open door to the officers' rec room. He walked straight in and found his superior officer reading the *Huksat Lao* newsletter.

'Captain Ouan, sir?'

'What is it?'

'The retarded man.'

'What about him?'

'He's gone.'

'Gone where?'

'We … we don't actually know, sir. When the trucks arrived he wasn't on any of them.'

The captain threw down his paper. 'You were supposed to be keeping an eye on him.'

'Yes. I'm sorry. He was in the habit of climbing up on to any truck he felt like. We got used to him just being there somewhere.'

'Oh, you did, did you? When was the last time anyone saw him?'

'Just before Xieng Ngeun. We stopped to shoot rabbits.'

The captain sighed. 'Well, he isn't likely to go far, is he, Corporal? Take a jeep back and find him.'

'Yes, sir.' He saluted but paused before leaving. 'Actually, it's "Sergeant", sir.'

'Not any more it's not.'

6

THE AMATEUR INTERPRETER
OF ENGLISH

The old Pathet Lao driver was at Siri's disposal for as long as he was needed. The jeep pulled up in front of the new regional hospital in Xam Neua at 8AM. Four years earlier, this capital of Huaphan province had been a pile of rubble and splinters. Not a house had remained standing after a dozen years of blitz. The non-combatant Air America forward air controllers had guided in the bombers and choreographed the destruction, but it was mostly Lao and Hmong pilots with their fingers on the buttons. It was a symbolic gesture. The civilian inhabitants had fled long before the city was flattened.

But now a new city was taking shape with pretentious boulevards as wide as the Champs Elysee and grand plans for another communist show town. The hospital was a temporary field of whitewashed barracks all waiting for a move to a more splendid home. The front office housed the administrators, and Siri and Dtui found Dr Santiago buried behind a rockery of files and books. He was a skinny man around Siri's age with a hairstyle modelled on that of Albert Einstein. He wore porthole spectacles with glass as thick as the bottoms of gin bottles. A cigarette burned in an ashtray beside him and he seemed to hover

DISCO FOR THE DEPARTED

there in its smoke. He was obviously used to people walking in and out of his office, because he didn't look up from his work when the visitors arrived.

'Dr Santiago?' Siri said when he spotted him through the canyons of paper.

'Da?' The old Cuban still pored over his lists. Siri wasn't surprised to hear him speak Russian. After almost ten years as head of foreign medical aid in Huaphan, Santiago still refused pointedly to learn Lao or Vietnamese. He spoke Spanish, English and Russian fluently and had reached an age when he considered himself sufficiently full of languages. He hadn't asked to come to Laos, or to work with the Vietnamese, whom he disliked. He certainly wasn't about to cross over the cultural divide. He was the expert and everyone had to make the effort to communicate with him. All in all, not unlike Siri, he was a stubborn but likeable old coot.

'Dosvidanya,' Siri said. It was his only Russian word and he wasn't actually sure what it meant.

Santiago finally looked up and squinted through his glasses. It seemed to take him a few moments either to focus or to place his old friend in his memory. 'Dr Siri? Is that you?' he asked in English. He jumped up from his chair and ran around the desk to embrace a respected colleague. They smiled and laughed a lot as they hugged, but Dtui noticed they weren't actually conversing. On the journey, Siri had told her how he'd worked with Santiago, on and off, for five years without the benefit of a common language. Siri spoke French and Vietnamese quite fluently and he too had reached his linguistic quota. When there was no English/Lao interpreter available, the two had merely observed one another's surgical skills and socialised with the aid of diagrams and mime. It had been such a peculiarly pleasant relationship, Siri wondered whether language might have spoiled it in some way.

Siri finally broke away and pointed to his assistant. 'Nurse Dtui,' he said.

'Hello, Dr Santiago. Pleased to meet you,' she said in English.

Both Siri and Santiago looked at her with astonishment for a few seconds before the Cuban went across to hug her also. It was a culturally inappropriate gesture that dropped into the spirit of the moment. He told her she spoke English well.

'I read and write,' she said. 'I don't really speak it.' It was true. She'd never used the language to converse. It was just a medium for study. In fact she was a little surprised to find it coming from her mouth so happily.

He assured her that whether she read it or spoke it, it was still the same language. And, from that moment, despite the fact that she'd never heard herself using it before, English became the language of communication and Dtui its novice interpreter. She knew her pronunciation was awful, but Santiago had no problem with that because his own accent was equally horrible. He too had learned English from American textbooks. Siri was full of admiration for his talented assistant.

Throughout the morning, the two old doctors caught up with each other's lives since they'd last met. Santiago was spending more time on administering Cuban aid, he told them, and had less and less time for the job he was actually trained for. Farmers continued to get blown up in their fields and there were fewer and fewer qualified medical staff members to care for them. There were under a hundred qualified doctors in the entire country so the PL medical staff was spread thinly to fill the roles of the royalist physicians who'd fled to Thailand. Santiago had funding but nobody to hire.

Through Dtui, whose confidence increased as time passed, Siri finally got around to the mystery of his concrete man. The Cuban thought about it for a moment and asked whether he was certain the incident had taken place early that year.

'January 21 to be exact,' Siri told him.

'Dr Santiago says that if it had been a few months earlier, he'd have had two very good candidates for us,' Dtui said. 'At least that's what I think he meant. But he reckons that by last October, they'd already gone back to Cuba.'

'They completed their tours?'

'Not exactly. He says it's a little complicated. They came in 1971 to help with the setting up of some project at Kilometre 8.'

'Xieng Muang.' Siri said. 'That's the hospital. It was an amazing project. They had to drill out the centres of two mountains. They built two complete hospital wards that were invisible from the air but were able to accommodate a thousand patients. It was an impressive piece of engineering. The Vietnamese military took care of the labour, the Cubans provided nurses and orderlies.'

'He thinks you probably remember the two men. Their names were Isandro and Udon.'

'Odon,' Santiago corrected her.

'Sorry, Odon. He says they were here from the beginning.'

Siri nodded his head. He'd only been invited in from time to time to help with surgery and he always brought his Lao team, but he did recall the sight of black orderlies running around the wards. He'd had no opportunity to talk to them.

'While the work was going on,' Dtui continued, 'Dr Santiago says they took care of the wounded in temporary caves here and there. Isandro and Odon were part of that project. They were the head nursing orderlies. When Kilometre 8 Hospital was ready they moved everyone into the mountains. The two boys finished one four-year tour and volunteered for a second. It seems that was quite unusual. Most of their people were in a hurry to get back home. But these two were good workers and they made friends with the locals. They studied Lao language, even got a taste for the local food. Of course, I might be making half of this up.'

'So, why were they sent back early?' Siri asked.

There followed a long spell while Dtui clarified points with the old Cuban.

'Apparently,' Dtui said, 'there were complaints.'

'Who from?'

'A senior Vietnam army officer said one of the men, Isandro, was making advances to his daughter. He made it very clear if he found the man anywhere near her again he'd shoot him.'

'And Dr Santiago passed this message on to Isandro and Odon.'

'He says he did but they defied him. They said they weren't afraid of Santiago or the colonel. He couldn't believe it. The situation just got worse and worse. The doctor couldn't have Cuban officials getting shot by a

Vietnamese for messing around with his daughter, so he didn't have any choice. He ordered them home.'

'And is he absolutely sure they went?'

'Absolutely.'

'And no other negroes went missing from Cuban projects?'

'He says this was the only one in the region.'

'Could you ask Dr Santiago to describe Isandro for me?'

Again Dtui and the Cuban went into a huddle.

'As far as I can make out,' Dtui said, 'he was built like a tree, tall and broad-shouldered like an American basketball player, and strong.'

Siri shrugged. This wasn't at all the description of their concrete man. Dtui asked about Odon.

'This is more like it,' she said. 'Odon was smaller. Santiago says he was ugly as a goat but had a permanent smile that endeared him to everyone. He says it's unusual for the natives, and I guess that includes you and me, to get along with dark-skinned foreigners, but Odon and Isandro really made the effort. Then he said something I couldn't really get – something like "more fool the natives" but don't quote me on that.'

Siri considered Odon a more likely candidate than his friend, but as they'd both left Laos, it appeared he'd either have to look elsewhere for their mummy's identity or prove that for some reason one of the orderlies got left behind.

Although there was an enormous refrigerator in one corner of the office, upon inspection, the thing was found to contain nothing but jar upon jar of culture specimens. It was a fascinating hobby, they all agreed, but not particularly fulfilling. So, Santiago invited his guests to join him for lunch at the new Lao Houng Hotel. He gladly abandoned his paperwork and seemed rejuvenated by this unexpected visit. As they were leaving the building, the Cuban stopped to speak to a nurse who looked too young even to have completed the nursing certificate. Siri noticed the old man take her hand in his and give her a rather unprofessional peck on the cheek. Although the girl blushed, she didn't pull away as one would expect of a Lao girl receiving an unwanted kiss. It appeared there was still a Latin fire burning in Santiago's grate.

They ate bland Vietnamese food beneath huge posters of unknown Chinese film stars, and joked about the new Oz of Vieng Xai. Then, as they drank warm lightly scented beer for dessert, Santiago turned his attention to Dtui. He asked her if she were a qualified nurse. When she said she was, he asked whether she thought her 'papa Siri' would be able to spare her for a day or two. It appeared that after the ceasefire they had moved the Kilometre 8 Hospital outside the mountain and back to some old French buildings that stood in front of it. It was still a hospital but nobody working there had more than six months basic medical training. Dr Santiago was expecting two new Cuban doctors to come before the weekend but, as things stood, he was desperate for somebody who could make decisions. The doctor went there whenever he was able, but he believed they really needed a big sister on the site.

She put the proposal to Siri.

'What do you think?' he asked.

'I don't know. I'm just a nurse.'

'Dtui, you'll never be just a nurse. I could probably play detective here by myself for a bit – but the decision's yours. The living always take precedence over the dead in my book. Just don't tell any spirits I said that.'

She turned back to Santiago and asked how certain he was the Cuban doctors would be there by the weekend. He told her he was positive. They were in the air even as he spoke. He stretched his arms to impersonate their aeroplane and Siri played at shooting him down. Santiago crashed onto the table. It occurred to Dtui that some little boys just never grew up. But she liked the old Cuban and when she told him she would help he was elated. She translated her decision for Siri.

'Good for you,' he said. 'I'll come by and lend a hand whenever I can. But I'm sure you'll have the place organised in no time. And Dtui … ?'

'Yes?'

'You won't forget these are live ones, will you? Don't go storing them in the freezer overnight.'

'Dr Siri!'

'Sorry.'

Mr Geung wasn't designed for walking. His ankles turned outward and his legs were short. But the notion had entered his mind that he should walk back to Vientiane. He knew it was far, but not that it was over three hundred kilometres by road. He knew he didn't have any money in his pocket to pay for a bus ticket, nor did he have a concept of how else he could get to the morgue and keep his promise. So, when the soldiers stopped to take a pee, he'd gone to the last truck in the convey and looked back at the road that snaked down through the mountains. He took a deep breath, as the doctor had taught him, and set off for home. Nobody noticed him go.

After only five minutes he was alone on the deserted road. Mr Geung wasn't one for doing things alone. He was good at joining in with others or doing what he was told, but he had hardly a trace of initiative. The trucks were barely out of sight before he realised he wouldn't be able to attempt such a journey by himself. He needed a friend. He needed a logical friend to keep him company. And, as if by magic, he looked back over his shoulder and saw Dtui just a few paces behind him. It was a relief. She was the most sensible woman he knew and he was sure she'd guide him back.

'I ... I'm sorry, little sis-ter,' he said and smiled at her.

She laughed and took his hand, and walked with him along the badly potholed road. At one point she whispered into his mind that the sun was directly overhead and they didn't have hats. They decided to walk through the groves of shady peculiar trees, keeping the road within sight. Having her beside him gave him confidence. As they walked, he reminded her of all the jokes she'd told for the past year. She was impressed that they'd remained stored in his memory. He didn't know where he'd be without Dtui's common sense there with him.

The image of Mr Geung appeared so clearly in Dtui's mind it was as if he were there in the room with her. She opened her eyes and looked around. Her clothes hung from the four posts of the bed like pall-bearers in the closetless room. The darned holes in the mosquito netting gathered the mesh like fairy stars, adding to her feeling that Guesthouse Number One was mystical in some way. The *klooee* pipe played its same dirge over and over in the distance and, even in late afternoon, the mist had begun to roll against the glass of the window. She realised she must have dozed and dreamed of her friend, but she felt uneasy for him.

She knew that but for the mystery guests on the far wing and the staff sitting around in the empty dining room, the guesthouse was deserted. Siri would be down on the veranda describing their visit with Dr Santiago to the small-minded security head. What a let-down he'd turned out to be. Until he'd suddenly turned into a raging communist Nazi, Dtui had even considered him a prospective mate. His cool smile and lean frame fitted her ever-shrinking list of requirements for a match. Unfortunately, she held firmly to the belief that any man for her had to have a mind of his own, and that had become an increasingly difficult order to fill. That was why she'd opted out of the evening's briefing downstairs.

But her room was overwhelming her with bizarre thoughts and feelings, so she decided to get away from it. She had two tasks that would keep her occupied for an hour or so. First she would try to get through to Vientiane on the one guesthouse telephone. About a month earlier, two men in old army uniforms with 'telephone company' written across the backs in laundry ink, had come to install a phone at Siri's bungalow. It was another Party reward for Siri's selfless contribution to the cause. Dtui knew if it hadn't been for her mother and the need to keep in constant contact with her, he would have told them where to stick their telephone. 'Another intrusion,' he would have called it.

Before the men had left, they wrote down the four-digit number, one that just happened to end in three nines, and assured them there would be a connection the following day. In fact it had been two weeks before they heard that distinctive Lao dial tone – a sparrow trying desperately to escape from a crinkly paper bag. Now, Dtui was able to check on her mother every few days. It put her mind at ease. Of course she had to yell her guts out to be heard. Siri was so impressed at the size of her lungs he'd wondered whether the telephone was actually necessary.

Another thing too had been worrying her – the autopsy. She took her sturdy Soviet flashlight downstairs and, after ten minutes of shouting over the phone, she walked out the back way and headed for the President's house. There had been no reason to lock the door of the meeting room. The body still lay in segments on the plastic tablecloth. The story of the Cuban orderlies had stuck in her mind. Certainly there was no way the body in front of her belonged to the amorous basketball player, but what about his goat-faced friend? What if he hadn't gone home? What if the smaller man had somehow been left behind and got himself into trouble?

With no logical alternatives in her head, she began to run the torch beam across the torso. She was used to Siri's ongoing discussions with his corpses during autopsies, so she began her inspection with, 'Excuse me, Mr Odon, I was wondering whether perhaps you had a little more to tell us than you have so far.' She'd noticed something at the initial inspection, three marks – almost parallel lines –

beneath the left armpit. At the time she'd merely noted them as 'interesting'. The pruning of the skin had left many such grooves, but there had been something strangely regimented about them. The memory had lingered in her mind and she wanted to satisfy her curiosity.

She shone the beam on to the right side of the chest. It was more deteriorated there, harder to recognise, but after pushing at the leathery hide with her fingers, she had no doubt. Three furrows in an identical position to those on the left – symmetrical. Nothing biological could explain such marks. The body had been scarred in some type of ritual. It certainly did have more to tell.

Siri had arrived at the point where he was prepared to wake up the guesthouse supervisor and complain about the damned noise. Three nights he'd been there, and every night the foreign devil music had blasted out at midnight. Surely the youth of Vieng Xai had better ways to spend their time. Surely the senior cadres of the region would clamp down on such bourgeois Western decadence. He couldn't work it out. Perhaps Huaphan had so few people left who really cared, the midnight dancers could do as they wished.

As sleep was hard to come by, he went over the points raised at the meeting with comrade Lit. They'd drawn up a list. One. Check the departure of Isandro and Odon last year. Two. Locate the Vietnamese colonel who'd made the complaint to Santiago. Three. Get information about any other projects in the region where dark-skinned foreigners were involved. Siri broadened the search to include Vietnamese mountain tribesmen even though he was quite sure the dead man was not Asian.

Somewhere between numbers seven and eight on the list, order finally gave way to sleep. The crow and the sparrow returned for a dream sequel, still on their wire above the valley, still preening one another. But slowly, one by one, other sparrows came to rest alongside them. One settled beside the first and attempted to flirt with her. She rejected its advances and returned to her crow. This caused a terrible kerfuffle in the sparrow community. They flapped and fluttered and squawked and it seemed an assault on the crow was inevitable. But, before they could attack, the crow enfolded the sparrow in his broad black wing and the two of them dropped. There was no attempt to fly away. They merely dropped like stones into the valley below and deep into the soft mud of the fields.

Siri was woken, not by the weak morning light through his window, but by the whimpering of a child. He thought of the girl in an earlier dream but the bunk opposite was empty. This was more real, and closer, so close he even raised his netting and peered under his bed. He went to the door and looked out into the empty corridor. But there was no doubt the sound came from inside his room. He touched the talisman at his neck. It could sense tricks from the malevolent spirits. They'd fooled him before. Their black magic had almost killed him on two occasions. But the white stone hung still and cool. This was no black magic. It was a sincere cry for help from some other troubled soul. But with no clues and no way of responding, Siri could only lie back on his mattress and listen to the feeble cries. The sound gradually climbed to

a higher pitch and became more hollow, and at some
point it blended with the sound of the bamboo *klooee*
that played its solitary morning tune.

THE CAVE OF THE DEAD

Mr Geung woke in panic just as he had the previous two mornings. But whereas on those other occasions he'd found himself surrounded by soldiers, today he was wrapped in a canvas tarpaulin like pork in a Chinese spring roll. He struggled to get loose, kicked and punched and panicked, but could find no way to free himself. His mind was blank. All the details of where he was and why he was there were gone. And so, although it didn't help a bit, he started to cry.

'And what, tell me, do you think you're doing in me firewood cover?' It was the voice of an old woman, that much he could tell. But he couldn't see her through the tunnel at the top of his spring roll.

'I ... I don't know,' he said, and continued to cry. He felt a tug on his cocoon and was sent rolling across the ground and flung loose from the tarpaulin onto the dry earth. An elderly woman and two giggling children were looking down at him.

'Grandma, he's a retard,' the smallest girl said.

'So he is,' the old lady agreed. 'What do you want here, retard?'

'I d ... don't know,' Geung answered truthfully.

'Then I should call the police and have you arrested,' she said.

'Yes, I th … I think so.'

'Or maybe I should get my gun and chase you away.'

Geung thought about that option. 'Y … yes, that would be f … fine too.'

The old woman laughed. Her betel-nut-stained mouth looked like a number of disasters he'd seen in the morgue. 'Eeh. You really are crazy. How am I supposed to threaten you if you agree with all I say, boy? Where you hail from?'

'Thangon.'

'Never heard of it.'

'Sorry. I have t … t … to go to Vientiane.' He clambered to his sore feet, smiled at the children and started walking.

'Wait. Wait there,' the old woman said. 'You think you're about to walk to Vientiane?'

'I p … promised.'

'Is that so? You hungry, boy?'

'Yes.'

'Well, you can't walk to Vientiane if you're hungry, seeing it's so far. And as …'

'Yes. I remember.'

'What's that?'

'The mo … mo … mosquitoes. I wrapped up so the mo … mosquitoes didn't get me. D … D … Dengue fever. comrade Dtui s … said you have to wrap up against the mo … mo … mo … mo …'

'MOSQUITOES!' the two girls chorused.

'Yes.' He smiled at the girls and they giggled back.

'All right,' the old lady decided. 'Come and eat and we'll see if we can get some sense out of you before your big march. And I think I can find you some home-made paste here that should keep the mosquitoes from your blood. It'll last for a week so long as you don't wash.'

66

'Thank you ma'am,' he said, and put his hands together in a polite *nop*.

'Well, I don't know where you're from or what you're about, but they taught you some nice manners.' They went into her solid wooden hut. This was the home of the caretaker of the pine plantation through which Geung had trekked during the first day of his escape. 'First thing you do is sit yourself down and take off them vinyl shoes. You wear them all the way to Vientiane and you'll be a cripple as well as a retard.'

'Thank you, m ... m ...'

'MA'AM!' the children yelled as if the circus were in town.

'Mother,' Geung said, and smiled again at the girls with his crazy-paving teeth.

Dtui's first day at Kilometre 8 Hospital was chaotic. It wasn't her fault. Chaos was the norm there. After only an hour she felt helpless. There was a staff of six, two of whom had no medical training whatsoever. The most senior medic had undergone six months of emergency field hospital training in Vietnam. Dtui, with a two-year nursing diploma, was their surgeon general. They all simply stopped making decisions and deferred to her judgement. She immediately mistrusted her ability to make those decisions. Never had she been in a situation that was so desperate.

By far the largest population in the fifty-bed hospital were *bombi* victims. Of all the wicked tools of war, the *bombi* was one of the cruellest. A shell packed with baseball-sized *bombis* was dropped from a plane. In mid-air the shell opened and the *bombis* rained down over the selected target. On contact, two hundred and fifty white-hot ball bearings exploded in all directions from each one, ripping through buildings and people with equal detachment. Some of the *bombis* were time-charged to catch out the survivors who went to care for their loved ones. But some just lay dormant for days, weeks, months or years to spring their deadly surprise on the innocent and ill-informed. The *bombi* had no sense of who its foe should be. A buffalo, a hoe, a child, a young mother planting rice, it mattered not. It took them all.

Every day at Kilometre 8 new victims arrived with truncated limbs bound to stem the flow of blood. They came on ox carts, on ponies, on litters dragged by their relatives. The hospital staff gave them generous doses of opium to remove any sensations, good or bad, and did their best to clean the wounds. Many had lost too much blood or were too shredded to keep alive. Those who survived did so mainly of their own volition. Every few days, Dr Santiago would come by to amputate whatever was unsaveable and perform whatever miracles it took to give people another chance at life.

There were no shifts at Kilometre 8. Staff slept during the rare moments of quiet, be they day or night. They cooked for those patients whose relatives weren't camped in the wards. They kept them full of a painkiller they knew would leave them addicted, and they stretchered the deceased up the slope to the cave of the dead, a crematorium on the skirt of the mountain. At the end of her incredibly long first day, Dtui estimated she'd lost four kilograms. Singsai, the senior medic, told her if she stayed a month she'd be so skinny they'd be able to store her in the closet with the mops. She enjoyed that image.

It had been a comparatively good day. Only one lady had made the journey to the cave of the dead. Dtui had personally been able to save the life, perhaps temporarily, of a ten-year-old child, and at two in the morning the residents at Kilometre 8 were all stoned into a restful sleep. Dtui and Singsai sat in front of the long rectangular prism that formed the main ward. They were too fatigued to sleep so they gazed up at the stars that made such rare appearances in the north-eastern sky that the medic saw them as an omen.

'Days like this make you realise how stupid you are,' Dtui said.

'You aren't stupid at all, nurse,' Singsai assured her. He was such a brown-skinned little man it was as if his words came out of the darkness from a floating set of teeth. He reminded Dtui of the mummy in the President's house.

'Okay, perhaps not stupid exactly, but ... lacking.'

'You've done a lot of good today.'

'But there's so much more I didn't know how to do. It's so frustrating. It makes me appreciate your Dr Santiago and my own boss that much more. They do this stuff day in, day out, year after year, just saving lives as if it were as natural as breathing.'

'I hope to be a surgeon some day,' Singsai told her, looking at the sky as if that were the only place such a hope might hang. He was in his fifties and unconnected so Dtui knew he had little chance.

She scrambled for a change of subject. 'Do you ever have any cases here that aren't emergencies?'

'One or two malarials,' he said 'We've a little boy with

chronic diarrhoea. They say that's the biggest killer of kids in the whole of south-east Asia. Most of them don't make it but we're fighting for this chap. He's been lucky. Oh, and then there's Mrs Duaning.'

'What's wrong with her?'

'Nobody knows. She's been in a coma for two weeks. We found her out on the road.'

'Nobody's come to claim her?'

'No.'

'Then, how do you know her name?'

'We don't, but we can tell she's Hmong. One of our Hmong interns christened her "Duaning". It means "nuts".'

They went to visit Mrs Nuts in a small block away from the others where the non-life-threatening cases lay. She was on her back with her eyes wide open, staring at the ceiling and muttering.

'What's she saying?' Dtui asked.

'The same thing over and over. She only started speaking the day before yesterday.'

Dtui leaned over her and listened. The old lady's voice seemed less gravelly than one would have expected from such a battered old crone. The words came from her mouth on a breath that smelled musty. 'Have to feed Panoy,' she said. 'Have to feed Panoy.'

'You don't suppose Panoy's her name?'

'This woman's? No. It isn't a very Hmong-sounding name.' He pulled up the single blanket to cover her and her feet were momentarily exposed. Both Dtui and Singsai looked at them in amazement. 'What the … ?'

The soles of the woman's feet were caked in some maroon substance. 'Has she been walking anywhere?' Dtui asked.

'No. As far as I know she hasn't moved. And this doesn't look like clay.'

Dtui scratched at one sole with her fingernail. She knew exactly what she was seeing. 'It's congealed blood,' she said.

'Why would she have ...? Are there any wounds?'

Dtui took a damp cloth from the basin beside the bed and rubbed carefully away at one foot. 'No.'

'Then how ... ?'

'It doesn't look random, Singsai. Look at this other foot. It's as if someone painted symbols onto her soles.'

'With blood? Whatever for?'

'That Hmong intern might have some idea.'

'Right. I don't want to wake him now, but in the morning I'll be very interested to see if he has an explanation.'

'Me too,' Dtui said. 'Me too.'

Two more emergencies during the night meant that Dtui didn't actually get to sleep until after seven. The breeze through her thin cotton curtain woke her at ten. Before heading for the main block, she stopped by to see Mrs Nuts. She still lay staring at the ceiling but her tune had changed during the night. Dtui leaned over her face to hear.

'Panoy is weak now. Panoy is weak,' she said.

'Who is Panoy?' Dtui asked.

'Panoy is weak.'

Dtui pushed back the woman's white hair from her face and put her palm on her cold brow. There was something dull about her skin as if she were covered in dust. Her pulse was slow. She wondered whether Mrs Nuts would make it through the day. Before she left the room, Dtui pulled up the blanket to look at her feet. The left sole, the one she'd wiped clean earlier that morning, was once again covered in dried blood.

Dr Siri was downstairs in the guesthouse dining room reading a month-old copy of *Pasason Lao*. There was a picture of his old friend Civilai shaking hands with some Mongolian diplomat. Both were smiling, neither convincingly. He could tell exactly what comrade Civilai, his only ally on the politburo, was thinking. It reminded him of an earlier time and two more idealistic people.

For years, Siri and his wife, Boua, had been members of the Lao Issara, the Free Lao resistance. But Boua was working her way towards a disciplined independence from the French rather than just being a nuisance to the colonists. She was the devout communist of the pair and it was she who led Siri to Hanoi and into the Nguyen Ai Quoc college. There he learned his Vietnamese and attended classes in communist ideology. He was baptised in red paint, held under until he breathed Lenin and defecated Marx. And with this new vital system he'd gone out into the Vietnamese countryside and convinced the farmers that nothing but communism could free them from the yoke of French colonisation. He worked in field hospitals throughout the north of the country, and even after eighteen straight hours of bloody surgery, he'd still find time to engage the villagers in ideological debates.

It was a period in his life he came to refer to as 'the years they borrowed my mind'. It wasn't until he met another enthusiastic cadre, a serious member of the Lao People's Party and lifelong communist called Civilai, that

Siri was able to put everything into perspective. Although he'd been trained to report comrades who strayed from the axiomatic straight and narrow, Civilai was so experienced and so obviously intelligent that Siri had no choice but to listen and re-evaluate his own clouded beliefs. Civilai loved communism. There was no question of his loyalty to the Party but he believed that communism should work without scaring the daylights out of people. For his opinions he was labelled an eccentric. He was too senior and too well respected by the masses to be kicked off the central committee, but he was kept backstage.

Siri had immediately warmed to Civilai's middle path so he too had become ostracised by the top men of the Party. While Boua soldiered on in her attempts to educate a nation of proletariat, Siri hung up his red flag and became a full-time doctor. That was probably when his wife's love for him began to dim. In Siri's heart, the love light never went out at all, he loved her until her death, but he knew she'd already begun to consider her husband a disappointment. Through all that time, only his friendship with Civilai kept him rational, and as the Party dumped more and more meaningless duties on Civilai, it was Siri who offered encouragement and hope to his friend.

This was a photograph of one more symbolic handshake with one more foreign official. It was another snap for the diplomatic album. Civilai told Siri he was becoming the Mickey Mouse of the new regime. He ...

'Comrade?' Siri looked up to see the guard from the upstairs partition standing drained of colour in the doorway. 'You're a doctor, right?'

'That's right,' said Siri.

'Come with me, quick.' He didn't wait for a response, just turned on his heels and ran back up the stairs four at a time. From his many years of experience, Siri knew that ten seconds saved by sprinting up a flight of stairs rather than walking rarely made a difference, apart from killing the physician as well as the patient. So he took the stairs one at a time and was met by the flustered guard on his way back down to see where he'd gone.

'Hurry up,' he said. 'It's a life-and-death matter.' Despite the urgency, he'd spared the time to relock the upstairs door before going for Siri. His hands shook now as he attempted to insert the key into the padlock. Siri reached the top landing just as the man burst through the first door and ran along the corridor to a second. That too was locked. Siri wondered what ferocious beast deserved such security. As he walked past the first room he looked in through the open door. Three expensive-looking leather holdalls sat full on one of the beds. On the floor was a large tray of seedlings and small pots containing cuttings.

'In here,' shouted the guard. 'He's not dead yet.'

On the only bed, convulsed in pain, frothing at the mouth, was a middle-aged man with greased hair wearing simple but expensive pyjamas. On the floor beside the bed, lying on its side, was a brown glass bottle. The label was in Russian but the universal skull and crossbones left no doubt as to its contents. Siri prised open the man's eyes and looked into his pupils. He then forced open the mouth to see the tongue and sniffed at the man's breath.

'They was cleaning the rooms after them others left. Stupid bitch must of left the cleanser in the sink. Don't know how he got hold of it. Must of been on his way back from the toilet and grabbed it without me seeing. Stupid bastard. It'll be me that gets shot if anything happens.' The guard was ranting, pacing up and down the room. 'Hospital! Can we get him to the hospital? Can you fix him up? Doc? Can you, Doc?'

'Listen, comrade,' Siri said, looking up at the frantic guard, 'I can't do anything with you stomping around like a rampant capitalist. I want you to go down to the kitchen and get the ladies to boil two litres of water. Stir in a handful of salt and about 30ml of cooking oil. Don't come back till it's all ready.'

'Right.' The guard abandoned all his locks and sped to the kitchen. The poisoned man still squirmed in agony on the bed.

'It's okay,' Siri said. 'He's gone. You can stop now.'

The man flinched for a second but then began to growl deep in his throat. 'Hos-pital.'

'You and I both know that isn't going to happen, don't we now?'

'Dy-ing.'

'Come on. You're no more dying than I am. In fact, I probably look in worse condition than you do. What on earth did you think this little show would achieve exactly?'

The man spat the remainder of the foam from his mouth and looked up angrily at Siri. 'Who in blazes are you?'

'Dr Siri Paiboun.'

'Egad. What are the odds of there being a bloody doctor in a place like this?' He sat up and shook his head.

'It was a good show. I doubt anyone else would have dared get close enough to smell the toothpaste. I imagine the staff would have thrown you in a truck and carted you off to the medical centre in Xam Neua. But I still don't see what good that would have done you.'

'No? Well, it's simple. There wouldn't have been security in a hospital. I could have sneaked out.'

'And gone where?'

'I don't know, man. Stolen a car? Headed south?'

'You obviously don't realise where you are. There's one road in the direction of Vientiane, and there are some hundred PL and Vietnamese encampments you'd have to pass through on the way. Are you really that desperate to get killed?'

'Better to die fast from a bullet than the slow torture your people have got planned for me.'

'How do you know what we've planned?'

'I'm not stupid. I know how you do it. Hard labour, basic conditions, no access to medicines.'

'I survived for thirty years in those conditions. Why couldn't you?'

'You obviously don't know who I am.'

'Oh, I know very well. But that doesn't answer my question.'

The man shook his head and looked at the window. 'I've never had to fend for myself. Just the merest sniffle and I was pumped full of drugs. I have no natural immune system, no resistance, no stamina.'

'You'd be surprised how quickly your body adapts.'

'No. It will kill me. I'm certain. Listen. The guard will be back as soon as he completes the ridiculous mission you sent him on. How about you and I come to some ... arrangement.'

'Surely you don't mean "financial"?'

'I have access to more money than you could ever imagine. If you could get me to Thailand, I c ...'

'What would I do with money?'

'Do? What would anyone do? Live a comfortable life. Be free.'

Siri laughed. 'If you don't mind my saying so, in your present predicament you're hardly a glowing advertisement for the combination of wealth and freedom. But, good try, boy. You know? You're quite unlike your father.'

'How would you know that?'

'We met. We spent a night together drinking rice whisky and sharing philosophy. I haven't exactly spent a great deal of my life in the company of royalty, unless you count playing cards, but I was impressed. He was a good deal more resigned to fate than you seem to be.'

'He's a defeatist.'

'He's a realist. He was here, wasn't he? And the Queen?'

'They took them away last night. Did you see the room they forced them to stay in? Disgraceful. Goodness knows what awaits them out there in the jungle.'

'You're afraid.'

'Don't be ridiculous.'

'It's nothing to be ashamed of. Fear helps us survive. I've spent a larger portion of my life being afraid than I have being in control. But here I am. Forget this escape idea, son. It won't help you or your family. Play the game. Find a tall tree somewhere, a tree that's survived all the coups and massacres of history. Go to that tree and dig a hole near its roots and bury your pride there. Invest all your royal heritage into the majesty of that great tree, stash it there and become the simple, humble person they'll ask you to be. Suffer the indignities and impress them with your will. Win them over with your humility. I know that's what the King and Queen will attempt to do.'

'I ... I can't.'

'You can. And it will have a deeper and longer lasting impact than any bravado, any heroics, any royal histrionics you have in mind. Show them you're a person with character. They won't know how to respond to that. There's nothing more disheartening to a bully than a man who doesn't get scared.'

Siri picked up the bottle from the floor. The Crown Prince looked forlornly ahead of him. 'Why did they separate us?'

'To break your will. You didn't actually drink any of this, did you.'

'It was empty.'

Siri laughed. 'You see? You're a very resourceful lad. You can survive a hundred re-education camps.'

The guard came running into the room. He held the handles of the steaming pot with rags wrapped around his fingers. The entire kitchen staff was behind him.

'It's done,' the guard said. 'What should I do with it?'

'Throw it down the toilet,' Siri told him. 'Better still, boil some decent vegetables for dinner.'

'What? But you said ...'

'I seem to have performed a medical miracle without it, and brought the prince back to life. There won't be any more problems. We won't have to boil him in oil after all.'

'Thank you. Thank you, Doc. Thank you.' The guard mumbled the words a hundred times. The thanks, of course, were for the preservation of his own skin. He had no interest in the wellbeing of his royal charge.

Before Siri left the room, he saw the bamboo *klooee* on the desk. 'Ah, so this is the weapon that's been inflicting pain on us since we got here. You only know the one tune?' he asked.

'And I can't even get that right.'

'When I see you next, you'll have a thousand tunes of the jungle, and you'll be playing them to the envy of the birds in the trees. Mark my words.' He gripped the prince's arm and smiled at him. 'Give my regards to your father when next you meet. He's an impressive man – with an impressive son.'

8

DIVINE IMPOTENCE

Mr Geung had left the forested mountain slopes and entered a valley that contained the first rice fields he'd seen on his walk. The rice stubble crunched under his feet. Everything seemed so dry, so dead. His country had been politicked into a drought. With every post-revolution month that passed, the Pathet Lao Government was learning how much more difficult it was to run a country of warm bodies than it had been on paper. For ten years in the caves of Huaphan the dream had always been to gain power. As few of the cadres honestly believed that dream would ever come true, no detailed ongoing plans were laid. No practical policy of public appeasement was worked out. Nothing spoiled a good popular uprising more than the presence of people and the need to satisfy their unreasonable demands.

In Laos in 1977, the population was becoming more and more dissatisfied. The new leaders had been given over a year to show what they were capable of, but successes were rare. Some people even dared to suggest that the communists were no better than the royalists. The euphoria of victory was slowly giving way to politburo paranoia, and the measures that resulted from it caused even more dissent. In an effort to discourage large public gatherings, festivals were either cancelled completely or greatly restricted. They were trimmed of religion, culture and superstition, which naturally left very little to celebrate. Dr Siri had compared this with allowing the wearing of spectacles but banning the use of glass lenses.

One such muted celebration had been the March Rocket Festival. Obviously, the combination of disgruntled villagers and large quantities of gunpowder was more than the authorities could tolerate. The government banned gatherings in built-up areas and restricted all the activities to remote fields policed by both uniformed and quite obvious plain-clothed soldiers. Female spirit mediums who normally gave the festival its meaning were barred from attending. There was no alcohol, no raucous music, and all activities had to be completed before nightfall. The amount of powder allowed for each bamboo shaft was so niggardly that many of the home-made rockets barely left their launch pads. They lurched a few metres into the air, then fizzled and fell to earth. There were spontaneous screams of panic from the fleeing onlookers but few cheers of delight.

The consequences of this debacle reached far beyond the disappointed villagers and their wasted day. The Rocket Festival was a fertility rite. The noise and gaiety should have woken the gods of lust from their year-long slumber. The spirit mediums would remind the roused deities that the time had come to send the rains and replenish the paddies. The phallic rockets would stimulate a heavenly orgy and the sexual juices would spill over onto the land. Thus could a rich harvest result.

This was what the villagers believed. The new leaders had no place in their soulless socialist hearts for such mythology. Marxist-Leninist doctrine had no time for fairy tales. Buddhism and animism were sins against rational thought, and logic would always prevail in a communist system. They'd see, these simple folk. The rains would come in April as they always had, and the populace would begin to believe in socialist order. As it turned out, only one thing would spoil that Party line.

The subdued April New Year celebrations passed with the same lack of enthusiasm as had the Rocket Festival. April gave way to May and the gods of fertility still slumbered. The skies remained clear and the rice fields cracked and turned to dust. By June the people had no doubt that the new government was responsible for this unprecedented drought. Socialism had a negative affect on the weather. This was clear in even the most simple of minds. The government's attempts at quelling dissent had only succeeded in exacerbating it.

All Mr Geung knew of this was that the fields crunched, but his new boots made light of the terrain. They'd belonged to the old lady's husband who had no use for them in his funeral pot. They were too small for her son but they fitted Geung to a T and made him feel proud to own them. She'd given him a large pack of dried food and smeared him with a foul-smelling ointment she promised would keep off even the vindictive dengue mosquitoes that plagued the land.

'W ... we should f ... f ... follow the road,' he told Dtui who marched beside him. 'But n ... n ... not be on it.' The old lady had dragged his story from him over breakfast and was sure the embarrassed soldiers would be searching for him.

'Stay close to the road but not on it,' she'd told him. 'If

a car or truck comes from your back that isn't the green of the army, beg them for a ride. Stay away from anything green. Got it?'

The words were embedded but some of the concepts hadn't taken root. 'From your back' was surely confusing, because if he turned round, his back could be anywhere. And as he always looked out through the leaves of trees, it seemed that everything he saw passing along the road was green.

Geung had walked for the whole day. The urgency of returning to the morgue was his drive. He ached. He wheezed. He felt his anxiety rise and fall as if he were riding to Vientiane on the back of a dragon. But when he heard the loud crack and saw the bloodstain appear on the front of his shirt, he was surprisingly calm.

'A ... a ... a bullet wound,' he said as if assessing his state for observers at the morgue. He stood still and watched the red rose grow into a country, one of the countries in Dtui's atlas that she tried to convince him contained millions of people. What tiny tiny people they must have been. The stain had grown to something like the USSR before Geung's eyes grew pale and he dropped like a fence post to the ground.

More panic. More emergencies and disasters. Soon, emergencies fell into a sort of natural seeding; drop everything emergencies, do what you can emergencies, and you'll just have to wait emergencies. Disasters too had their own ratings; unavoidable, did-the-best-we-could, my fault/your fault. Then there were godly moments when a decision had to be made as to who most deserved to die. By the afternoon of her second day, Dtui wondered whether her heart had shrunk. She felt less. People had become less human. Death had become less of a tragedy. Her patients weren't blacksmiths or housewives, they were percentages. 'With this little ability and this little pharmaceutical back up, this patient, let's call her number seven, has a forty per cent chance of survival.'

It amazed and saddened her that, in order to do her job properly, she had to stop caring. With all his years of battlefield surgery, she understood now that Dr Siri must have been working the percentages for a long time. It hadn't made him cold, just philosophical. The burden was less if he lost patients when the odds were against him. Dtui had to play it that way too at Kilometre 8.

The lull came mid-afternoon. They'd sent two up the slope. They'd stabilised three. Dtui was on an adrenalin high that lifted her like a flying carpet. Tired though she was, a sledgehammer to the head couldn't have put her to sleep. She prowled the wards like a large unblinking polar bear. She bullied patients to stay alive, ordered medicines to work. At the end of the ward, the Hmong orderly, Meej, was searching without hope for a vein on the chopstick-thin arm of a patient. Meej was a stocky, good-looking man in his twenties. Like Dtui, his natural expression was a smile.

Dtui massaged the patient's arm until a faint bluish shadow appeared which she speared with the hypodermic. Within seconds the patient was connected to his drip and she steered the intern outside.

'How you feeling?' she asked.

'Drowned,' he confessed.

'You and me both. Just keep a score of the ones you save.

That's how I do it. Don't count the others. They would have gone anyway.'

'All right. Thanks.'

'I wanted to ask you about Mrs Duaning.'

'Is she dead yet?'

'Weak, but holding on. What I was curious about was the blood on her feet.'

'Ah, that. It's an old superstition. The relatives daub blood on the feet if there's something seriously wrong.'

'Medically wrong?'

'Sometimes, or mentally. It keeps the evil spirits out.'

'But this blood appears all by itself.'

Meej laughed. 'No, it doesn't.'

'You know something I don't.'

'The young girl's been here since the day before yesterday. I don't know if she's a relative or just someone from the village. They'd been looking for the old lady. She wandered off one day. The girl arrived here looking for her. She only spent a minute with her then ran off home. She came back a few hours later with three pigs and a machete.'

'How come I haven't seen her?'

'She isn't that comfortable with white medicine. She stays hidden out back. Her role's just to keep the feet bathed in blood till it's all over.'

'Does she know what's wrong with the woman?'

'She didn't say.'

'Do you know where she is?'

'Yes.'

'Can you bring her to me?'

'Well …'

'What's wrong?'

'Could you change out of your white uniform? She's quite certain you're a ghost.'

Dtui looked down at the only uniform she'd thought to bring with her and smiled. It wasn't exactly white any more. 'They make ghosts this big up here? All right. Bring her into Mrs Nuts's room and I'll change out of my ghost disguise.'

Ten minutes later, Meej prodded a girl of around ten into the little ward block where only three heavily drugged patients and Mrs Nuts stayed. The girl was carrying a jam jar in the bottom of which was a fresh batch of blood. Dtui smiled but the girl recoiled at the sight of her even white teeth. 'Do you speak Lao?' Dtui asked.

The girl looked at Meej. 'She doesn't,' he said.

'Then can you ask her what happened to make her run home to get the sacrificial pigs?'

He did. Dtui noticed how all the questions were long and the answers short. 'She says the woman's possessed.'

'How can she be so sure?'

The girl pointed to the woman's mouth, still repeating her weakening chorus. 'That,' she said.

'That what?'

Mrs Nuts was still repeating her lines, over and over in perfect northern Lao dialect.

'She said the old lady can't speak Lao. Not a word of it.'

Dtui raised her eyebrows in surprise and whistled low. 'I see.'

'And there's something else,' Meej told her.

'I doubt it could get any weirder.'

'It does, Nurse Dtui. She said this voice, the voice the old lady's using – it doesn't belong to Mrs Duaning. Someone else is speaking through her mouth.'

Comrade Lit arrived at the guesthouse in the middle of the afternoon and found Dr Siri on the veranda. 'Good health, comrade Doctor.' They shook hands. 'I heard about your miracle cure of our ... houseguest today.'

'Nice to see that the grapevine is still up.'

'I'd like to thank you. It would have been quite difficult if anything had happened.'

'It was nothing, really.'

'Nevertheless, the Party offers its sincere thanks, and ...'

'Out with it.'

'It would be greatly appreciated if the identity of our visitors remained confidential.'

'Darn, and there I was just about to make an announcement over the national radio network. Who in blazes am I going to tell?'

'Particularly, I think it would be beneficial,' he lowered his voice, 'to keep it from your nurse.'

'She's already a security risk?'

'Not ... no, she ... Please.'

'I'll see what I can do. Now, you have some news for me?'

'More than I expected to have,' the tall man said, sitting himself down opposite the doctor. Siri poured him a cup of tea from the flask and left it to cool. 'I've just been speaking to the Immigration Police in Hanoi. I called them yesterday and gave them the names of your Cuban interns. It's taken them all this time to go through the files. You know what it's like. It appears neither man left on the flight they were booked on. In fact there's no record of them leaving at all.'

'But they *were* shipped to Hanoi?'

'They made it that far. They had a military escort. I talked to the driver. He remembers it clearly.'

'So, could we assume they turned round and came back?'

'I don't know. If they did they had to be noticed by someone. I've got my men asking around.'

'Anything about the Vietnamese colonel?'

'His name was Ha Hung. I'm afraid I've come to a dead end on that investigation – literally. The colonel was killed three months before the path was laid.'

'What were the circumstances?'

'Hmong ambush.'

'And what happened to his daughter?'

'I don't know. They told me his family went back to Vietnam after the old man's death. They won't be easy to trace.'

'Could you try for me?'

'Certainly. Anything else?'

'Dr Santiago will be dropping by here on his way to Kilometre 8 Hospital. I've asked him to take a look at our mummy. See if he recognises him.'

'Hmm. I doubt even the great Dr Santiago could identify what's left of that. I'm sure he'd be too busy chasing around young girls barely old enough to be his grand-daughters.' Siri noted the animosity but wasn't really interested enough to dig down to its roots. Lit looked around. 'I can't help but notice the absence of Nurse Dtui at our last two meetings. I hope it doesn't have anything to do with my putting her straight the other day.'

'Son, let me put it this way. You may very well be able to domesticate a gibbon by repeatedly whacking it over the head with a hammer, but people respond less kindly to concussion.'

'It's one of my duties to educate.'

'You don't beat people up with a philosophy, young fellow. You warm them to it gradually.'

'You think I was a little too heavy-handed?'

'I'm sorry to say you're mired in the shattered cranium school of mentoring. Take it a little easier in future and I'm certain you'll have more success.'

'Was Nurse Dtui upset? Is that why she isn't here?'

'Dtui's got a much thicker skin than that. No, she's helping out at Kilometre 8 until the new Cuban doctors get here.'

'She is quite remarkable.'

The comment surprised Siri. 'I thought you didn't like her.'

'On the contrary, Doctor. I've been more than impressed from the very beginning. I admit she lacks discipline, but …'

Siri waited for the 'but' to go somewhere but it just dangled. 'I'll be sure to tell her when I see her this afternoon.'

'You're going out there?'

'I'll go with Santiago. I'd be interested to see where the Cubans were billeted, ask around, you know?'

'And you'll be sure to let me know if you find anything?'

'Of course.'

'The Central Administration was most distressed to learn the victim might have been Cuban. Their delegation naturally wants this cleared up as soon as possible. There's a politburo member coming from Havana for the concert. I'd like to have the culprit locked up by then. I think I should come by and see you this evening.'

'Actually I'm planning to stay out at the hospital tonight.'

'What on earth for?'

'Oh, I might be able to help a little bit, and it would be nice to get some sleep. That confounded discotheque dance has managed to wake me up every night since I got here.'

Lit laughed. 'Doctor, this is Vieng Xai.'

'So?'

'So there hasn't been a dance here since the senior members all left for the capital. That's why next week's concert is such a big deal.'

'Comrade Lit, I hear it. I feel the vibration of the speakers.'

'Perhaps it's a radio or someone's record player. What type of music is it?'

'That annoying American rubbish. The type they used to bounce up and down to in the hotel nightclubs in the old days.'

'Well, I'll look into it for you, Doctor. We certainly don't want our youth polluting their minds with decadent Western pop. But believe me, Dr Siri, there never has been a discotheque in Vieng Xai and as far as I'm concerned, there never will be.'

At the wheel of his yellow jeep, Santiago arrived at Kilometre 8, like every good swashbuckling hero, with a screech of brakes and in a cloud of dust. The beleaguered interns came out to greet him all sighing with temporary relief. Only one person there knew who the little white-haired man in the passenger seat was. While the rest of the staff gathered around Santiago, Dtui strolled over to Dr Siri.

He smiled at her ruffled look. 'How's it going, Nurse?'

She laughed a sort of desperate laugh. 'How many years did you do this?'

Siri climbed from the jeep and wiped the dust from his face with an old towel. 'It gets easier after the seventeenth year.'

'This is my second day and I'm a wreck.'

They walked into the ward and Siri briefly summarised those two days from his point of view. 'And Santiago seems quite certain the body is that of Odon, the smaller of the two interns.'

'Did you ask him about the parallel scars?'

'I pointed them out to him and I noticed a look of ... I don't know, not fear exactly, but some darkness came over him. Don't forget we can't speak to each other so I'm looking forward to your translation later tonight. Meanwhile, what's to be done here?'

Siri and Santiago were a formidable team. Dtui followed them on their rounds and assisted them in the four operations they performed. Everything seemed so much more straightforward in their hands. By eight, the wards were settled and the staff was sitting around a table eating a dinner of baked lemur and sticky rice. Santiago preferred to save his comments about the tribal markings until the three of them were alone, so Dtui entertained them with the story of Mrs Nuts. Both surgeons were so fascinated by the tale they went to the sleeping ward the second they'd finished their meal. Dtui was saddened to see how pale the old lady had become. Still she spoke in her stolen voice although now the words floated painfully on laboured breaths. They had to lean close to catch them and her breath was rank with decay.

Santiago asked what she was saying.

'She says "almost too late",' Dtui told him.

'What is?' Siri asked.

'I think she means she won't be around for much longer.'

But Siri believed otherwise. The amulet around his neck was warm against his skin. It seemed to vibrate as if it were receiving an incoming call. The doctor was starting to recognise its signals. He took the old woman's hand in his and held the amulet in his other. Images fell into his mind that he knew weren't his own.

'Dtui, remember what I say,' he called, and began to describe what he saw. 'Bushes, chest high. I'm falling. Water trickling. Concrete. All of this surrounded by darkness. A door, a very thick metal door, green, too heavy to budge. Hands. Small white hands. My own, like I'm looking down at myself. There's blood on them.'

And then, as if the line were suddenly cut, Siri saw nothing at all. He opened his eyes and the old woman was silent. He knew she was dead. 'What did I say?' he asked Dtui.

'You don't know?'

'Not at all.'

Dtui went through the list as accurately as she could, then translated for Santiago, who seemed to have no idea what he'd just witnessed. She told him she'd explain everything later but wanted to know whether anything Siri had seen sounded familiar to him. He shrugged and concluded that bushes and water could be any place.

'All right. Let's start with bushes.' Siri took control. 'Is there anyone on staff who's lived here all their life?' After a consultation they came up with Nang, a jittery nursing orderly who still fainted from time to time at the sight of blood. She seemed delighted to discuss something that wasn't related to surgery. What Siri wanted to know about was fruit. He didn't have the sample with him but he was able to describe the berry he'd crushed in his room at the guesthouse. The others all looked on bemused as the two tried to give it a name.

'Monkey ball plums,' said the girl. 'That's what you're talking about.'

'And where can they be found?' Siri asked.

'It's all over if you know where to look. It grows on the karsts. They pay well for it at the market so a lot of village people go looking for them. More than a few people have been blown up out scrounging for monkey ball plums.'

'Can you get it around here?'

'Of course, at certain times of the year. All the mountains at Kilometre 8 have bushes.'

'Do you want to share what this is all about, Doc?' Dtui asked.

'Clues,' Siri told her. 'We mustn't ignore any clues. Like the green door. Ask Santiago again if there are any green doors in his memory.'

She did just that and watched the Cuban flick mentally through all the doors he'd known in his life. At last he asked her whether she was sure it was green and not blue. She asked Siri but he had no recollection at all of his vision.

'If we say blue,' Dtui asked, 'would that make any difference?'

Santiago told her that indeed it would. The bomb doors at the old hospital were heavy metal, but they were blue.

'And where is the old hospital?'

He pointed through the window to the black shape of the mountain. It stood out from the indigo sky, looming over them like a giant crow.

She translated for Siri, who knew the hospital well. They'd moved everything down from there to the original buildings and shut up the old place. There was no way in. The bomb-proof doors had been locked to keep out inquisitive children from the middle school down the hill. But in his mind all the pieces fitted together, the berries, the water and the concrete.

'Who has the key?' he asked.

Still confused by events, Santiago took them to the administration office, unlocked the desk drawer and rifled through the bunches of keys till he found the one that should have opened the old hospital padlock. From the store cupboard he took a machete and three battery packs that powered headband-mounted lamps that would leave their hands free. He led the way along the overgrown path that snaked up to the nearest entrance to the hospital. The door was twenty centimetres thick and hadn't been opened for a few years. It took the combined effort of all three pulling on the handle to budge it enough to squeeze through the gap.

A sad, musty odour escaped as they entered. The secret vents drilled above had clogged with weeds and the air they walked into was old. The histories of the hospital's victims still clung to the place. But Siri recognised something else deep inside its unrelenting blackness – the smell of a recent death. Dtui took a little longer to identify the scent, but she soon came to realise they were too late to save whomever had breathed their last in this cold man-made cavern. She and Siri switched on their batteries and the three headlight beams swept back and forth across twelve hundred square metres of grey stone. The old doctors had spent many hours inside this hidden chamber so the only thing that surprised them was the absence of sound, no scurrying of animals, no chirping of bats. It was as if nature had been too afraid to take over the vacated premises.

But Dtui stood open-mouthed at the sight before her, amazed that in wartime, under a barrage of bombing, such an incredible feat of construction could have been achieved. In the concrete floor, conduits allowed natural water from the surrounding mountains to pass through the cavern. There were operating rooms and offices off the main chamber and cleverly designed latrines that allowed effluent to flow away from the ward. Then, the beam of her lamp caught a shape in the centre of the vast concrete floor. It was a body, crumpled. Its limbs were bent in impossible angles. As they walked towards it they could make out a woman in her early twenties. From the state of her they could tell she'd been dead more than twenty-four hours.

Directly above her, weeds dangled from one of the engineered vents, a perfectly round hole some two metres across. Siri knew the vent angled upward to a spot on the mountain slope, invisible from the sky, where fresh air would be drawn into the hospital by means of a pump. The pump was long gone, and all that remained was a hole, an unseen hole into which some unsuspecting woman collecting berries might drop.

Santiago bent over the body and looked at the dead woman. Dtui translated the words he spoke.

'The doctor's very impressed. He really wants to know how you were able to find her. But he's sorry to say that your clever trick was too late to help Miss Panoy.'

'No,' Siri said, strafing his beam across the cavern. 'This isn't Panoy. I'm certain it was the spirit of this woman reaching us through the old Hmong, but she wasn't talking about herself. She had to be dead to communicate. There must be someone else here.'

Dtui passed on the message to Santiago. Without questioning, he joined them in a continued search. The water in the old aqueduct had been diverted to the village at the foot of the mountain but the open drains still remained. Water still trickled through them. In some spots they were a metre deep, and that was where Panoy lay. Santiago found her. He called her name and immediately dropped down into the channel beside her. She was about four years old. She was seriously injured and weak from hunger, but miraculously she was still alive.

Santiago called up to the others that he believed she could be saved. He climbed from the trench with the girl in his arms and walked quickly through the blue door. Dtui and Siri couldn't keep up with him. They stood at the entrance and watched the energetic old Cuban scurry down the slope to the hospital. Dtui put her arm around Siri's shoulder and smiled at him.

'Nice one, Dr Siri. How do we explain all this to Santiago?'

'Much as I appreciate the benefits of a good lie, I fear we may have to tell him the truth.'

'You sure? Lying might be easier.'

'Oh, I don't think that skinny old lion will have a problem with this. I get the feeling he's seen it all before.'

She turned her head and her light beam drilled into the metal door beside them. 'Tell me something. What colour's this, Doc?'

'Green.'

'You're colour blind, aren't you?'

'If this isn't green I suppose I must be. I dread to think what else Mrs Nuts might have passed on to me.'

Panoy was remarkably resilient considering what she'd been through. There wasn't much they could do about her cracked ribs but they reset both of her arms and an ankle, stitched a couple of large gashes, and put her on an intravenous drip that would slowly replenish her lost energy. Meej stayed with her to check her vital signs through the night.

Siri, Santiago and Dtui sat beneath the night sky. It was cold enough for jackets but not so uncomfortable they needed to light a fire. The rice whisky worked well enough to keep the blood flowing. Siri had sat like a bystander while Dtui with her hard-worked dictionary and a flashlight had attempted to explain Siri's connection to the spirit world. She told Santiago about the thousand-year-old shaman called Yeh Ming Siri unwittingly hosted. She told him the spirit was patiently waiting for Siri's peaceful and natural death so he could retire from the shaman business. She told him about the teeth and the dreams and the white talisman he wore to keep away the evil spirits. All Siri could do during this confession was watch the reaction of his old friend. It was difficult to read, as if he were organising the information into compartments. At the end of it, the Cuban looked at Siri for a few seconds with an expression of pity, the way you'd look at someone who'd lost a relative. He pulled the perennial cigarette from between his lips and surrounded his head with a halo of smoke. Then there was a glint, perhaps of admiration and, quite out of the blue, Santiago began to laugh. He refilled their glasses and patted his colleagues on the back as if this were the best news he'd heard in a long time.

Then, Siri was once again sidelined for a good five minutes while Santagio took his turn to tell another story. Dtui interrupted often to clarify points, looked shocked here, fascinated there, and at the end she sighed and raised her eyebrows. Then, there was silence.

'What? What is it?' Siri said, notably flustered at being left out.

'Oh, hello, Doc. You still there?' She smiled. 'Look, I tell you what. I'm a bit tired...'

'Nurse Chundee Vongheuan, if you don't tell me right this minute I shall slap you with a damp possum.'

She giggled. 'Only joking, Doc. Keep your toupee on.' She took a sip of her whisky and settled back to begin Santiago's story. 'It looks like now the old fellow knows how weird you are, he suddenly feels confident enough to tell you what really happened here. It seems there was more to the two orderlies than meets the eye. He was afraid if he told you everything you'd think he was nuts, so he's happy we can all be nuts together now.' Santiago obviously couldn't follow her translation but he smiled and looked at Dtui as if he were enjoying the story anew. He threw back another mouthful of whisky like a fire eater about to blow forth a torrent of flames.

'The way I read it is like this,' Dtui said. 'In Cuba they have their own shamans and strong connections to the spirit world. There are a lot of big cults and little cults. Many of the priests for these cults are phony. But there are some that really communicate with the spirits.'

'Does Dr Santiago actually believe this?' Siri asked.

Santiago laughed again when the question reached him.

'So he says. He strongly believes in the spirit world. He says he's seen too much in his life that has no scientific explanation. He says if you like he could spend the next two weeks telling you all the rites of Palo and, what was it? Santeria?' She looked at Santiago who nodded. 'We don't want him to do that, do we?'

'I think not.'

'Good. Then I'll just keep to the point: why he sent the Cubans home. It wasn't only because Isandro was fooling around with the local girls. That was a good excuse, something he could write in a report without them laughing at him in Havana. But there were other reasons. He was happy with the work they did, so obviously the things he found out about them had to be serious enough for him to sacrifice two valuable nursing assistants.'

She stopped.

'Well, what were they, these reasons?'

'He didn't tell me.'

'What?'

'He says he'll take us to their cave in the morning and show us for ourselves. Frustrating, isn't it?'

'Painfully so.'

No amount of pleading and sulking would force the Cuban to change his plan, so all three finished their night-caps and retired to their allotted sleeping spaces in the nearby middle-school classrooms.

Siri had been shown his spot earlier where several nylon quilts were laid out for him at the front of a year-two class-room at the school. Someone had chalked 'welcome visitor' on the blackboard. But as he approached the room now, he noticed that the door was open and he heard peculiar sounds from inside. Desks were being shifted. Something dropped to the floor and broke. Breaths, deep inhuman snorts. He considered going for help but realised he didn't know what he needed help from. He grasped the amulet through his shirt and strode to the doorway.

In the light of a small orange candle someone had left burning for him on the teacher's desk, Siri saw a most bizarre scene. There were five buffalo in the small room each apparently vying for a position at the front by the blackboard. One creature had leaned against the chalk and was branded with the message 'welcome visitor'. Two had already claimed their places of honour and lay on the dirt floor either side of Siri's quilt like enormous Dutch wives. All five looked up at him when he entered the classroom and, as far as creatures with no upper teeth are able, they smiled.

9

A WART ON THE HOG

Mr Geung's eyes opened slowly. There were no sharp edges anywhere. Colours seemed to bleed together. He knew it was morning because a cock was crowing and the sun was throwing out threads of light like a spider building the web of a new day. He'd woken with the sunrise for most of the mornings of his life, but never here, never like this. This was, what? Not a house because there were no walls – but a roof. People were sleeping around him. He shifted, but one side of him was stiff. He ached numbly as if something heavy had slept on half of his chest. He looked down to see himself fully dressed – boots and all – to the waist. His upper body was naked except for a long dirty pink bandage that wound tightly around his chest, his neck and his upper arm. He touched the bandage tentatively, knowing it didn't use to be there and wondering what it was for. When his fingers reached a place by his left shoulder he winced. Something serious had happened there. He didn't remember the shot or the blood, only that he had to get to Vientiane to look after the morgue. He sat up.

'Hey, Kum,' he heard. 'He's up.'

One of the bodies sleeping under the wall-less roof stirred from its place on the ground and came to Geung's side. He was a man of around Geung's own height with sun-darkened skin and short spiky hair. Across his shoulder was a belt of bullets which Geung considered must have been terribly uncomfortable to sleep in. The man's voice sounded bruised.

'How you feeling?'

'I ... I'm good,' Geung told him.

The man turned his back and yelled across to the colleague who'd spoken first. 'He says he's all right. He can talk.'

'Yeah, some of 'em do,' came the reply.

Spiky Hair spoke slowly as if Geung were of another species. 'I shot you. Do you understand?'

Geung looked at the pink bandage and nodded. The memory was slowly returning.

'I'm sorry,' the man continued. 'It was a mistake. I thought you were ... Well, no. I didn't know what you were. I just shot. If I'd known you were ... like you are, I would never ...'

'Get him to forgive you,' came the floor-bound voice. Slowly, other bodies were beginning to stir.

'I need you to forgive me,' Spiky Hair said. 'I can't afford to lose any more credits. You understand? You could really mess up my karma. Buddha's pissed off enough already that I've resorted to thieving. But he was getting used to the idea till you come along. Now I'm back in the shits. You forgiving me would really help get me back in the good books.'

Geung didn't really have a clue what the man was talking about. 'Who ... o ... o're you?' he asked.

Spiky Hair sat beside Geung and sighed. Forgiveness always came at a cost. 'I used to be a soldier,' he whispered. 'Except I was on the wrong side. Now, I'm ... now we're what they call opportunists. You know? We wait for trucks and convoys that aren't too seriously guarded and we sort of ask them if they can help us out with a few *kip*. We were lying in wait in the field when you crept up and spooked me. You know? I thought you were after us. I didn't know you were ... how you are, honest.'

'C ... can I go?'

'Go? Go where?'

'Vientiane.'

'That's a damned long way.'

'I promised.'

'Look, I'm not sure you're up to that journey, brother. I mean there's no infection. The bullet wasn't that big and it went right through you. You hollered like a wild sow when we scrubbed at it with white spirit but I reckon we cleaned it up all right. You're going to ache for a while.'

'C ... can I g ... go?'

Spiky Hair shouted back over his shoulder. 'He wants to go.'

'Then let him go.'

'What if he dies on the way?'

'Not your problem. Once he's out of here you're off the hook.'

'Why don't you just forget all that religious crap,' someone else said. 'You're a bandit. You'll never get close enough to sniff nirvana.'

'No. Don't say that.' Spiky Hair looked desperately at Geung and asked again, 'Do you forgive me?'

'Okay.'

'Really? Thanks. That's big of you.'

To show his gratitude, Spiky Hair put together some rations and walked a few kilometres with Geung. The effects of the opium started to wear off and Geung grimaced with each step. Soon they were picking their way through thick vegetation that teemed with insects and wildlife. Lizards scurried out of their path and squirrels climbed out of reach.

'Where's the r ... road?' Geung asked.

'Road? You don't need a road. I thought you people were like dogs, just followed your noses.'

Geung turned to him, bristling. 'I ... I'm no dog.'

'Okay, take it easy.'

'No dog.' His face turned pink with indignation.

'All right. Gee. I'm sorry. Listen. If you follow the road it'll add another hundred kilometres to your trip. Understand? The thing winds all over the place. Just keep the sun on your left shoulder blade in the morning and your right tit in the afternoon. That should put you on a straight line.'

'I'm no dog.'

'I get it. You aren't really paying attention, are you?'

'Well, I ... I'm not.'

They walked on but it was another twenty minutes before Geung forgave Spiky Hair for calling him a dog. Shooting him was one thing. Calling him a dog was another thing completely. By then the guide had come up with a plan to make the instructions clearer. The supplies he'd prepared for Geung were in a cloth shoulder bag on a long strap. As the gunshot wound was on the right, he hooked the bag over Geung's left shoulder to hang at his right hip. He explained that the sun should climb up the back of the strap in the morning and down the front in the afternoon. He made up a little song that just happened to rhyme.

'The sun wakes up and climbs my back,
At evening drops into my sack.'

They must have sung it a thousand times by the time they reached the foot of the Kuang Si Waterfall. Spiky Hair still wasn't sure the boy had got the idea, although he certainly knew the song well enough. He filled a canteen from the clear stream and put it in the pack with its stolen food and a supply of opium for when the shoulder started to act up. He made Geung promise not to take all the opium at the same time but Geung reminded him he wasn't stupid.

'No, of course not,' said Spiky Hair as he turned back and left Geung to his own devices. 'Keep to the footpaths,' he said. He had little faith the boy would make it to Vientiane but it didn't matter. The bandit had made enough merit to compensate for that. Even a donkey would have more sense than to set off on a two-hundred-and-fifty kilometre trek on a day as dry as a dead man's scrotum.

Panoy made it through the night. Her breath was shallow but her vital signs looked promising. Dtui felt confident enough to leave her for an hour and walk with the doctors to the complex that had once housed the Cuban workers. During the height of the bombing, some two hundred villagers had also spent their days in this network of caves that riddled the large karsts about a kilometre from the hospital. Nowadays only the front section was used – for storage and for keeping fodder dry in the rainy season. The rest was deserted.

As they neared the caves, Santiago told Dtui about the resilience of the locals in the face of massive offensives. The natives always seemed to have smiles on their faces during the air raids. He laughed as he told her how, early in the conflict, the American Secretary of State had described Vietnam as a hog. When asked about Laos he'd said the place was no more than a wart on that hog. 'But look,' Santiago said, 'how much trouble that little wart made for the great Americanos.'

When they arrived at the front of the cave, Santiago introduced them to the Sheraton. It was even chalked there on the overhang: *Sheraton de Lao*. They'd brought their headlamps with them once again and they switched them on as they walked through reception. It was a large high-ceilinged cavern where most of the locals had stayed. Santiago led them through to a smaller room that was once the home of the Cuban contingent. It was empty now and there were no posters or mementos or signs of life other than a few chalk calendars here and there.

Santiago had stayed here when the work was going on at the hospital, he told them. It was a joint Vietnamese–Cuban project but the Viets had their own cave and they didn't mix very much with the Cubans. It was on this project he first met and locked horns with comrade Lit. Before he was promoted to become the head of security for the region, Lit had been the overseer for the Vietnamese engineers. The Cubans had arrived with skills and a good deal of knowledge, but from the beginning, Lit seemed to treat them like country bumpkins – no better than assistants. When his superiors informed Lit he was supposed to take orders from Dr Santiago, that the doctor was to run the hospital project, he lost face. It was the doctor's view that Lit had never been able to forgive him for that.

Dtui was having trouble keeping up with his asides so Santiago agreed to simplify both his language and his explanations. He told them how, in the beginning, he hadn't seen the *negritos* as much more than friendly men, always in a happy mood. They worked hard and were good at their jobs. But Santiago had started to hear rumours, bad rumours from his staff. His country had a tradition of black magic all the way back to Africa. He told them about a belief known as Palo Mayombe. It was a popular myth in Cuba that Palo remedies could cure all ills. They could find you love and even change the ugly into the beautiful. Dr Santiago joked that he obviously hadn't sampled that particular remedy.

In general the remedies did no harm. A lot of Cubans tried them just as the average person in Laos might read a horoscope. Many visited their shaman for counselling and an excuse for a chat. There were some famous Palo Mayombe shamans who were known to perform incredible miracles. Most did only good for their communities. But there was a small cult, a branch of Palo, which was very dark. It was known as Endoke, a word derived from the name of the darkest spirit. It was here that the practices of sacrificing and bloodletting became common. Santiago told of patients he knew who had suffered as a result of Endoke practices. He swore he had never seen anything so cruel.

Standing, as they were, in an eerie cave where the only light came from their own foreheads, and the sound of water dripping echoed all around them, Santiago's story was starting to give Dtui the creeps. Her translation suffered accordingly.

'So,' Siri said. 'The rumours were that the two men, Odon and Isandro, were practising Endoke in some way.'

Dr Santiago said that was exactly what he'd heard. At

first he did nothing about it. He knew how Cubans liked to make up stories, just like the Lao or the Vietnamese, to entertain their friends around a campfire, or to scare the children to keep them from wandering off. But one day, one of the nurses came to him and led him deep into the mountain in which they now stood. Santiago told Siri and Dtui to follow him and walked off into the darkness.

The caves spider-legged back into the karst, getting narrower as they went. Dtui looked forlornly at Siri. Only a few months earlier the pair had been involved in a horrific case that took them into tunnels such as these. Very few sane people would knowingly set off down dark passages again before that trauma had worked its way out of their systems. Siri paused and looked back at the nurse.

'Are you up for this?'

'You know me, Doc. Anything for a laugh,' she answered without convincing either of them. They scurried after Santiago's retreating light beam, Siri bringing up the rear. Fortunately, they didn't have to venture too deep into the mountain. Santiago seemed to know his way around the caves and they soon found themselves at their destination.

The Cuban stopped and stood back, letting the light beam do the explaining for him. They were at a dead end that formed a natural altar with a ledge. Unreadable symbols were chalked on the wall and mud had been fashioned into a sort of ornate frame around them. Siri took a step forward and shone his light onto the ledge. He leaned over and sniffed at the dark stain that began on the shelf and dribbled down in parallel lines from its edge.

Santiago confirmed that it was blood – this was a sacrificial altar. When he'd first seen it there had been other artefacts around it. There had been some sort of cauldron, he said, but someone seemed to have removed everything.

Dtui scrunched up her nose. 'Well, at least this ledge isn't wide enough to sacrifice people on.'

Santiago told her there was no need. For the most basic Endoke spells all they needed were chickens and pigs.

'So, apart from cruelty to animals, and depletion of food stocks,' Dtui suggested to Siri, 'Isandro and Odon weren't exactly dangerous.'

But when she translated her comment for the Cuban, he became quite heated. He took Dtui's hand in his and told her that to realise just how dangerous they were, she had to understand some of the magic of Endoke. The blood from the animals that they sacrificed was fundamental for their curses. These spells were heavy black magic, often arising out of the desire for revenge. Endoke was a magic of vengeance. If you stole a man's wife he could put a curse on you. If you killed a man's brother, he could damn you in a way that was even worse than death. Never should you cross an Endoke priest.

Dtui had just asked whether Santiago believed these two men were priests when, from the corner of her eye, she noticed Siri's hand reach for the amulet beneath his shirt as he stared back into the darkness. Santiago was looking towards the altar when he replied and missed this move-ment. He told her he believed that the markings she found on their mummy were known as 'the scratches'. They were a symbol of those who practised the dark arts. He said that he'd been able to learn many things about Isandro and Odon once he'd discovered the altar. He had finally confronted them in his office one day and forced them to show him the marks on their chests.

'How many?' Siri asked. He'd removed his flashlight band and was squinting back in the direction from which they'd walked.

Dtui didn't even bother to translate the question. 'Three on each side, Doc. Come on. Keep up. I've told ...' She suddenly realised the question wasn't directed towards her. Siri wasn't involved in their conversation at all. She shone her head beam back into the empty tunnel. The light seemed to snap Siri out of a trance.

'One of them is coming,' he said, this time to Dtui.

'One of who?'

'The spirits of the *negritos*.'

She was reluctant to translate this but she owed it to Santiago who was confused by the distraction. The old doctor seemed to take the news even worse than she did. He backed up against the altar, his olive black eyes flitting back and forth across the darkness.

'Should we do anything?' Dtui whispered.

'No,' Siri told her, still looking back into the empty tunnel. 'She says there's nothing for us to worry about.'

Dtui didn't even want to know who 'she' was. She took hold of Siri's arm and held her breath. Behind her she could hear the Cuban muttering. She moved her head from side to side but her flashlight was useless for what took place next. Only Siri could see the visitor. He was naked and black as pitch. His face was a gathering of ill-matched features. He came loping urgently towards Siri and stood in front of him. Although Siri assumed this was the smaller of the two, he still had to tilt his head upwards to look into the man's empty eyes. And there they stood, neither seeming to know what to do next. The black man grew angry with frustration. For some reason he seemed to be looking over

Siri's shoulder at Dtui with unconcealed fury. He slowly raised his fist as if to strike her and bared his teeth.

'Dtui, step back with Santiago,' Siri shouted.

She did as she was told even though all she could see was Siri standing with his neck craned upward and his arms out to his sides. He clenched his fists and shuddered slightly. The shudder grew in intensity, more like the vibration of a silent truck engine. She and Santiago looked on with astonishment as Siri started to shake with such violence they knew there had to be an external force exerting itself on him. Fearing for his safety, Dtui stepped forward again and threw her arms around the doctor. All the strength she could muster didn't stop the shuddering.

Then all at once, he went limp in her arms and she lowered him to the ground. There were several seconds during which there was no movement, no sound. Dtui put her hand in front of Siri's mouth but felt no breath. Then, just as suddenly as he had collapsed, his eyes opened and he gave her a friendly smile.

'Nurse Dtui, you really will have to resist these urges to throw yourself at me.'

'I have a weakness for men who wobble,' she said.

Santiago, pale as limestone, came over to take a look at his old friend. He checked first Siri's pulse, then his own. Siri looked as if he'd been in a fight. There was a mysterious bruising about his face that stood out against his drained white skin. Dtui looked into his pupils. As she held him, his strength gradually returned and, before her eyes, the bruises faded.

'Now, that was an impressive recovery. I think you'll live, Dr Siri,' she said.

'Sorry about all that.'

'You saw something, didn't you?'

'Yes, indeed I did.'

'What did it say?'

'Nothing.'

'But it did something to you.'

'Dtui, I may be wrong about this, but I do believe one of our Cuban friends just took up residence in me.'

That, she didn't translate.

There were three things Spiky Hair had forgotten to mention when he sent Mr Geung off on a beeline for Vientiane. One was that the reason the road took such a mammoth detour was to avoid the Kuang Si foothills, some of which had a gradient too steep even for goats. No sooner had Geung huffed and puffed his way over one, another loomed ahead of him.

One more thing Spiky had omitted was, given that Geung was orienting himself by the sun on his bag strap, what he should do if the sky became overcast. In the beginning he just stopped, sat, and waited till the cloud passed. But as he got higher the clouds got thicker and his guiding sun made fewer and fewer appearances. His waits got longer to the point that by 3PM he'd stopped completely. It was a dilemma. He knew he had to keep moving but not in which direction. Every hill looked the same. Any one of them could have been the one he'd just crossed. There were no landmarks. Every tree looked the same.

And then there was the third thing. It was a whopper, and was probably the most costly omission. Despite the efforts of hungry villagers and traffickers and traders in animal pelts or exotic organs, these hills still teemed with wild beasts. If ever they should meet him, most of them would be more afraid of Mr Geung than he was of them. But the tigress that had stalked him from the waterfall wasn't afraid at all. She had cubs to feed and she'd travelled far to find game. The human was meaty enough and he was heading almost directly towards her lair. It was as if she'd ordered room service and it was delivering itself.

10

THE MILLION-SPIDER ELVIS SUIT

Siri returned to Guesthouse Number One. Santiago dropped him off and, as usual, said several things that Siri didn't understand. Siri said something equally incomprehensible and they parted company with a friendly handshake and a lot of laughter.

While they were still together with Dtui at Kilometre 8, Santiago had submitted all the circumstantial evidence that had combined to convince him that Isandro and Odon were dabbling in ugly magic. It was quite compelling. Two cases specifically were particularly hard to explain away. The first was that of a Vietnamese woman who had come to Vieng Xai with the Vietnamese engineers. She cooked for them and did their laundry. As it turned out, she was an incurable racist. She believed that black-skinned people were barely a rung above the ape on the ladder of evolution and had no qualms about voicing her opinions. Whenever she saw the two Cubans around the hospital area she would quite proudly call them monkeys. As she believed they lacked the intellect to speak her language she even went to the trouble of miming her views for them.

She was an average-looking woman with an unpleasant personality, but lonely men in a foreign country tended to overlook such flaws. So it transpired that the woman fell pregnant. She claimed it was a miracle, a divine conception, and as none of the men stepped forward to voluntarily claim paternity, one by one the local people started to believe her. After all, they thought this would be the perfect opportunity for her to finger some randy soldier and blackmail him into marriage. Yet she swore to the last she was still a virgin.

Santiago had been away on the early morning she was carried into the hospital. It was her seventh month and something had gone horribly wrong. The young Lao surgeon on duty that night believed the only way to stop her haemorrhaging was to remove the foetus. It was his call and nobody later came to question his judgement. But the woman had died on the operating table. When Santiago returned, the Lao surgeon was inconsolable. He found the boy drunk mid-morning and ranting. Nothing the old doctor could do was able to calm him. He knew this was far more than a doctor's grief at losing a patient. There had to be something more. Santiago talked to the staff nurse. She told him how the surgeon had ordered her out of the theatre before she could get a look at the foetus. He'd carried it himself up to the cave of the dead where it was to be cremated the following night. Santiago, intrigued by the story, had gone up to the cave and there he found a burlap sack small enough to contain the Vietnamese woman's baby. What he discovered inside was not human. In the sack was the incomplete foetus of an ape.

Both Siri and Dtui felt they'd been spun a late campfire horror yarn, but the teller was impressively calm and sincere. His second tale was no less peculiar. A Party cadre had come from Havana to make an official appraisal of how Cuban aid was being spent in one of the country's few overseas humanitarian projects. He was due to stay for a week, check the books and return. It was quite straightforward, but he was an observant man and not without some experience of Palo ways. It also appears he had some sixth sense which he chose not to develop. He was committed to the Cuban Communist Party and had no desire to complicate his life with magic. The Party had taught him that shamanism was one more opiate for a people who would be better off drunk on socialism.

In Vieng Xai, the bookkeeper evidently saw something that concerned him and he decided to discuss it with Santiago. They had an appointment to meet one evening at eight, but at seven Isandro came to Santiago's office to tell him the bookkeeper had been struck down by some affliction. He was clutching his throat and unable to speak. The director went to the man's bedside and could see he was in agony. They rushed him immediately to the theatre where Santiago performed an emergency tracheotomy. There was no evidence of disease or trauma in the respiratory tract so the surgeon had to conclude the man's breathing was laboured as a result of some intense pain. After several more exploratory incisions, Santiago found the cause of his problem. The bookkeeper's epiglottis had turned to wood – more accurately, some hard substance like the stone of a small peach. The surgeon had no choice but to remove it. They sent the bookkeeper home in a deep coma. When they were putting together his belongings to ship back to Havana, they found a slip of paper in his bag. On it were the names of the two interns, and beside them the man had doodled various Endoke symbols.

Although the monkey foetus story had been second-hand

and, to some extent, conjecture, the doctor had seen this other bizarre happening for himself. It was shortly after this that Santiago discovered the altar, confronted Isandro and Odon and insisted they return to Cuba.

Siri had wanted to know, if the two men were so powerful, why Santiago wasn't afraid of retribution himself. The Cuban had smiled broadly and slowly begun to unbutton his shirt. Siri and Dtui were astounded by what they saw. A necklace of talismans hung there like a mayoral chain of office against his undershirt. This esteemed man of science was adorned with a lei of talismans, dried flowers, nuggets of metal, teeth and carefully placed knots. It was a wonder he could stand upright under its weight. Siri's single white amulet paled by comparison.

Santiago openly admitted his fear of the two Endoke priests. He was only too aware of what retribution they could wreak on him. Siri had felt oddly comforted that he wasn't the only man of learning forced to use magic to stay alive.

In his room, Siri began to undress before heading down to the shower. Since his experience at the altar he had felt peculiar. Strange desires were welling up in him. Normally he spent as little time out of his clothes as he could, but today he felt an odd hankering to look at himself in the closet mirror. This was something he'd avoided doing for a number of years. He was no picture. They wouldn't ever cast a statue of him. But, for some reason, he felt a surge of pride as he looked at his solid frame. If he dyed his hair he could pass for, what? Sixty? Fifty-five? He was strong, virile even. Today, for some reason, he believed he could break rocks with his bare fists, rip the husks off coconuts with his fingers.

He let his grey PL issue undershorts drop to the floor and he strode up and down the room, straight-backed and butt naked. He let his penis swing from side to side, flexed his biceps, bared his teeth at ...

'Can I get you some more tea?' The kitchen lady was standing in the doorway. He hadn't heard the door open. In her hand she held a thermos. She looked at him sadly as if he were a dementia victim who had lost track of his trousers. 'Are you all right, uncle?'

Siri grabbed the quilt from the spare bed and wrapped it around himself. 'I'm fine. Thank you.'

An hour later, respectfully dressed now but no less embarrassed, he was back up at the President's house. Once more he was standing over the dissected mummy. He'd never revisited a body so many times, but this particular victim continued to change personality the more he learned about him. Two things still worried Siri. If the *negritos* had been sent home, what was Odon doing back at the President's cave a month later? And, if you were being violently beaten and held under concrete, what would possess you to hang on to a key? Surely you'd need both hands free to protect yourself.

Siri fished the key from his pocket and went out onto the balcony of the new house. First he enjoyed the splendid view across the valley. Then he went to the back of the building and strained his neck to look at the very top of the karst cliff. It was from there the boulder had fallen and unlocked the secret. Odd that it should fall exactly where it did ten days before the concert. He went to the start of the pathway that led up to the old cave. The broken sections and the boulder were halfway between the house and the cave entrance. *What were you doing there, senor?* he wondered.

Once the old cave dwellers' houses were complete and all the documents and personal belongings moved into them, there had been no reason, none at all, for the senior cadres to go back into the caves – no more than the Count of Monte Cristo would have to pop back to Elba to reminisce over the happy times he'd spent there. So, the caves were locked to keep out animals and preserve what might some day become neo-historic sites for tourists. *What better place?* Siri thought. *What more unlikely hideout could there be than the disused caves of the President himself?*

He walked up the path, rounded the removed section, then rejoined it to arrive at the front door. There was an actual door in a rectangular frame set back from the rock face. Siri had a delightful sense of the absurd – he visualised ringing a bell, peeking through a letterbox and wiping his feet on an ass-hair doormat. But the door was barred and locked, and it would have taken a small brigade of very persistent firemen to break through it. He walked around the rocks to the right of the door heading upwards but quickly came to a dead end. He passed the door again, heading south, rounded a small outcrop, and came to what must have been a back door.

At first glance, this too was locked and barred. The cursory inspection of a night-watchman would have ascertained as much. But Siri stepped up to the door and looked at the wooden planks that were nailed across it. A thick metal chain with a padlock was wound around two links connecting the door to the frame. It looked impenetrable. He stood back and stared at it like it was a puzzle that had something else to tell. Once he'd taken in the whole scene, he smiled. Before him, he knew, was an optical illusion. He took hold of the handle and tugged at it. The door, complete with its nailed planks and its frame and its metal chain, swung open on oiled hinges as quietly as a dolphin turning a somersault under water.

Before going inside, Siri reached into his cloth bag for his torch. He paused briefly to admire the brilliance of the faux-locked door then let it shut silently behind him. PL caves were part natural, part sculpted. Where alcoves didn't exist, rooms were constructed of plywood to give the feeling of a rather claustrophobic motel. Each cave had an airtight room with a pump and fallout shelter doors in case of chemical weapons attacks. For some reason, perhaps because the Americans really didn't know they were there, the Pathet Lao in their Vieng Xai caves had escaped such vulgar weaponry.

He followed his torch beam through the stone age apartment. This home he'd only visited once when one of the President's sons was taken ill. It had been more homely then. There had been pictures and carpets and ornaments. With the generator lights and a good imagination you could have been in a bungalow on the Black Sea. Now it was a cave. Siri opened the last door off the old meeting room expecting to find it just as empty as all the others, but the door nudged something. He shone his light inside and took a look. It was crammed with all kinds of ill-matching objects like a jackdaw's cache.

Somehow he knew. This was where Odon had stayed after his return from Hanoi. He imagined him holed up here under the noses of the LPLA. The stone grate in the corner, directly under the air vent, still had a sooty black pot on the grill. A long, straw nest was his bed. A green plastic pail with a broken handle still contained drinking water, and standing against the wall was the only piece of furniture in the entire place, a tall wooden wardrobe. Even before he walked towards it and tried the door, he knew it would be locked and that the key in his hand would open it. Even so, he tugged at the handle first and thought he heard a sound from inside. The key turned easily in the lock and he pulled open the door. Although it appeared empty at first glance, something fled past his ear from out of the darkness. He was too slow to catch it in the beam of his lamp but he sensed rather than heard the soft flapping of wings.

Given the setting, he assumed it was a bat but it was already out of the room before he could turn. He looked back into the wardrobe – a simple rectangle with a shelf at the top and a rail for hangers. That was it, no clothes, nothing. There wasn't even a mirror on the inside of the door. He wondered why on earth a man would lock an empty cupboard and hang on to the key even when he was under attack. Even when he knew his life was about to end.

Siri ran his hand around the back edges and corners inside the old wardrobe to find the hole or gap through which the bat had entered. When he didn't find one he started again, more carefully this time, pushing at the wood to find a spot that might give way. He tapped the solid teak of the sturdy old structure and stood back scratching his head. There was nothing. There was no possible way for the bat to have entered that wardrobe. None at all. Of course, that made no sense. The key was in the hand of a man buried in concrete six months ago. For the bat to have survived that length of time, there would have to have been large amounts of food in there with it. Even if it had managed to eat all that food, it would still have done an awful lot of shitting in six months. There was no sign, visual or olfactory, to suggest that had happened. Not for the first time in the past two years, Siri was flummoxed.

'All right,' he said aloud, his words bouncing around the inside of the cave. 'Then there had to be another key in someone else's possession. Whoever that was, and let's for argument's sake say it was Isandro, took out whatever it was from the cupboard and put a bat in its place. Perhaps it was an accident and he didn't see the creature fly in. But why would he bother to relock an empty wardrobe?' Siri was no expert on the eating habits of bats. All he knew was that they tasted like duck and were very good for your health. But he assumed a bat could live no longer than two weeks without food or drink. That would have to suggest that Isandro was still in the cave several months after his friend was killed.

He knew there were more holes in his hypothesis than there were pots in the Plain of Jars. But at least now he had one, it gave him something to work from. He spent the next half-hour searching through the belongings in the room. Everything was veiled in a shimmering layer of spiders' webs that reflected the torchlight like a frost. There was one kitbag, small piles of clothing, a shaving and washing kit, some Spanish-language books, candles, two Soviet-issue Makarov Pistolets – both unloaded – small packets of dried rations, tea, coffee, powdered milk, a tray of what had once been vegetables – now fossils – matches, and an old flashlight whose batteries had leaked and left a crusty white layer on everything around it.

If Santiago had been right and the sacrificial items had been removed from Kilometre 8, there was no sign of them in this room or anywhere else in the President's cave. If

Odon had continued with his black magic upon his return, he'd practised it somewhere else. Siri was surprised to find the passports of both men inside an old tin can on a makeshift shelf. With them were bundles of Lao *kip* rolled in rubber bands. They were beautifully printed with a broad-jawed, crew-cut king glaring defiantly from them, but, as a result of two devastating devaluations and a switch to the watery liberation *kip*, they now had no value beyond the aesthetic.

Siri had seen enough and he was feeling a little claustrophobic. He went back to the side door and stepped into the glaring daylight. As his eyes got used to the dazzle, he looked down to see that his dark blue safari shirt and black trousers had picked up a thick layer of white dust. He was about to slap away at himself to shake it off when he noticed the dust was moving. He scooped the side of his hand against his sleeve and looked more closely. He was surprised but not startled to find that he was covered from collar to cuff in tiny white spiders. As he'd cleared away their webs to search the room, the owners had attached themselves one by one to his clothing. He looked admiringly at himself – millions of tiny spiders reflecting the sunlight like a slowly shifting Elvis Presley suit.

Siri arrived back at Guesthouse Number One to find Lit's jeep parked out the front. He wondered why it was that he was doing most of the work on this murder enquiry himself while the head of the security division made brief guest appearances and took a lot of notes. As he was climbing the front steps, an answer of sorts came to him. Lit, just as Santiago had suggested, was an administrator.

He was faithful to the Party and was being promoted vertically; this month, Head of Security, next month, Head of Sanitation. It had very little to do with ability and everything to do with trust. He'd never been a policeman, had no investigative training and didn't have a clue how to handle this, his most serious high-profile crime. He had men under him who may have been competent police officers, but he couldn't be seen to be relinquishing control over anything so important. So, Siri was his solution.

'Dr Siri, I didn't think you'd ever be back,' the chief said, rising from his seat to shake the doctor's hand.

'Comrade Lit, you could have come to Kilometre 8 at any time. You knew where I was.'

'Didn't want to disturb you all. I know how hectic it can get out there. Come to the dining room. I brought us some Vietnamese beer. I can't wait to hear how our investigation's going.'

The beer turned out to be a mistake. It was warm and slightly flat and Siri knew from experience he'd have a thumping headache the following morning. Their debriefing had been pleasant enough. Omitting only the encounter with the spirit of Odon and the bat, he told Lit everything exactly as it had happened – the altar, the sacrifices, the secret hideout in the President's cave. Lit took notes and looked impressed. That seemed to be the sum total of his contribution to the meeting. He'd had no luck locating Colonel Ha Hung's family and hadn't found anyone who'd seen the two Cubans returning from Hanoi. Siri wondered whether the man was trying at all.

One thing that had been niggling Siri was why anyone would spend a lot of money on a nice pathway from the President's house to his cave, given that it was deserted and nobody had shown a second of interest in it since it fell vacant. Lit reminded him that this was an historic site like Lincoln's cabin or Hitler's bunker and that in the not too distant future large parties of tourists would be travelling on pilgrimages to Vieng Xai to see where the proud and glorious republic had taken shape. That reason had curiously satisfied Siri although he had trouble imagining bus tours to Vieng Xai. They'd drunk their beer from tea cups and Lit drove off into a mist that had arrived along with the night.

Siri found himself sitting on the veranda with a strong coffee. He missed the sound of the *klooee* playing its single tune. The upstairs guard was gone, the plywood partition was disassembled, and the rooms were empty. None of the staff seemed to know, or was prepared to say, where the royal family had been moved to, but he doubted he'd ever see them again. The kitchen people had gone to bed and made Siri promise to take his cup to his room when he retired. The cups, like the plates and cutlery, were numbered and had to be accounted for at the end of each month.

After two days at the hospital he was enjoying the late night peace of Vieng Xai. Despite having the makings of a city, it was still inhabited by country people who went to bed early and rose with the sun. He enjoyed the feeling of cold, and a damp sky so low you could stand on a chair and reach into it. He enjoyed the distant crowing of badly tuned cockerels and the barking of lemurs high on the karsts. He felt a marvellous peace. And then, as if the god of unhappiness had caught him enjoying himself, the blasted discotheque started up. It was no record player, no radio broadcast. The ground beneath him trembled from the base. He heard youths whooping along to a chorus they didn't know the words to.

He hadn't yet had the opportunity to go to his room so his bag with its torch was still beside him on the seat. Something urged him to go and see for himself – to follow the beat and see where it led him. An echo in a valley littered with stone outcrops can be deceptive, but he guessed the sounds were coming from the direction of the military cave complex. It was about a kilometre away beyond the football field. He emptied the grounds of his coffee and put his cup in his bag. It was a walk that would have proven difficult without the torch. There were no stars, no moon, and with all the guesthouse staff in bed, no lights from anywhere to guide his way. Only the throbbing of the ground beneath his feet and the loudening music gave him direction. But something odd began to happen as he pursued the sound. He got rhythm.

Siri and Boua had slow-danced in little student cafés in Paris during their studies. When they returned to Laos they'd enjoyed the drunken *lumwong* circle dances, the slow-motion swatting of mosquitoes to music. But none of these demanded a great sense of rhythm, which was just as well because Siri didn't have one to speak of. He wasn't a natural head-nodder or foot-tapper yet here he was, amazingly, walking in time to the beat. His hips were actually swaying. The middle finger of his right hand began to strike repeatedly against its thumb like a match on a damp box. It was a bizarre, but not totally unpleasant experience. He felt some inexplicable connection to the music that he wouldn't previously have believed possible.

He crossed the potholed football field and headed along the dirt track that led to the general's house and the army caves behind it. He'd been there a number of times. Above were the cave apartments of the military hierarchy. Below was an enormous natural cavern that had been converted into an auditorium. There was a concrete stage at one end with a deep orchestra pit in front of it. The ground rose in gentle tiers to the rear wall where the mouth of the cave was wide enough to let in natural light during the day and a current of cool air at night. It had a flow of spring water to quench the thirst of concert-goers and acoustics to shame La Scala.

This was to be the site of next week's Friendship and Cooperation Concert, an all-star event to mark the signing of the Lao–Vietnamese Twenty-Five-Year Treaty of Cooperation and Friendship. All the old cave dwellers would be returning for a nostalgic weekend. They'd be entertaining their foreign guests in the smart new houses, and on Sunday night bringing them to this underground marvel to watch the top Vietnamese dancers and musicians perform. Then, they would *lumwong* themselves to rice-whisky oblivion, before being carried back to their lodgings. Siri had asked Lit why all the entertainment was Vietnamese. Geographically, Huaphan province protruded into its neighbour like a large lady's bottom sticking out of a bathroom window, but as far as the doctor knew, it was still Laos. Lit recited all the appropriate propaganda, 'showing respect to its Vietnamese guests', 'learning from more experienced performers', but he hadn't been able to explain why Laos couldn't produce one act to impress its visitors.

These thoughts were going through Siri's left-right bobbing head as he reached the vortex of the noise. He told himself this was a rehearsal. They were testing the sound system, checking the acoustics for the microphone. Disco music was all they had on tape. It was a logical explanation and he could probably bring himself to forgive them.

He'd spent the last thirty years around soldiers to whom the phrase 'following orders' overrode all social and moral considerations.

The thick gooseberry bushes that had once disguised the mouth of the cavern had been cleared, so Siri walked unhindered up to the entrance. There was a high stile fashioned out of stone he had to climb over before reaching the steps that led down into the hall. But from the top of the rock he was able to see all the way to the stage. His breath left him. He sat on the stile with a bump just in time. A second later and his legs would have certainly given way. The concert hall was full – full to spillage – full to rib-crushing, jumping insanity. He had no idea where the music was coming from. There was no DJ on the stage, no visible sound system, but the music was loud and throbbing. He tapped his foot to the beat and scanned the assembled throng in disbelief. These weren't trendy young kids in wide-collared shirts and flared trousers. They were common folk. They were farmers, mothers with babies strapped to their backs, old men. The only teenagers he saw were in stained uniforms with confused expressions as if they'd stumbled there by mistake. Rarely in Huaphan had such a diverse crowd assembled in one place to share an experience so enthusiastically.

Apart from a fondness for jazz, Siri had no interest in American music and would have failed the simplest quiz on its origins and genres. But either from Dtui or the other nurses at Mahosot, he'd heard the word 'disco'. He'd been amazed at how it could squeeze through the gaps of anti-American feeling. After he'd learned what it was called, he heard it often in Thai radio broadcasts. It was for sale on the black market trade in commandeered US belongings.

Lao bands sneaked numbers into their repertoires and fooled the government spies into thinking it was ethnic tribal music. And here it was now in the concert cave in Huaphan.

The circulation had returned to Siri's legs and they were swaying like windscreen wipers to the music. His brief feeling of panic had turned to excitement. He'd known immediately what these enthusiastic party-goers had in common. They'd all been deprived the opportunity to enjoy life without fear. They were the innocent victims of the endless war. All they asked was to live their simple lives, but they'd made one mistake. They'd been born in a province that had become a political front line. For reasons they didn't really understand, they were the enemy and what good is war, what is its point, if nobody suffers for it? The dancers at the disco cave concert had all suffered to varying degrees, then the suffering had stopped. They had died. Siri had never been exposed to anything like this magnitude of spiritual boogie. He was a relative novice. He'd heard voices but never seen such a sight as this. Three ghosts were a crowd to him.

A week earlier, he would have smiled and gone home at this point. There would have been nothing gained by staying. But tonight he found himself walking down the steps to join the dancers. He knew he was hosting a spirit with rhythm and who was he to begrudge the man his final bop? There was no hostility towards the old doctor. Nobody paid attention to him. In a way it was as if he were the only one who wasn't there. He pushed his way politely through the crowd without actually making contact and began moving in ways he'd never moved before.

A half-hour later he was still there, still dancing. He was exhausted but he couldn't stop. He knew the anatomy of the human body intimately and could account for aches in every one of his muscles, but he was just the vehicle tonight. His failing breath wheezed like a Bulgarian air conditioning unit. The music seemed louder, thumping against his ears. People crowded in on all sides. Flashing lights from nowhere blinded him. One spotlight seemed to pick him out – spot prize – top dancer – crowd recedes – he struts his stuff alone – the microphone, 'Hey!'

He said, 'Hey.'

'Hey, comrade.'

He said, 'Hey, comrade.'

'What do you think you're doing?'

He said, 'Wha ...' Siri looked into the bright spot and beyond it. There was now just the one light. It was being held by a man in an army jacket several sizes too big for him and a knitted hat. He was directing his flashlight directly into Siri's face. The doctor looked around at the cold, deserted limestone cavern.

'You got no right to be here. What are you playing at alone in the dark?' the old watchman asked. 'You drunk or something?'

Siri stood bent forward with his hands on his knees struggling for breath. His body had just completed the hill section of the Tour de France. He knew he wouldn't get it out of bed in the morning. But, as soon as he had the breath and the strength, he started to laugh. The watchman was sure Siri was unstable and took a step back.

'Sorry, comrade,' Siri said at last. 'Rehearsing for next week's show.'

'You don't say. That doesn't seem right to me, making an old fella like you perform. They should be ashamed of themselves.'

'I'm a lot younger than I look, brother.'

'Well, I suppose you must know what you're doing. Don't you stay here all night, now.'

'I won't. Thanks.'

The beam swung around and the watchman followed it into an ominous tunnel across the auditorium. Siri remained standing in the centre of the huge, people-less discotheque feeling more than a little silly, but somehow invigorated.

11

A THOROUGHLY DECENT PROPOSAL

Mr Geung had been in the tree for eighteen hours. He could tell the time quite well but his watch was hidden safely under a loose tile beneath his bed at Mahosot. So, eighteen hours was a guess. It could have been three hours or a week. He still had food and some water, but he was missing sleep. He hadn't been able to work out how to catch a little shut-eye without falling to the ground. His shoulder ached but he'd changed the dressing as instructed and the wound looked free of infection. He was something of an authority on the look of wounds but only now realised how badly they hurt. Climbing up the tree hadn't helped in that regard. He was quite proud of himself that he'd been able to get as high as he did with one arm. He'd never been much of a tree climber, but then again he'd never had such an incentive.

The tiger hadn't chased him up the tree, not in the sense that the animal runs, is about to pounce, and the prey is forced to scurry up to a high branch in panic. That hadn't been the way it happened. Geung had been sitting waiting for the sun to return to his shoulder strap when he noticed the tiger at the edge of the clearing. The only time he had ever seen anything like it was at the last New Year show. It had been apparent then, from the reaction of the audience, that large cats with fangs were fearsome creatures. By the end of the show, he'd been as nervous as all the other onlookers. The sense of danger is contagious, and that is just as well, for, without it, he might very well have approached the animal to make friends. If the tiger had been of a mind, she could have attacked and devoured Mr Geung during any one of his eleven attempts to get up the tree. It was, however, daylight, and her prey was still strong. She had him cornered and weakness would soon overcome him.

Dtui and Geung sat there in the tree exchanging jokes and laughing at their predicament. They kept each other awake. Once, when the tiger attempted to climb up after them, Dtui egged on her champion as he poked at the drooling mouth of the cat with a dry twig. It was fun having his friend there. Only the fatigue and discomfort stopped it from being a most enjoyable adventure.

Dtui was in the sleeping ward. Again the image of Geung came into her head. If only there were a telephone in the morgue she might have phoned to see if everything was well. The bed vacated by Mrs Nuts was now being used by little Panoy. She still hadn't regained consciousness but her pulse was as strong as a horse's. Dtui could recognise all the signs of a fighter in her. She'd already made up her mind to do all she could to reunite the girl with her relatives and see her settled back into some semblance of a normal life.

She stroked Panoy's hair from her forehead and turned from the bed. To her surprise, comrade Lit was standing in the doorway. With the sun at his back, he looked positively godlike. The new epaulettes on the shoulders of his uniform glinted like wings. For a second she almost forgot she didn't like him.

'Nurse Dtui,' he nodded stiffly.

'Comrade Lit. Can I help you?'

'I'd be grateful if you could spare me a few moments.'

'Shoot,' she said.

'I was thinking perhaps outside.'

'Comrade, these patients are so drugged you could drive a truck over them and they'd smile at you.'

'Even so …'

'Look, it's hot out there. This room's twenty degrees cooler … and, I'm on duty.' He annoyed her. She wanted him to get whatever it was over with and get the blazes out of there.

'Very well,' he said and walked into the room. Dtui stood with her arm crooked against her waist waiting for some lecture. But she noticed now that the head of security had apparently forgotten to put on his suit of arrogance. He seemed rather frail, almost, one could say, timid. He continued to hold himself upright but it wasn't without effort: more like a wall-hanging than a signpost. Dtui found his silence disconcerting.

'The sooner you start, the sooner I can get back to work,' she said. She was confused by the look of uncertainty on his face. His gaze was cast over her shoulder to some point on the wall beyond her.

'Yes,' he said. 'That's quite right. The plight of the downtrodden and oppressed takes precedence over the personal issues of we servants. The patients should quite rightly be our priority.'

'Good,' she said. 'In that case I'll go and look after the downtrodden. If you'll excuse me.' She walked past him and headed for the door. There was something unnatural about the situation.

'But ...'

She turned to him. 'But?'

It was at this point he began his speech. It had obviously been written beforehand and memorised. But there was no doubt in Dtui's mind that comrade Lit had spent many hours composing, decomposing, rewriting and practising this recitation. Even with occasional lapses into engineering analogy, it was unquestionably the most beautiful thing anyone had ever said to her.

At school, she'd had what could possibly be termed *boyfriends*. At least there had been a culture of pairing up and going out. But the boys that she'd paired with had been well down the pecking order. They'd been more interested in her breasts than her soul. On thinking back to those disastrous dates, it had occurred to her once that her boys had all been the shades of fruit; the pale pink of lychee, the tan of sapodilla, the orange of sweet mango, and, like fruit, they'd all gone off in the hot seasons. And, as she listened to Lit make his presentation like a fifth grader reciting the national creed, she plummeted instantly and hopelessly in love with his words. Once he'd finished, she could recall very little of the detail because she'd been too stunned to record any of the words on her memory.

There had been mention of his first impression of her on the day they'd unearthed the mummy. He'd confessed to thinking about her constantly and made some comparison between her eyes and stars. It may have been a line from a well-known song but she could forgive him for a lack of originality. The fact that he'd even noticed she had eyes was enough for her. He had summarised his financial status and prospects, and, almost in the same breath, come straight out with his atomic bomb blast. He'd said he would be delighted if Nurse Dtui would be kind enough to be his wife – just like that, straight to the temple without even a hint of sampling the goods beforehand.

Something like that can have a profound effect on a woman, particularly one to whom such a proposition had never before been made. A man – fully sighted, and with a complete set of limbs – liked her sufficiently to commit his life to her. It was enough to momentarily erase all the negative thoughts of him that lingered in her mind. It was enough to make her knees wobble so violently she had to sit on the edge of a bed. She couldn't bring herself to speak. He, in turn, had come to the end of his script, so the two of them remained there mute in the dark room with only the clicking of one old man's unconscious tongue against his palate as an accompaniment.

At last, Dtui found her voice, or part of it. 'I ...'

'You'll probably need time to think about all this,' he interrupted. 'So, I'll leave it with you. If it helps, the regional Social Relations Office has already given us the go-ahead for our engagement. It's all signed and stamped. Right then. I'll see you later.' He didn't actually salute before leaving, but it was a very military nod that he gave her before marching triumphantly out into the sunshine.

Few things in life could stop Nurse Dtui from speaking. It was her forte. She had smart responses for every situation – a witty comment to brighten even the most difficult of times. But for a full five minutes, she sat in the shadow of the ward of the unconscious, and could think of nothing at all to say. She was as delirious as all the patients around her. Indeed, she might have remained in that state for a good deal longer if Panoy hadn't chosen that moment to come out of her coma. Dtui jumped up when she heard the sound. She turned to see Panoy sitting upright with her eyes staring directly at her. Slowly, the little girl's voice issued forth with a stream of Hmong, a language Dtui couldn't understand. What was clear, however, was that this wasn't the voice of a child.

Once all the guests had vacated Guesthouse Number One and their belongings had been successfully pilfered, there was no longer a role for the guesthouse truck. The staff didn't see any harm – as long as he put his own petrol in the tank – in Siri borrowing it for the day. He'd heard there was a Vietnamese unit stationed up near Sop Hao at the border. That same unit had been in Laos before the well-publicised but temporary Vietnamese troop pull-out. It was the same unit to which Colonel Ha Hung had been attached. Siri decided it wouldn't do any harm to visit the place.

He was enjoying the drive. Whereas the rest of the country was dying of thirst, the north-east still had enough rain to replenish the water in the hillside paddies. The late morning sun reflected from them like broken pieces of a mirror stacked in jagged pyramids. Little girls, straight from their baths at the local pond, too young to be ashamed, walked naked along the dusty roadside wearing their sarongs as hats. A truck overtook him, carrying small pigs in light cane cages on their way to the abattoir. Their beady eyes streamed with tears.

The rice fields on either side were neatly laid out and well tended. Big spoon blossoms and itchy fruit lined the hedgerows. He passed a single temple with its doors padlocked. Hill tribe people carried baskets of twigs high on their backs and strapped around their foreheads. Ponies with bells warned nobody in particular of their coming. A young man in the middle of nowhere hoisted a guitar over his shoulder. Without exception, every buffalo he passed looked up from its munching and watched the doctor on his journey. He felt happy to be surrounded by this unprecedented peace. He smiled to himself and his shoulders rocked to some disco tune deep in his soul.

At one point he found himself driving along a newly laid road which he suddenly had to leave in order to cross a bridge five yards off to the right. Once over it, he had to drive along another dirt track to get back on the road. It was a fine bridge and the road was straight and level so this lack of construction coordination troubled him. He stopped to talk to the owner of the nearest shack who explained that in Huaphan province, the Soviets were now responsible for bridge building. The Vietnamese had the road portfolio. Each resented the other's involvement. The Vietnamese weren't the fastest of road builders whereas the Russians had their bridges in place at exactly the contracted time. On roads that were merely upgraded, this wasn't a problem. But on new roads, the Vietnamese engineers sometimes arrived at a river with their road trailing behind them, only to find they'd missed the bridge by several metres. The Vietnamese refused to re-route the road, the Russians had no intention of rebuilding the bridges. As Civilai often said, 'The monk is in no position to give back the alms if he doesn't find them to his taste.'

By the time Siri had found the discreet unsignposted unit of Vietnamese infantry it was already mid-afternoon. The Lao sentry at the turn-off swore on his grandmother's grave there was nothing but trees at the end of the dirt drive he protected. Siri had the unit number and the exact kilometre marker, both provided by Central Command in Xam Neua, so he ignored the man and his shouldered rifle and turned into the drive. It was unlikely a solitary old doctor would be shot for attempting to invade a compound of militia.

Two kilometres further on he found the camp: a well-organised, tented expanse that clearly housed more than just the one unit. He was stopped by a real guard in uniform at a weighted red-and-white barrier. The soldier was sharp with the doctor and within a minute was yelling Siri's ID information into his walkie-talkie. As he waited, Siri looked ahead at the sight of foreign troops on his soil and felt resentful. The war was over, won. Why were these Vietnamese still here? He'd trained in Vietnam and done most of his doctoring there. Yes, Laos had a debt of gratitude to repay. Yes, it was true, she probably wouldn't have defeated the royalists without Vietnamese help and the present administration wouldn't be sitting where it was. But, enough.

A reply crackled over the wireless. The guard pointed out the officers' tent and raised the barrier to let him pass. He drove down a slope and then up the rise upon which the invaders were billeted and noticed permanent buildings here and there in various stages of construction. As soon as he skidded on the loose gravel in front of the main tent, a captain strode out to meet him. Siri recognised him.

'Dr Siri.' The soldier smiled and shook his hand warmly.

As always, Siri's Vietnamese took a while to warm up. 'Captain Vo Chi. They didn't tell me you were here. How have you been?'

'Alive and well, thanks to you, my good friend. I thought you'd have been put out to pasture a long time ago.'

'I was there, comrade. I smelled the daisies. I could almost taste the grass. Then I felt the lassoo round my neck and I was hauled back to the knacker's yard.'

In the mess tent, they ate and reminisced over the year or so Siri had travelled with Vo Chi's division as its head field surgeon. But Siri wasn't there for nostalgia. He had a long drive back and a lot of information to gather before then. Siri gave Vo the name of the man he was interested in. Vo confessed he'd only vaguely heard of the colonel but recalled there was an old sergeant major at the base who had been with the commander for much of the campaign. Vo sent an officer to find him and bring him to the mess tent.

Although Siri was unable to place the face of Sergeant Major Giap, the old warrior recognised the doctor as soon as he entered the tent. He even remembered his name. There had been many battles, many units, many transfers and so many men. Siri could hardly be expected to recall all of them. He got straight to the point.

'How did the colonel die?'

'In a Hmong ambush, Doctor,' the sergeant major replied directly, but Siri noticed him cast a glance towards his captain. He wondered whether this was the official account of the demise.

'When Colonel Ha Hung was stationed in Vieng Xai,' Siri continued, 'I believe his family was with him.'

The sergeant major seemed much more relaxed about answering this second question. 'Yes, comrade. His wife and daughter.'

'No one else?'

'No. Well ... they had a *moi* maid that came over with them.' 'Moi' was the derogatory term for the montagnards. They were to the Vietnamese what the Hmong were to the Lao: minority, ill-treated, unloved. Siri noted in the timbre of the sergeant major's voice that he had no respect for them.

'And you met the wife and daughter?' Siri asked.

'Oh, yes. Certainly. It was a long-term posting. We had the option of bringing our families along. My old lady was here at the time, too.'

'What was the daughter like?'

'Gorgeous. Hong Lan, her name was – Pink Orchid. She must have been about, I don't know ... seventeen at the time. She had more troops after her than the Hmong did. A little cracker.'

Siri's fingertips tingled. 'And did anyone catch her?'

Again, Giap glanced at his captain. 'The colonel and his wife were very strict with her. Very possessive, the colonel was. He made it very clear early on that he'd shoot any man that laid a hand on her. And he was a scary man when he got mad. He frightened me lots of times, I don't mind admitting.'

'And do you believe he would actually have killed anyone who touched her?'

'How can you tell a thing like that, Doctor?' He turned and smiled at the captain whose face remained blank.

'Right,' Siri said. 'Of course. So, as far as you know, nobody made any official – I mean, appropriate advances directly to the colonel?'

'I don't think anyone dared, except for ...'

'For who?'

'Well, there were rumours. But I'm sure you aren't interested in camp gossip, are you, sir?'

'I'll take anything I can get right now.'

'All right. There was this time when the girl got very sick. I mean, very sick. Some woman's thing I heard it was, and they had her in the hospital for a couple of months. Some Vietnamese doctor operated on her. The colonel wouldn't let any of them foreign doctors anywhere near h ... Oh, sorry. No offence to you, Doctor.'

'That's all right. Not every day you get the chance to be an alien in your own country. So, she was out in the hospital at Kilometre 8?'

'Correct. And she pulled through, much to the relief of her parents. But she had to have, what do you call it? Convalescence. They couldn't move her for quite a time. And, while she was up there in the caves – and this is where the rumour starts – she got friendly with one of them interns. Cuban fellow he was. Don't know whether he stuck his old fellow in her there in the hospital or ...'

To his own amazement, Siri lunged across the table in the direction of the sergeant major and sent cups and plates flying. He seemed intent on striking the old man. Both soldiers jumped to their feet and stood looking down at the doctor in shock. It was no less of a surprise to Siri.

'I ... I'm terribly sorry,' he said, groping for an explanation. 'I ... I have this nervous tic. It does that sometimes. Please forgive me.' He began to gather the bakelite cups from the floor.

The sergeant major laughed. 'That's all right. Frightened the life out of me, though. Thought you must be squeamish about sex or something.'

'Are you all right?' Vo asked.

'Just fine,' Siri told him, weaving his fingers together on his lap. Odon had to be controlled. 'Please go on, Sergeant Major.'

'Right then. Where was I? Oh, yeah. So, this "thing" happened with the intern and I suppose the guy thinks all his birthdays have come at once. He meets a pretty Vietnamese girl, knows they make the best wives in the world, so he decides he wants her. He goes up to the colonel – had to have balls like coconuts to do that – and he asks for his permission to go out with his daughter. The colonel couldn't believe his ears.'

'Why not? It sounds like the correct thing to do.'

'Why not? I'll tell you why not, Doctor. This intern was black, wasn't he. Black as a monkey's asshole.' Siri fought down his hands. 'Black as a …'

'Yes, I get it. He was black.'

'You know how it is. One of them fair weather communists from the Caribbean. Natives that join whatever army pays best. And, the way the story goes, the colonel laughed in his face. But the blacky just sat there. Colonel told him to get out but he didn't budge. So the colonel took a switch of bamboo to him. He still couldn't get the bastard out of his office. It took a dozen men with coshes in the end.'

Siri was developing a strong disrespect of his own for Giap and his storytelling. 'And what happened?'

Giap hesitated. 'I guess that was it. They took the girl away from the caves and put her in a place where the nurses were women and wouldn't do any twiddling about while she was unconscious. I hear she got better.'

'And she didn't see the Cuban again?'

'Couldn't imagine so. If she did, he'd be dead by now.'

Siri wondered whether that might indeed be the case. 'How did they communicate?'

'Say what?'

'The intern and the girl. What language did they use?'

'No idea, Doctor. But she was a smart girl. I know she understood Russian. She might have spoken African for all I know.'

The interview continued for another half-hour. There were several other things the sergeant major was ignorant about. But, most importantly, he didn't know what happened to the mother and daughter after the colonel's death. Siri began a trail of mundane, unnecessary questions and waited for Vo to lose interest. As it turned out, the only time he left them alone was when he paid a brief visit to the latrine. Siri pounced.

'Listen, brother. I promise you this information will never get back to your superiors. Please trust me. I need to know exactly what happened at the ambush. How did Colonel Ha Hung die?'

Giap looked at the tent flap, considered the question for a few seconds, then crouched across the table towards Siri. 'He went instantaneously insane, Doctor. Really. We were there in a valley. Our outriders got butchered but we were in armoured trucks. We could have held out there for days. What usually happened was the Hmong would pin a convoy down for a few hours, pick off whoever they could, then run off into the jungle to boast about it. The Yanks had deserted them by then so they didn't exactly have unlimited ammo to throw at us. It would have passed.'

'But?'

'But,' he lowered his voice. 'Something came over the colonel that I'd never seen in him before. He was always

Colonel Cool in battle. Never saw him lose it. But this particular day he says something like, "You deserve this!" A deep scary voice he used. He takes out his handgun and jumps down off the armoured car. Just leaps out like a cowboy. And he shouts out "Charge!" Now, I tell you, there wasn't one of us dumb enough to charge in a situation like that. But he wasn't really expecting us to. He just headed off across the clearing. He hadn't gone but ten steps. He swatted off the first couple of hits but I bet them Hmong were singing up there in the trees. A uniformed officer? I bet that got 'em some points. They peppered him.'

Siri was astounded. 'So, in your professional opinion, that wasn't the action of a man in control of his own faculties?'

'Every surviving man of us agreed the devil had got into him that day, Doctor. Every single man of us.'

12

BEHIND THE TEAK WARDROBE

Mr Geung rejoined Route 13 at Kasi. Naturally, he didn't know it was the same road he'd left four days earlier. All roads looked alike. But the sun was prodding him south and he knew this road was now heading in the same direction as him.

In his hand he held a pointed stick. It was a weapon against wild beasts. It had been a much larger stick that killed the tiger, but that branch had been too heavy to carry. A stick was a stick. A dead tiger was a dead tiger.

It had been getting close to morning and he still hadn't slept. The tiger was resting directly below him, waiting for him to tire, to drop from the tree like a ripe mango. Several times she'd tried to climb up after him and failed. On one occasion, Geung had kicked out at her. His boot against her teeth caused her to lose balance and fall to the ground. He felt guilty about that. From then on, frustrated but ever patient, she slept with one ear pricked up like radar. Whether she heard the crack before he felt the branch give way was something he came to ponder later. All he could be sure of was that he and the branch suddenly dropped, very quickly. There was a second crack and a thump that sent a bolt of pain from his bottom to his shoulder and back again several times. He was thrown into the thick grass where he lay hurting, waiting for the tiger to come and eat him. But she didn't come.

He looked to his side and saw her close, and dead. She was such a beautiful creature. Her eyes were mascara'd like the girls behind the Hanoi Road market. (He'd only looked, not touched.) Her fur was thick and prettily patterned. He reached over and ran his hand through the soft coat. He cupped her sad face on its twisted neck. And he put his cold nose against her warm one, and he wept.

Apart from the cockroaches in the morgue and several million mosquitoes (Dr Siri had assured him they were unfeeling and certainly unworthy of pity), Mr Geung had never been directly responsible for the death of another living creature. He was truly ashamed of his first murder. He understood death. He worked with it every day. He knew it was the end of people. They wouldn't come back. This lovely animal wouldn't come back either and it was because of him. He also knew what happened after death. He'd been to temples with the nurses and watched dead people being readied for their trip to nirvana. Although he never actually saw any of them leave, he was certain that's where they were going. The nurses said.

He had to honour the tiger in the same way. It was the least he could do. Despite his own injuries, he spent much of the morning collecting kindling from the forest to build the pyre. The animal was incredibly heavy – so heavy he hadn't been able to lift her onto the sticks. He had no choice but to rebuild the rude structure on top of her. He doubted Buddha would mind too much if a body arrived upside down. With the matches from his bag he lit the dry twigs and sat beside the fire as it quickly engulfed the pyre which collapsed onto his victim. The cooking meat smelled delicious and Geung's stomach rumbled, but his mind didn't let him know how inappropriate such a connection might be.

He didn't have the words the monks used, but he knew it was appropriate to chant. There was a song in his head and, in a deep voice, he sang it over and over the way the monks would have.

'The sun wakes up and climbs my back,

At evening drops into my sack.'

Mr Geung didn't know just how long ago all that had been. But knowing the sun would always be on the tiger's back certainly made him feel better. And besides, it was her destiny. He'd tramped over endless hills since then with his flat feet. Whenever he came across a stream, he'd taken drinks but resisted the temptation to bathe. 'Don't you dare wash it off,' the old lady had told him while coating him with her mosquito balm. He didn't dare. So, in all this time he hadn't washed and he knew he was starting to smell bad. But he'd promised the old lady. His skin was flaking, not only on his neck where the sun baked him, but inside his clothes too he was itchy and uncomfortable.

As if things weren't bad enough, he found that he was going deaf. It had happened before in his life. He'd been told it was common for people such as himself – a build-up of fluid in his ears. But here in nowhere land he had no nurse to make him hear again. Of course he had Dtui, but she was only in his head.

'Never mind. To Vientiane,' she told him, and he started to march down the centre of the potholed road at approximately five kilometres an hour. He was still 200 kilometres from home.

Dtui needed Siri more than she'd ever needed him. It wasn't about the medical problems that queued up like shoppers in a Moscow breadline. She could just about keep on top of those. No. She needed Siri to help her with two absolutely baffling emergencies that weren't likely to be found explained in a medical textbook. In the once-quiet sleeping ward, a four-year-old child sat wide awake babbling in the voice of a seventy-year-old woman. Meej had listened to her for an hour. The language was certainly Hmong, although the child was Lao Thai. According to the intern, she was reeling through an oral history of the life of the seventy-year-old. He said it was like listening to a recording of everything she'd ever said, starting around 1940 – played fast-forward, too quick to catch it all. Dtui was in no position to doubt Meej's appraisal.

And, as if that mystery weren't confusing enough, still there was the proposal. It sat heavily on her mind like the carcass of an overweight sloth. She had developed infinite respect for the underpaid staff toiling around her at Kilometre 8, but, no matter how much she liked them, she wasn't about to discuss her intimate feelings with them. She needed a cynic. She needed someone to put her thoughts into perspective. Comrade Lit was tall and gangly, but certainly worthy of a hug. He had a kind, strong and – at a stretch – handsome face that would be nice to wake up beside every morning for the rest of her life.

Indeed, it was only the being-an-ass issue that presented any obstacle at all to her falling into his arms and cooing, 'Yes, yes, my love. Take me.' Was being obnoxious really that much of a stumbling block to being a good husband?

Would it take much of a change on her part to fit into his two-dimensional, brainwashed, personality-deficient life? Surely, if a pig could mate with a dog, Dtui could become a good Party wife: the wife of a man who does the paperwork for marrying a woman before he asks her. There was no doubt about it. She needed Siri to slap her a few times to help her see sense.

Siri was, in fact, back in the President's cave sitting cross-legged in the Cubans' hideout. Something didn't feel right about this whole story – the relationship between Isandro and the girl. If they actually had the magic to kill her father, to make monkey babies and peach-stone larynxes, then surely they could enchant the hospital-bound girl and have their wicked way with her. Why would Isandro go through the humiliation and loss of face of asking her father for permission to woo her? The sergeant major's rumour didn't make any sense at all.

Siri decided, spiders or not, he had to go through Odon's things once more. He had to be sure he hadn't missed anything. He burrowed deep into the kit-bag, felt below the straw mat, flipped through a shelf-load of books whose titles meant nothing to him. But, there wasn't a thing – no evidence that Hong Lan, the Pink Orchid, had touched on the lives of the Cubans at all. Yet, they'd come back. Why? They'd given up their tickets home and put themselves in a dangerous situation as conspicuous outsiders in a hostile land. For what?

Siri was champion at asking himself questions. All he needed was another voice that could answer them. There was never a helpful spirit around when he most needed one. The ghost of Odon, assuming it was still inside him, hadn't done a damned thing of any use. Dancing and

swaying weren't going to get them anywhere. Siri didn't
need rhythm at this moment in time, he needed solutions.

He shone his torch around the cave for the umpteenth
time; the humps of clothes, the fireplace, the bed, the big
teak wardrobe that stood ominously against one wall. He
thought back to his brief visit here ten years earlier. What
had this room been then? He closed his eyes and retraced
those steps through the cave. The son and mother had been
visiting from China. The boy had picked up hepatitis
somewhere on the journey. It wasn't serious. He was strong
and the right diet and rest would see him through it. They
had isolated him.

That had been in one of the plywood rooms. The living
room was down from it, the bedrooms were ... That was
it. This wardrobe had been in the President's bedroom
then, all the way at the other end of the complex. This had
been the business end, where meetings were held and plots
hatched. What on earth would possess anybody to go to
the trouble of lugging a heavy old wardrobe to the other
end of a cave when the thing had obviously been so heavy
they hadn't even bothered to take it down to the house? It
had been left behind. But Siri was certain it wouldn't have
been moved before it was abandoned. He was sure the
Cubans had manhandled it here themselves. Now, why
would they have done that?

He walked to the beast and stood in front of it. He'd
already given it a thorough internal examination and
found nothing. He decided to dedicate more time to its
outside. He closed the doors and scanned his light across
the front. He looked to the right side of it and found
nothing. He was walking around to the left when he
stepped on something that sent him skidding forwards. It

almost floored him. He heard whatever it was ping against the wall in front of him then roll back in his direction. He slowly regained his composure and waited for his breathing to return to normal.

He shone his torch on the floor. There he saw the cause of his skid. The floor was dotted with ball bearings – the type used in truck or tractor wheels. Hundreds of them sat on the ground in no particular pattern. When he'd visited the room earlier, he hadn't noticed them. Nobody would have, unless they'd bothered to go around the wardrobe. But, once he saw them, he knew immediately what their function was. It was a simple set-up, but brilliant. He knew it was conceived by the same minds that created the optical illusion back door. He went back to the right side of the wardrobe and pushed. It didn't take a great deal of effort. The massive wooden cupboard glided majestically on the ball bearings beneath it as if it were on ice.

Siri stood back to admire his discovery. In the wall of the cave there was an aperture large enough for a man to clamber through. His heart was beating fast. It was like discovering a pharaoh's secret chamber in an ancient pyramid. He went to the opening and shone his light inside. Here it was. This was the Cubans' temple – a room no bigger than an air-raid shelter. Here was their sacrificial altar, their cauldron, their paraphernalia. A feeling of foreboding fell over him. He had little doubt that this was the centre of their black magic.

He removed the white talisman from inside his shirt and allowed it to hang openly around his neck. He breathed deeply and climbed inside the chamber to get a better look. There were two more beds in there, woven more carefully than the others in the first room, one covered in a stained cloth. There were various pots and jars of unidentifiable pastes and powders. In one corner there was a stack of dried fudge from tapped opium plants. In that state, the drug would maintain its potency for years. He recognised the unmistakable odour of dried blood and went over to the sacrificial altar. It was broad, easily wide enough for a body. Behind it was some display, what looked like photographs, but as he reached out to touch them, the talisman began to tremble against his chest.

He wondered what wickedness had been conjured up here, what evil spirits had been awakened inside these walls. He sensed something lurking in there with him, high in the shadows pressed against the cool stone. But it was nothing you could use a flashlight to see. His instincts told him to leave. He hosted a dark Cuban spirit and that made him susceptible – open to attack. Panic took hold of him, but even so, he somehow willed himself to reach out again for the photographs that were taped behind the altar. As he ripped them free, a high-pitched scream seemed to emanate from the rocks all around him.

He hurried for the aperture and flung himself through it. On the other side he lay on the ground trying to catch his breath. His lungs were weak and useless now in times of crisis. Once more he'd ignored the advice of the shaman, 'Do not subject the spirit of Yeh Ming to danger. Protect your ancestor and yourself at all cost.'

Siri wondered what there was about his character that made him gravitate towards these whirlpools of dreadful excitement. He was a terrible disappointment to himself. With his breathing almost regular, he rolled the wardrobe back in front of the secret annex, sat with his back against the cupboard doors, and shone his light onto the pictures.

One was slightly larger than passport size. It showed a handsome black man in one of those humourless poses a photo studio might insist on for an official portrait. The other was larger, about forty by forty-five centimetres. It was also a studio picture but the girl Siri took to be the colonel's daughter, Hong Lan, had been posed looking high and to the left of the photographer. She was a long-necked beauty with a shy, Mona Lisa smile. In her hair she wore a pink lotus.

Siri could certainly see how Isandro had fallen for her. Any red-blooded man would have. But this was wrong. The pictures as the centrepiece of the sacrificial altar pointed Siri to one unavoidable conclusion. The Cubans had used their magic to beguile the girl. Her heart had been hijacked and she had been forced to love this man against her will. Odon was dead. The living didn't have the facility to haunt. But he knew not why the black magician was using him as a vehicle. Again, he had only his imagination to answer this question. He was afraid the Endoke priest needed Siri's body to complete whatever process had been set in motion in this temple. He knew he had to find Hong Lan, but was afraid that this was exactly what Odon wanted him to do. By making contact with the girl, would he be bringing danger back into her life? If Odon had been killed by the girl's family to protect her, would it not be better to keep these skeletons safely in their cupboards in order to keep her safe?

13

THE SMALL BLUE PEUGEOT

In July 1977, the average yearly income in Laos was a little over eighty dollars. Some things people in the West considered necessities were unattainable in Laos – luxuries you read about in foreign magazines. Petrol was one of these. Most people who owned a car and hadn't been quick enough to flee to Thailand now considered their vehicle to be a permanently immobile thing – a small wheeled shed or an outside cupboard. On the roads, the majority of transport had some government connection or was owned by foreigners. Anyone who could afford to run a private car and claimed not to be in one or the other of these categories had to be viewed with some suspicion.

Mr Geung had made every effort to leave the road whenever he heard an engine approach. He was exhausted. His feet were blistered and the muscles in his legs were screaming for him to stop and rest. But he had to get to the morgue. Dtui had helped him fashion a hat from banana leaves that kept off the sun and made him look quite decorative. She was with him most of the time now, giving advice, urging him on. He certainly couldn't have made it this far without her, however far this far might be.

As his hearing slowly faded, he found he was catching the sounds of approaching trucks later and later. But for the last hour or so, nothing at all had passed him on the highway. It was almost as if the road were running out of strength along with Geung. The asphalt had gradually turned to gravel which had now become sand. The sun was still on his shoulder so he knew he was still heading in the right direction, but the road beneath him seemed to have lost faith that it could make it to Vientiane.

A car – a small blue Peugeot – suddenly darted out of a side track a hundred metres ahead of him. Mr Geung was in the centre of the road and there was nothing but open clearing on either side. There was nowhere to run, so he continued walking. There was nothing to worry about. Only army trucks had to be avoided. One thing he was sure of was that the army didn't drive little blue cars. He expected the driver to ignore him and go past but the car stopped beside him. The driver obviously expected Geung to stop also and talk to him, but the little man continued on his journey. After a few seconds of silence, the car dropped into reverse and rolled backward till it was travelling parallel to Mr Geung.

The driver was a middle-aged man with dyed black hair and a cigarette hanging from his mouth. 'Good afternoon, comrade,' he shouted above the sound of the whiny engine.

'I … I'm walking,' Geung told him.

'That, brother, I can see. Are you walking because you like to, or because you have no choice?'

'Yes.'

'Yes, which?'

'I … I'm w … walking to the morgue.'

'Oho. Don't be so negative, brother. Nobody died from walking. Where you headed?'

Mr Geung thought it was funny that the car could go

backwards along the road. It made him laugh. It was the first time he'd laughed all week. 'Vientiane,' he said.

'Well then, maybe it will kill you. Especially seeing as you're on the wrong road. Route 13 took a left turn some fifteen kilometres back. You missed it.'

'I have to go … go straight.'

'You'll end up in Thailand if you do that. Listen, comrade, I'm on my way to Vang Vieng. That's halfway to Vientiane. It'll take a big chunk out of your journey.'

'Vang Vieng.' Geung had heard of that place. He didn't know where it was but people in his village used to talk about it a lot. If it was near his village, it couldn't be that far from Vientiane.

'All right,' he said, and stopped walking. The driver opened the passenger door. Geung noticed a pistol on the spare seat that the man hurriedly put in the glove box.

'Nothing to worry about,' the man told him. He stopped the little car and watched Geung climb painfully into the front seat. When he was in, the driver leaned over and slammed the door shut. His passenger smelled like a latrine. He introduced himself as Woot. Geung introduced himself as comrade Geung, and they shook hands. Woot's fingers were sticky as if he'd just eaten glutinous rice and not bothered to wash them. That thought reminded Geung that his supplies were gone and he was hungry.

The little blue Peugeot went back along the old road, then, just as Woot had promised, they turned right onto Route 13. Geung had seen the sign earlier but ignored it because the sun had wanted him to go straight. A few kilometres further on, there was a tall signpost listing the names of the places the road would take them. The driver slowed down as they approached it.

'See, brother?' he said. 'That there, halfway down. That says Vang Vieng. Can you read that?'

But Geung was more excited about the final name on the list. He recognised the characters for that one. He smiled at Woot then looked back at the sign.

'Vvvv ... ien ... tiane,' he said. 'Vvvvientiane.'

It was the happiest word he'd ever spelled. He couldn't get the smile off his face. When the car sped up, he looked out at the passing rice fields and bared his teeth to the warm air that blew in through the window. He was happy. He thought how great it would be if comrade Woot could go all the way to Vientiane. But what he didn't know was that comrade Woot didn't even plan to go to Vang Vieng.

Siri sat alone in the guesthouse restaurant and stared into a mug of coffee so thick you could lose an anchor in it. It was his second mug. He missed Vientiane baguettes and omelettes and fresh-caught river fish. Here they were in a part of the country where there was no drought. Things grew naturally in the north-east. Civilai had once said you could drop a lemon-flavoured lozenge up here and within a week you'd find a lemon tree growing. So, Siri couldn't understand why the only dish on the Guesthouse Number One menu was *feu* rice noodles and cabbage.

The coffee was to take away the taste of the cabbage and stimulate his leaden mind. He had lots of little clues but he wasn't able to put them together in an order that explained anything. The previous night, the disco had kept him awake till two. Some infernal bongo drum had willed him to go back there, but he fought off the temptation. He'd been hoping for a dream, but when sleep finally came there was nothing to see. At least, there was nothing he could remember.

He'd woken again later when it was still dark. He had an urge to go to the bathroom. It was an annoying urge because the bathroom was downstairs and dark. But he'd arrived at the age when a man's bladder has risen through the hierarchy of bodily organs to become all powerful. It made the rules. He slipped on his sandals and walked down to the communal lavatory. The air was still and cold. Smelly water squelched under his feet. He'd left the torch on top of the partition wall. His memory was good enough to have no need for a spotlight on his business. The beam was directed back into the shower booths.

The sound of water dripping behind him gradually became a spurt, as if someone had turned on a shower. He lowered his sarong and turned. The water beneath his feet had risen drastically. The shower opposite was gushing, throwing forth impossible torrents of water – far more than could ever logically pass through a lead pipe. Siri had learned how to overcome fear during moments such as this. It was his reverse twilight, the time before sunrise when he was neither awake nor asleep. It was a time to observe and learn. There was no need to panic.

The water poured now from the ceiling of the shower booth like a mountain waterfall. It continued to rise past his knees. It had no temperature, no substance. He was vaguely able to make out a shape beneath the surface two metres away. He took up his light and directed the beam down into the water. There, lying flat on the bathroom tiles, was Isandro. He reclined like a cadaver prepared for burial with his large hands spread, one on top of the other on his chest. He looked serene, peaceful – complete.

DISCO FOR THE DEPARTED

The next thing Siri knew he was being woken by a
banging on his door. It was an angry banging. His door
didn't have a lock but he'd wedged the chair under the
handle, and the maid who walked in ten times a day
without warning was taking it personally.

'Who is it?' he asked sweetly, knowing the answer full
well.

'Your breakfast,' she snapped, 'is in the bowl. If you
aren't down in five minutes it'll be cold.'

'You are an angel in brown burlap dungarees, comrade,'
he shouted through the door. 'The Party extends its gratitude for your keeping me in sustenance.'

He'd learned from experience, if he took five or fifty-five
minutes, it would still be cold. So he took his time going
down, picked at the tepid noodles and considered his
mystery. And still, an hour later, here he sat with his second
mug of sea mud, still contemplating the vision he'd had in
the bathroom. If Isandro had died peacefully, why was
Odon's spirit this restless? What was the connection with
water? Had he drowned? Why couldn't Siri's spirit
colleagues just put up a blackboard with all the answers
chalked on it? Why did it all have to be so cryptic?

'Good morning, Doc.'

Siri looked up in surprise to see Dtui walking into the
dining room. Her once-white uniform looked like she'd
offered it up as a canvas to some modern artist from
Hungary. In her arms she carried little Panoy who,
despite her splints and bandages, was looking quite rosy.
The sight of them erased the puzzles from the doctor's
mind.

'Morning, Panoy. Morning, Nurse Dtui, what are you
doing here?'

'The Cubans have landed. They got in last night. I've been excused.'

'How did you get here?'

'The truck that brought the new doctors gave me a ride back.'

'And should I assume you've become a foster parent?'

'I found out what village her mother was from. As soon as we get her back to earth I'd like to take her there.'

'That's nice of you. I doubt the fractures will take long to heal. I imagine we could take her any time.'

'Er …'

'Yes?'

'It isn't really the fractures we need to worry about.'

He felt the child's forehead and looked into her eyes. 'Has there been some complication?'

'You could say that. The truck ride quietened her down a bit, but I reckon she could start up any time now.'

'Start up what?'

The spirit of Mrs Nuts had a marvellous sense of timing. Even as Siri stared at the girl, she seemed to change to a different gear. She smiled and giggled once as a four-year-old, then continued where she'd left off in the voice of a grandmother.

'Oh, I say.' Siri raised his bushy old eyebrows and watched in surprise. 'We seem to have a few wires crossed here.'

'Tell me about it.'

'I'm not sure I can. If she were a radio we could just twiddle with the antenna a bit. But this isn't going to be easy. Not easy at all.'

*

Mr Woot, the spy, the bounty hunter, the chicken-counting *Khon Khouay* representative for the region, was sitting in the office of the regional Insurgency Intelligence Unit eight kilometres from Vang Vieng. He still had that Darkie Toothpaste smile on his face, just like the minstrel on the tube, but it was beginning to fade. His capture of the day was safely in his cell, and all Woot wanted now was his bounty money. Once he was paid he could be back out on the streets hunting down insurgents, discovering double agents, weeding out royalist sympathisers. But the Unit director still hadn't handed over the reward.

'Woot,' he said. 'You know? I don't think I can sell this tale to Vientiane.'

'What are you talking about?' Woot said indignantly. 'I caught him red-handed taking notes at the airfield.'

'You didn't bring me any evidence.'

'Ooy, I told you. Before I could get to him he'd swallowed the paper. I wasn't about to reach down his throat and fish it out, was I now?'

Captain Bounyasith was an old drinking buddy of Woot's and he got a percentage of all the bounty money he handed out to his field agents. He was trying very hard to make the story fly, but it was still too heavy to get off the ground. 'Plus,' he said, 'there's the fact that the airfield down there hasn't been used since Air America left.'

'Reconnaissance, comrade. Reconnaissance. The insurgents have obviously got it earmarked as a future invasion site. Come, on. Work with me on this, brother.'

'I'm just telling you what Vientiane's going to say to me. That's all.' The tired old captain sighed and dipped his Vietnamese biscuit into his tea. All but the pinch between his fingers broke off and sank beneath the surface. He swore under his breath. It was a crumbly, soggy type of day all round.

'Okay,' Woot conceded. 'But we do have the actual insurgent locked up.'

The captain fished around in the tea with his pen. He could find no evidence at all that the biscuit ever existed. 'Have you not noticed what he is?' he asked. 'Don't you think they'll notice that at the interrogation?'

'It's a front.'

'A front? You mean he's pretending to look the way he does? You mean he doesn't actually have speech and hearing problems? You mean he doesn't have flaky skin and flat feet and stink like a field latrine?'

There were a few seconds of silence.

'He's good, I'll give him that.'

Captain Bounyasith leaned back and emptied his tea out of the open window into the yard. They heard the chickens cluck towards it in a frenzy. 'No, Woot. It isn't going to work. Nobody's going to believe it.'

'Shit!' The spy, who everyone in the province knew without doubt was a spy, stood up and cursed his luck. 'What are you going to do with him?'

'Give him a bite to eat and let him go.'

'Did he have any money on him?'

'Not a brass *kip*.'

'Shit. I can't even get the petrol money back. What a day.'

14

MRS NUTS GOES HOME

Mrs Nuts's village was only five kilometres from Vieng Xai but there was no road. To get there, Siri, Dtui and Panoy had followed their guide along a narrow track that wound slowly through a gentle valley past rocky outcrops that poked up like fingers making rude signs. The village itself sat ridiculously on top of a high knoll as if, one day in its distant history, it had fled there to escape a flood. The final fifty metres of pathway seemed to climb vertically. Panoy weighed no more than a wish, but Dtui had carried her all the way and she was certain this final stretch would be the death of her. Fortunately, the girl who had daubed Mrs Nuts's feet with blood recognised the big nurse and came running down to relieve her of her burden.

They were welcomed with some confusion by the villagers and led to the hut of the shaman. They discovered him swaying in one corner. He flapped his arm slowly as a gesture for the strangers to come in. He was a man of around forty, muscular and kindly, but he was so laid-back, Siri and Dtui almost fell asleep listening to him. He had apparently invented a cocktail of local herbs which, he claimed, dispensed with the need for food if taken three times a day. It also left him in a state of perpetual bliss – one which he was reluctant to disturb with work.

'You see?' he said in a slow drawl. 'Organising an exorcism takes many many many days. Weeks, sometimes. Years.' He obviously didn't know to whom he was speaking. Dr Siri understood only too well, given the right frame of mind, an exorcism could be patched together in an hour or so. He just had to find that frame of mind in the stoned shaman.

'Great and respected witch doctor,' Siri said. 'Of course, you're right. But here in your village you have a poor unfortunate lady wrapped in betel-nut leaves who can't be cremated until her soul has been reunited with her body. And we have brought that soul in the body of this little girl. It's barely an exorcism – more like replanting a yam in a different garden. It couldn't be any easier.'

Of course, it wouldn't be quite that easy, but all Siri needed was for the shaman to bring together the tools of his trade and Yeh Ming would probably oblige with the service. The shaman sighed long and deep and started to list the difficulties. Siri didn't really have time to hear them. He decided it was necessary to give the man a small prod. He reached out for his hand and gripped it firmly. All those present noticed a change come over the shaman. He seemed to be witnessing events nobody else could see. It was as if he were being filled with information like a tyre being slowly pumped full of air. But before he could burst, Siri released his grip.

'Well, why didn't you say so?' the shaman smiled. 'Welcome.'

Within an hour, the paraphernalia was ready. The shaman was dressed in red and had a hood pulled back from his face. It was a humble affair. Apart from the two main participants, the shaman, Siri and Dtui, there were three witnesses. One of these appeared to be the shaman's wife, who played various percussion instruments, making them all sound like kitchen utensils rattling together in a drawer. Something within Siri bemoaned this lack of rhythm.

Siri had seen this all before on a much grander scale, but it was Dtui's first paranormal ceremony and she wished she'd had the presence of mind to bring the morgue camera. She studied the tray of assorted stones and ornaments, the dagger, the offering of food and cigarettes. The cone of banana leaf origami she'd seen often at weddings and funerals but never decorated as lavishly as this. Threads of unspun white cotton looped down from the display and were long enough to drape across the supine bodies of Panoy and Mrs Nuts. For everyone's sake, the village women had treated the old lady's body with musky oils and scents. These had the effect of dulling the putrid stink of death long enough for the ceremony to take place.

For twenty minutes, the shaman sat cross-legged in front of the display chanting a well-worn series of mantras. A ceremonial dagger jutted from the lightly packed earth at his feet. Siri held his amulet lightly. A tingle of nervous apprehension climbed the back of his neck. At his last exorcism, the *phibob* had killed the shaman and all but drained the life out of Siri also. He was better prepared now, but still hoped the malevolent spirits weren't tuned in at such an early hour.

The shaman, already one or two paces closer to nirvana than most, was quick to enter his trance. His wife lowered the hood over his head and Dtui wondered how he was going to see what he was doing with no eyeholes. But he didn't need his eyes. For the next few moments, all his movements would be guided by some non-being. Siri had seen mediums thrown across the room by the spirits that possessed them at this stage. He'd seen shamans hit themselves violently with their own fists or rise into the air. But there were no such histrionics for this gentleman. His visiting spirit seemed as lethargic as its host.

He rose to his feet as smoothly as smoke rising from a mosquito coil and walked once around the spectators. His feet barely touched the ground. He sighed and kneeled by the body of Panoy who still muttered in a stranger's voice. She lay on a straw litter beside Mrs Nuts. He leaned down to her head, cupped his hand around her ear and began to whisper. Siri knew by this stage that the shaman would need no help. All was under control. After two or three minutes, the little girl's body jerked slightly. Only one person in the audience saw what happened next. The spirit of Mrs Nuts rose from the girl's body, looked around the room, then crossed over to her own. She woke the spirit of the little girl who slept in her place and watched as she stumbled sleepily back to her own body. Mrs Nuts then curled up in her old carcass, oblivious to the smell. It was that simple. Like changing beds in the middle of the night.

Little Panoy's eyes opened. She looked at the threads that lay across her body like spider's yarn, then noticed the red hooded shape beside her. She jerked away, and, like any normal four-year-old, began to wail. Dtui rushed to comfort her, but none of this noise or movement had any effect on the shaman who was now in a deep sleep.

Later, Dtui and Siri and the guide took tea beneath a straw canopy. The sun was harsh but a breeze skimmed across the top of the knoll. Siri stared at the pretty girl who'd brought them the cups and was now sitting beneath the leaves of a banana tree. There was something about her that drew him to her.

Dtui's voice pulled him from his reverie. 'Of course, it was interesting. I'm not saying it wasn't. But I have to say I was expecting something more – more violent. You know? Blood and screaming and people going crazy.'

'That does occasionally happen,' Siri told her. 'This was the soporific version.'

'When will the shaman fellow wake up?'

'Judging from his normal relationship with consciousness, I'd say sometime around November.'

'So, we should get going.'

'Hold on a while.'

'What for?'

'There's something else here.'

'What?'

'I don't know. But there's a connection. There's always a connection. I feel we shouldn't leave just yet.'

'You're the boss. I'll go see how Panoy's doing.' Dtui clambered to her feet and walked off to the hut where the little girl was sleeping off her ordeal. Siri sipped his tea and smiled at the teenager. Her features were finer than the other women of the village and her skin darker.

'Little sister,' he called over to her. She smiled shyly. 'Where are you from?'

'From Vietnam, uncle.'

'You're montagnard aren't you?'

She seemed pleased that he'd not used the derogatory word *moi*. 'My mother's Hmong, my father's montagnard. He came here with his family when the Viet Minh started to …' She stopped herself.

'I'm Lao, not Vietnamese,' he told her.

'My father's people had sided with the French colonists against the communists. When the war was lost, the Vietnamese made them suffer for it.'

'There can't be many montagnards here in Huaphan.'

'There are a few.'

'Tell me about them.'

She seemed delighted this old Lao doctor was showing an interest in her people. She came across to sit beside Siri and told him about one young man who was a porter for the military, and about a family she knew that was working on the Vietnamese roads, and on she went. There was an amazing grapevine. In spite of her isolation here, she could reel off the details of all the expatriates from the central highlands. At last she got to one that pricked Siri's interest.

'Then there's H'Loi,' she continued. 'She's married to a Lao. She used to be the maid of a big Vietnamese soldier who died. Then there's ...'

There it was: the connection. Siri interrupted her gossip. 'Do you know what happened to the family H'Loi worked for?'

'The soldier's family, you mean? No, uncle. All I know is she found herself stuck here without a job. But she got lucky and caught a local chap.'

'Do you have any idea where they live?'

'Of course.'

'Is it far?'

'About half an hour. Do you want to go there? I can show you.'

*

Siri sent Dtui back to the guesthouse with Panoy and the guide. Dtui seemed anxious to talk to him about some other pressing issue, but she decided it could wait. He had a feeling it was something serious and promised he'd be back as soon as he could. He set off across the rolling hills closely at the montagnard girl's heels. Very few hikers in Huaphan strayed from the well-trodden paths. In fact, even the well-trodden paths were known to explode from time to time.

At a village so simple it made the previous hamlet look like Manhattan, they met H'Loi. She was a plain jolly woman in her thirties who lived with an extremely ugly Lao man much older than herself. The marriage had given her legal status. Necessity, for the victimised montagnards, was the mother of invention. The woman had already been fluent in French and Vietnamese as well as two local dialects. Since her marriage, she'd mastered Lao. In any other society she'd be a highly sought-after personal assistant or interpreter. In this village she made babies and cooked. She knew there was no point in arguing with her fate.

She sat in her simple house with Siri and was happy to discuss her time with the colonel and his family. She'd been recruited by the colonel's wife when they were at their previous posting in Ban Methuot in Vietnam's central highlands. It wasn't as if she'd had any choice. She was lucky to have any kind of work at all. The fifteen-hundred kilometre journey here to Huaphan was for their next posting. Although the wife could be something of an ogre, the daughter, Hong Lan, was sweet and, in H'Loi's charming phraseology, as smart as a bath full of judges. Apart from being the maid, cook and tutor, H'Loi had also been the girl's companion. They had become close.

When Hong Lan fell sick, H'Loi had gone to the hospital every day. Often she stayed there overnight. Hong Lan used to tell her it was just a little stomach pain, but the doctor had confided once that it was more serious than that and she had to have two operations to make things right. Hong Lan was in the Kilometre 8 Hospital for over a month, recovering. Then, one day, the mother turned up out of the blue and had her transferred to a military hospital just outside Xam Dtai. That had been too far for H'Loi to travel every day so she didn't see Hong Lan until the girl returned home.

Hong Lan hadn't been herself at all after that. She was still very weak but everyone said the operation had been a success and it wouldn't be long before she was her old self again. But H'Loi wasn't so sure. All that positive talk didn't seem to change Hong Lan's condition one little bit. They talked a lot in those days. Once the girl confided that she'd fallen in love during her stay at Kilometre 8. That came as something of a shock to H'Loi because she'd never suspected anything of the sort. Although Hong Lan didn't ever tell her who the man was, she talked about him as if she knew him intimately. She said there was good reason why she couldn't mention his name.

But, by then, H'Loi had already started hearing the rumours. She knew about the black magicians and their love potions and hypnotism and their sacrifices. H'Loi's people had its own share of occult practices so she knew how dangerous they could be. In spite of her love for the girl she'd nannied for nine years, H'Loi was certain she didn't know what she was saying. She'd been hexed. She'd never before talked of love, never shown an interest in men. Then, suddenly, after six weeks in a cave, she'd fallen head over heels in love with a man she hardly knew: a man who was totally wrong for her. When she finally confronted Hong Lan with her suspicions, H'Loi didn't pretend to mask the hatred she felt for the Cubans. It didn't matter whether they were black, pink or cobalt blue. They were bad. She told Hong Lan they were devils, and the relationship between the girl and her nanny soured.

The colonel's death was so unexpected it left them all stunned for some time. The war was over and the family had dreams of a normal, happy life. As a military family under the Viet Minh, they'd never had a permanent home. But just when they were so close to their dream the old soldier goes and gets himself killed. After the funeral, Hong Lan's mother started preparations for their journey back to Vietnam. They had a small army pension, enough for a little house. Perhaps Hong Lan could even go to college.

But, just before the departure, the girl was kidnapped. She was taken right from their wooden shack in broad daylight. At the time, her mother had been away making the final arrangements for transport. H'Loi was out picking fruit for the journey. When she got back to the house, Hong Lan was gone. There were signs of a struggle. A strongbox had been broken into and the housekeeping money was missing. According to H'Loi, everyone knew who was responsible. There was a huge search. The colonel's old regiment was mobilised. They scoured the whole province. After two weeks when there was still no sign of the girl or the Cubans, everyone assumed they'd taken her out of Laos. The mother returned to Vietnam leaving H'Loi to fend for herself.

Siri had so many questions about this amazing story he didn't know where to begin.

'Why didn't you return with the mother?' he asked.

'She didn't ask me to. She blamed me for not watching her daughter that day. She just vanished with all their belongings and my wages, what little there was of them. I didn't have any money to go anywhere. The regional command sympathised and they kindly found me a husband.'

'Very nice of them,' Siri said. 'And you didn't hear anything else of Hong Lan?'

'Oh, there were stories. This is the world capital for rumours. I'm sure you know that, uncle.'

'Were there any credible ones?'

'Not really. There was one that they'd murdered her and buried the body. Another was that the blacks had smuggled her to Cuba to use as a sex slave.'

'And what do you think happened?'

She gave him a look as if it had been a very long time since anyone had sought out her opinion on anything. 'I really have no idea, uncle. I'd like to think, spell or no spell, that she enjoyed this love she thought she had, and that she's still living in blissful ignorance somewhere.'

'How was Hong Lan's relationship with her mother?' Siri asked, again catching the woman by surprise.

'I suppose there's no harm in telling you. I doubt I'll ever see the old witch again. You know? If they were close, they wouldn't have needed me. It was as if she'd done her national duty, produced the child the colonel expected, then left it to grow by itself. The mother was politically active. She ran seminars and organised this and that. But I never once saw her hold her daughter. I wasn't the first nanny. The girl had half a dozen before I came along.'

'Yet, she turned out okay?'

'She turned out lovely. That's what happens when you have a montagnard looking after your child.'

'I'll bear it in mind when I have my next.' They both laughed and the husband poked his ugly head in through the window to see what was happening.

H'Loi ignored him. 'I often wonder whether she would have been so susceptible to the magic if she'd had a little more love from her family.'

'The day of the kidnap ... whose decision was it for you to go and pick fruit?'

H'Loi laughed again. 'Do you really expect me to remember such a thing? I'm just a simple housewife, remember?'

'Madam,' Siri said, in all sincerity, 'I have met many simple housewives in my life, and, believe me, you are not one of them. You are a very astute, intelligent woman.' She looked at him with her mouth open, astounded. Never in her life had she received such a compliment. The fact that it had come from a man of letters, a physician no less, made it all the more incredible. All the more profound. A solitary tear gathered momentum in the corner of her eye and rolled down her cheek.

'I suppose it had to be Hong Lan,' she said, wiping it hurriedly away.

'What did?'

'Who suggested I pick fruit. She was the only one who ate the stuff. I'd never seen anyone get through so much fruit without spending the day in the toilet. Her mother lived on a diet of rice and pork rind for years. That was probably the root of her nastiness.'

'Do you believe Hong Lan might still be alive?'

'Doctor ... honestly, I don't feel her presence any more.'

Siri got lost three times on his walk down from the hills, but as anywhere down would lead him to the only road he was never in a state of panic. He arrived at the guesthouse just as the day ended. He found himself mesmerised by the setting sun. He saw it as a huge bullet puncturing the horizon in slow motion. The horizon bled, its red seeping from the entry wound and oozing across the landscape. It occurred to him that forensic pathology might be damaging his appreciation of nature.

Before even reaching the front steps of the building, he saw Dtui and Panoy under a *don soak*, the sad tree. He walked over to them.

'Hello,' he said. 'Having a picnic?'

'They won't let us in,' Dtui told him.

'In what?'

'In Guesthouse Number One.'

'Why on earth not?'

'They say this little girl here' – Panoy looked up and smiled and tried to reach for Siri's eyebrows – 'is illegal. They say they can't allow guests who are not on the official Party register.'

'But she stayed here last night.'

Dtui put on the strict tone of the guesthouse manageress. '"That was an absolute infringement of regulations for which somebody will be punished." If they'd known we'd smuggled her in they'd probably have shot us on the spot.'

'I take it you've already argued the point?'

She smiled. 'Isn't my face still blue?'

'Then let us once more attempt to champion the cause against silly rules.'

They walked to the steps and the manageress, still in her apron and army fatigues, stood at the top with her arms folded. It appeared she'd anticipated this second foray. Siri took a moment to weigh up the enemy. She'd never formally introduced herself, though Siri had noticed her lurking in the background of every meeting, meal and melee. She was fortyish and formidable, but Siri had battled worse.

'Good evening, comrade,' Siri smiled.

The woman responded with a line she'd obviously been rehearsing. 'I'm sorry, Doctor. She can't come in. There are rules. I've already reported last night's infringement.'

'She doesn't need a room,' he tried.

'She isn't registered. She can't come in.'

'This is a guesthouse.'

'Not that kind of guesthouse, it isn't.'

'You mean, the kind that admits guests?'

'Only guests that are on the list.' She was an immovable object. 'Rules are rules. Where would we be if we all went around bending them?'

'Quite right. And what is your stance with regard to evidence?' said the irresistible force known as Dr Siri.

'I ... you what?'

'Evidence, comrade. I'm the national coroner. I've come north to collect evidence for the President.'

'Evidence is things.'

'It certainly can be "things", as you rightly say. It could be photographs, or even the spoken word. Or, it could be a person who bears evidence.'

'I'm not sure I understand what you're getting at.'

'This little girl' – he dragged Dtui forward with Panoy in her arms – 'is covered in fingerprints.'

'She ...? There aren't fingerprints on people.'

'Obviously you haven't been keeping abreast of world issues on forensics. Why do you think we didn't let her shower yesterday evening? According to the law, and I'm also a barrister so I know what I'm talking about, this little girl is not technically a person. She's *corpus delicti*. In short, she's my evidence. Naturally, if there were some way to remove the fingerprints from her and take those to the justice department, I would do so. But I'm sure you realise how nasty that would be. She is the evidence that carries the prints. So you don't have to worry about her being registered, do you?'

'I ... I don't?'

'No. Because by the letter of the law, as she isn't a person, she can't be a guest.' He winked at her and smiled. He doubted she was silly enough to believe such rubbish but he had given her a way around her rules.

'I ... I suppose.'

'I'm sure comrade Lit of the security division will confirm this when he gets here.'

The woman's left eye looked first at Siri, then at the child. The right eye did so a split second later. Both eyes eventually settled on Dtui. 'Why didn't you tell me this?'

Dtui shrugged. 'I'm in medicine. Law's way above my head. I wouldn't have known where to start. I was sure, as legal adviser to the President, comrade Siri here would be able to clear things up for you.'

'Well, yes. I mean. If only I'd known.'

Panoy was sleeping soundly on the spare bed in Dtui's room. Siri and Dtui were sitting out front with their feet up on the balcony wall. She'd just finished explaining her dilemma. Siri grunted.

'I mean, it is a marvellous compliment,' she said, looking up at the cliff that towered over them like a purgatorial mother-in-law. 'I mean to say, it isn't as if he doesn't have choices. He's somebody. He'll probably keep climbing till he's … what? Prime Minister or something. Women like men with power. But, if he got that far, I doubt he'd want me spurting on about his politics. It's sure to annoy him. Perhaps I'd be able to tone it down a little. I could run the house and leave the country to him.' Siri took a sip of his tea and smiled.

'I mean,' she went on, 'he'd have to make changes too. That's what a good marriage is – compromise. Right? I'm sure you and Boua had to make compromises. And look, you were together for a hundred and some years. It just takes a little work.' She sipped her tea also.

Caught in the light from the balcony, they watched an egret swoop down from a ledge and perform an almost perfect loop-the-loop before continuing its glide downwards. It was worth a comment but Dtui was preoccupied. 'I mean, how many offers like this is someone like me going to get? Perhaps I should think about that. If I passed this up, there I'd be an old maid with varicose veins and a moustache always rueing this lost opportunity.'

A little girlish sigh escaped from Panoy's dream. Dtui let it fade away, then continued. 'I suppose the question is, which would I regret more, marrying him or not marrying him? My ma says a man is never going to be sweeter than he was on the day he proposed to you. She said that's the best you get. Once you're deposited in the wife bank he never has to make that effort again. He really knocked me flat with his speech, but I wouldn't be surprised if he got a sub-committee to write it for him. I didn't exactly see any emotion. He recited it like he was making a presentation to the grand assembly.'

She swung her feet down from the wall and stood with her hands on the balcony railing as if she were about to address a large gathering. 'And the damned permission form.' She almost spat out the words. 'What arrogance. What spinelessness. Would he have to get Party permission before every decision he made? Everyone at the Regional Office knew he was going to propose before I did. Is that how he'd run his personal life? "Dtui, darling. I think it would be nice if we made love tonight. I'll just pop down to the Social Order Committee sub-office and fill out an F27b."' She blushed. 'Ooh, sorry, Doc.' He raised his eyebrows in forgiveness.

'I mean' – she appeared to be on the last lap now – 'what kind of a creep wouldn't have the backbone to stand up to a room full of bureaucrats? And who does he think he is – negotiating me into a marriage without any flirting or wooing? Surely a girl deserves that? Perhaps he knew I wouldn't have had any of it. I'd have knocked him back at the first glimmer of a "come on". The shock marriage card was the only one he had to play.

'But, this is all academic, Doc.' She looked over her shoulder to see if he was still there. 'You know why? Because, when I get married, it's not going to be to some-body who's suitable or well off or looks good in a uniform. I'm going to marry someone who turns my insides to soya paste. I'm going to marry someone I hate to leave when I go to work in the morning: someone I miss all day. I'm going to marry someone I love and I'm not going to settle for anything less. I could no sooner love comrade Lit than I could learn to like this horrible creepy building. No, you self-assured Party machine – go find yourself another "suitable" woman to appoint to the wife position. I'm out.'

She heaved a sigh of relief and sat heavily back onto her chair. Siri put his hand on hers.

'Thanks, Doc,' she said. 'I knew you'd sort it all out for me.'

'Glad to have been of service,' he told her.

15

LAONESS

Mr Geung had followed the coastline of the Num Ngum reservoir for twenty kilometres. He'd spent the night in a disused fishing hut on the bank. The first thing he noticed when he woke was his own smell. He could hardly remember why he was coated in this dark brown gunk that had hardened to a shell, and the clear water was right there in front of his door. He walked fully dressed, apart from his boots, into the reservoir. It was a wonderful feeling. Not till he was in up to his neck did he undress. His shoulder stung a little but the cool water soothed his aching muscles, soaked his flaky skin, and washed away his only protection against insects.

What makes the dengue mosquito so deadly is the clock. Once the sun dips below the horizon, people know that this is mosquito frenzy time. They wear long sleeves, put on repellent, and light their coils. At night they sleep under nets. It's a type of unspoken contract between man and his bloodsucking foe. But the dengue mosquito is a contract breaker. She strikes in broad daylight when you're sweating in the fields, when you're swinging on your hammock in the shade, even when you're sitting stark naked beside Num Ngum reservoir waiting for your clothes to dry.

The incubation period for the disease is five to seven days. A little after that you'll know whether the strain is one that will make you violently ill, but not kill you, or whether you've contracted the bleeding fever which will usually finish you off painfully but quickly. Even without the rains, tens of thousands of lives had been claimed by the wicked daytime blood thieves this year. The epidemic had originated in the north of Vientiane province, probably in the area around the dam.

Geung slapped at his arm a fraction too late. He picked his attacker from his skin. She was a tiny thing, black and white striped and bloody. He wondered how such a small thing could bleed so much.

People had been incredibly kind to the odd man who passed through village after village on his long march down the western shore of the reservoir. Before the days of political deception and fragmentation, this had always been the Lao way. If a stranger came to your house, you would offer him what you had to help him on his way. Even families with barely enough food for their own children would break off some of their sticky rice and prepare a separate bowl of spicy vegetable sauce for a visitor. There had always been trust and respect.

In the large cities, that feeling was all but gone. But in the small villages the elders still held out hope that Laoness wouldn't be destroyed by politics. They fed Geung, gave him balm for his skin, dressed his blisters and offered him a bed for the night. They had to shout loudly now to be heard because all sounds had become an underwater buzz to Geung. Although they all tried, no one could dissuade him from his foolish desire to complete his walk to the capital. They yelled a 'good luck' and watched him limp his way south. Everyone doubted he'd live long enough to complete the trip.

Mr Geung was getting a bad, bad, feeling too. He'd walked more than he ever had in his life. Already he could feel his strength draining away. He couldn't count how many daybreaks he'd woken to or how many flat footsteps he'd trodden. Strange things had begun to happen in his head. He felt sure he was becoming a moth. The only thing in his mind was the electric light bulb of Vientiane. It dazzled him away from his actual surroundings and filled his head so completely he often didn't know where he was or who he was talking to. Every woman he met, he called Dtui. Every man he addressed as comrade Doctor.

Siri and Dtui sat silently on the concrete path not far from the broken slabs. The 'evidence' continued to sleep off her trauma under the watchful eye of the guesthouse maid. There was no sun and the sky promised a depressing period of rain – not a good old central-plains monsoon, but a slow drizzly rain that could soak into a man's mind and dampen his mood. A line of red ants had found Siri on their proposed parade route. Before heading back in the direction from which they'd come, each ant stepped forward to take a look at the doctor like visitors at a mausoleum.

'Perhaps we're looking in the wrong places,' Dtui said at last. Siri had taken her to see the Cuban hideout and the eerie altar room. They'd found no new clues at either.

'Or not looking in enough right places. I feel perhaps we aren't talking to the right people.'

'You're right. Let's get talking,' Dtui agreed.

'Any suggestion as to where we might start?'

'Right here under our backsides' – Siri raised an eyebrow – 'Look at all this concrete. How long do you suppose it took to build this path?'

'A couple of men? One or two weeks.'

'And the Cubans were right here in the cave behind them all that time? Don't you wonder if they might have seen something?'

'Excellent. Yes, indeed. That's the kind of ... concrete thinking that will get you to the Eastern Bloc.'

'Doc ...'

'I'm sorry.'

The guesthouse truck arrived in Xam Neua an hour later. Tracing the contractors had been comparatively simple. There was one main team that did most of the concrete work on government projects. They were presently working on the new police station down by the bridge. The foreman of the team was an old soldier who Siri knew from several campaigns. In Laos, the odds of bumping into people one knew were far from astronomical. In fact it happened all the time. The concrete layer's name was Bui and he had the type of face and build that doesn't undergo any drastic changes between sixteen and sixty. Dtui was impressed at how everyone, excluding high-ranking bureaucrats, was truly delighted to be reunited with their old friend Dr Siri.

They all sat together on the newly dried concrete floor of a room that would soon house a police lieutenant. Bui wished he had whisky to welcome the doctor, but they had to settle for warmish water that smelled vaguely of paint thinner. Once they'd caught up with one another's news, Siri told the old man why he was there in the north-east and asked whether Bui might have any information that could help them. He could never have expected the response that he got. Dtui's instincts had, as they say, hit the bullock right in the balls. As they sipped at their water, a light drizzle floated down from the clouds, and Bui told them the story of what had happened one day in January.

'It was a Tuesday if I remember rightly,' he began. 'The reason I know that is because the President's footpath was the last one we did and some inspector was due in on the Wednesday flight to check we'd got it all done. There were only two flights a week then. Well, we were only just on schedule. We found ourselves working late into Tuesday evening to get it done. So, it turned out we were walking back down to our huts in the dark.

'There were three of us and we were all tuckered out, looking forward to a good meal and our beds. We'd just got to the football field. As usual, there was a mist, one of those that makes you shudder just walking through it. That was when we saw them.'

'The Cubans?' Siri asked.

'And the girl.'

'Hong Lan? The Vietnamese?'

'Couldn't be sure it was her, but we'd all heard the stories about the black magic and the kidnapping and all. The bigger of the two, he had the girl in his arms, you know? The way you carry an old person. She looked drugged.'

'Or dead?' Dtui asked.

'Could have been. Her arms were dangling down and

her head was hanging back. They just walked out of the mist about thirty yards ahead of us. Me and the boys froze. It was like something out of one of them Hong Kong ghost films. The big guy was in front with the girl walking slow. About five paces back was the little one, and I swear he had this knife, more like a sword really. Whatever it was, it looked like it could do a lot of damage.'

'Did they see you?'

'If they did, they didn't let on. But, to tell the truth, it was as if they couldn't see much of anything – like they were in a trance.'

'Where were they heading?' Siri asked.

'Straight for the military complex.'

'The concert cave?'

'In that direction. So we waited till they were gone, long gone, before we were game to say anything. Even then we whispered. Sound carries on the mist. We got into a huddle and decided what we ought to do. We knew the Vietnamese had been looking for the girl, but the mother had left already – gone back to Hanoi I heard. So, one of the boys rode his bicycle over to the army post – the one that used to be up at the Xam Neua intersection. You remember that?'

'It was still there? I thought all the Viet Minh pulled out at the end of '75.'

The old soldier laughed but didn't bother to explain away that particular PL trickery.

'And what happened?' Dtui asked.

'Well, that was it.'

'What was it?'

'We didn't hear anything else about it.'

'Didn't you ask?'

'We went back to Xam Neua the next day and were busy with the inspector. He wanted this and that changed. You know what they're like. Afterwards, nobody seemed to know anything. We sort of forgot all about it.'

'Hell! If it had been me, I would have exploded with curiosity,' Dtui told him.

'It's true,' Siri agreed. 'I've seen Nurse Dtui explode with curiosity, and I have to tell you, Bui, it isn't a sight you'd want to witness twice.'

There were still a couple of hours of daylight when Siri and Dtui got back to Vieng Xai. They stopped at the guest-house only long enough to check on Panoy and pick up two torches and a kit of assorted tools. There were three messages from Lit waiting for them. Each asked that they get in touch. They ignored them and headed off to the caves.

Dtui was amazed to see the concert hall hidden within the karst. It seemed even larger now to Siri without its midnight crowds.

'Something's been drawing me here since we arrived in Huaphan,' Siri confessed. 'I should have paid more attention.'

'It's enormous,' Dtui said. 'Where do we start looking?'

'Up top are the chambers and the general's quarters. Down below we have this space, then there are various alcoves and there's a long tunnel that leads to the other end of the mountain where we should find the dining and kitchen area. I suppose we should just poke around till something sparks our instincts.'

'Doc?' Dtui looked around at the high arching walls,

her torch made ominous shadows behind the irregular overhangs. 'We are ... you know? Alone here, aren't we?'

'We should be,' he told her honestly. 'Until about midnight.'

'What happens then?'

'The disco starts.'

He walked towards the stage leaving her wondering whether that was a Dr Siri joke or if she should perhaps keep an eye on her watch. Together they scoured the walls for any icons or symbols similar to those they'd seen at the altar. They saw none, and the question remained, why would they bring her here for a sacrifice when they had a temple set up inside the President's cave?

They went through the auditorium inch by inch without results, then began working through the alcoves. Here the military had plotted its strategies, learned the art of bomb-making and guerilla warfare, and played ping pong by candlelight. There was one small room where male nurses, trained by Dr Siri, had administered medicines, and one more that had served as an armoury. But none of them gave up any secrets.

'So, I suppose we should go through to the kitchen,' Siri decided as they neared the narrow tunnel drilled fifty metres through the solid rock. They stepped over a natural underground stream that had been steered into a concrete conduit. Once it had been used as a collection point for drinking water. Siri led the way into the tunnel, then suddenly stopped. Dtui stumbled into the back of him.

'Hey,' she said.

'Dtui, back up.'

She did so. 'What is it?'

Two things had caused Siri to stop. The first was a

feeling as if someone else's legs were inside his own, walking in the opposite direction. The second was a recollection – the vision he'd seen in the guesthouse bathroom – Isandro lying serenely in water. He turned back to look at the trough through which the water flowed. It was no more than two metres long, designed to channel the naturally flowing water to one side of the walkway, then release it on the other side. Once free to find its own level, the stream spread out rapidly before disappearing beneath the rock face.

'Shine your light down here, Dtui.' The ground sloped gently downwards for three or four metres. The earth was a mixture of clay, sand and fine gravel. It was one of the few sections of floor, presumably because of the running water, that wasn't concreted. Without taking off his old leather sandals, he squatted in four centimetres of water.

'You see something?' Dtui asked.

'I'm not sure. Would you mind going back along the chamber a few metres and shining your lamp from a different angle?' She did what he asked. 'A little higher, perhaps. Splendid. Can you see anything?'

She tried to. She squinted and jiggled the light, and willed herself to see something, but apart from the uneven ruts, there was nothing unusual. Unless, the ruts ... She raised the light even higher, then walked slowly back towards Siri. At last she'd seen what he'd seen. It could merely have been the different quality of the soil, or the packing of it, or the slight ridge, but there were two distinct shapes. They were oval, side by side, too neat and regimented to have been caused naturally.

'Dr Siri. I see them. You don't think ... ?'

'Only one way to find out.' He went to the concreted area

and swung his old army pack from his shoulders. It contained the tools they'd brought with them from Vientiane. As they hadn't known what to expect, they had an interesting collection of just about everything they might need. There was a short-handled garden spade which he gave to Dtui, and a concrete trowel which he took for himself.

First they confirmed that the area around the ovals was more tightly packed than that within them. This increased their belief that something was certainly buried there. They dug vertically down at the centre of the first oval which was a more sensible and less tiring method than attempting to empty the entire space. After a depth of about two hands, they began to dig with more care. If a body had been buried there, it wasn't likely to be very deep in these conditions.

Down they went, three, four, five hands and still they encountered nothing. The clear water filled their hole and caused small avalanches to frustrate their work. Before they knew it, both of them were sopping wet and getting colder as the night mist enfolded the giant karst.

Suddenly, Dtui stopped digging and sat back. 'Dr Siri ...'

'I know,' he said.

They were seven hands deep and had hit tightly packed mud. What they'd both expected to be a grave was in fact empty. Dtui felt an odd sensation. She was aware that something had happened to her sense of decency over the previous year. Before this, she would never have dreamed of digging into wet earth hoping – yes, she had actually been *hoping* – to find a body. She knew Siri had been hoping too. What kind of person had she become? She was a ghoul, a macabre ...

'I suppose we shouldn't be disappointed,' Siri said, mirroring her own feeling.

'Hardly worth trying the other one,' she added.

'Not much point.'

'It's getting late. We really should take a look through the other chambers before ...'

'The disco?'

'Right.'

But they both looked at the second oval the way children, already full, might stare longingly at one more sweet goat's-milk *roti*, wondering if they could perhaps make a space for it. Without a word, they were soon on their damp knees scraping away at the top gravel. At three hands, Dtui's fork met something solid.

'Doc?'

Immediately water filled the hole they were digging and something floated up to the surface. It was a wooden shirt button. Without a word, they pulled back to broaden their excavation site. For another hour they worked carefully to exhume the body that lay beneath the stream. They scraped away the gravelly sand and piled it behind them so it wouldn't collapse back into the grave. When at last the body was completely exposed, lying in a bath of crystal-clear water, Siri and Dtui stood on either side of it shivering in the dank cave. Their torch batteries were almost expired and the faint beams of light shimmered onto the horrifying scene before them.

'Dtui,' Siri said at last. 'I doubt you or I will see anything like this again as long as we live.'

People still spoke to Geung but he no longer heard them. They looked at him kindly but he hadn't the humour to return their smiles. He concentrated the last of his effort into putting one foot in front of the other, one foot in front of the other. Left, and then right. Left, and then right. His aching head was dipped, watching his boots. Responsibility. The morgue. Left – right – food from somewhere – water from somewhere. Insects biting. Left – left, no, that wasn't it.

One town, then another, then one more. How many more towns could there be? How many kilometres of road? Was the sun at his back? He no longer had his bag straps. Where did they go? Was the sun somewhere, dropping into his sack? In the morning ... strap ... what was the song? Then, the road ... just stopped. One minute it was there – then it wasn't. Instead, a wide, slow-moving river. A group of people, their mouths moving at each other, moving at him, laughing. A ferry comes, a flat slab of metal, so heavy, so unlike a boat you could never imagine it on water. Under it, yes. But not floating. Something ... was ... familiar.

The group, like one big crab, with many heads, steps onto the slab of metal. So familiar. Amazingly they float, the crab, the car, the dozen motorbikes. A boy comes. He prods Mr Geung in the chest and holds out his hand. He prods again. Geung looks into the boy's eyes and sees himself reflected there.

The slab of metal runs into the far bank as if it isn't expecting it to be there. The crab lurches forward but keeps its feet. Geung is thrown to the deck. Hands collect him, shuffle him forward. The road re-emerges. People come to stand in front of him – around him. So many mouths moving, so many teeth. They steer him like a bicycle piled high with sugar cane. They steer him off the road and the sun is off his shoulder, onto his nose, in his eyes. A face eclipses it, blocks the sun, switches off the electric light over Vientiane. It is a face without features that leans into his, a ping-pong bat all in black. Mr Geung blinks. Why is this bat holding his shoulders, brushing the hair from his forehead?

They turn, he and the bat, in an odd tango. And by some miracle, the bat acquires a familiar face – the face of Mr Watajak, the man who'd gone to all that trouble to father seven children, only one of whom was a moron.

16

THE WHITE NEGRO

In the kitchen of the military cave complex, an area once covered in camouflage netting, but now open, comrade Lit, Dr Siri, and Nurse Dtui stood around a trestle table upon which lay the almost complete cadaver of Isandro Jesus Montano. Comrade Lit wasn't feeling his best. In fact he'd already thrown up once and was planning on doing so again. It's true he was nervous because in less than four days the entire politburo would be attending a concert not thirty metres from where the body was found. It's true he was nervous because the woman whose name he'd already submitted to the Social Relations Committee to become his betrothed, the women who still hadn't displayed any gratitude for this fact, was standing no more than a metre from his side. Yet, daunting as these two facts may have been, it was undoubtedly the sight of the body that was causing his stomach to churn.

He had seen the other Cuban of course, even handled the mummy. But that had been inhuman, more like a knotted tree branch. This ... thing, this was obscene. So much alive it could almost rise from the table and take hold of his throat. And how could a man who had been black all his life become so white? There were tints of green and yellow, but much of the bloated skin was ashen like the flesh of the Chinese Buddha. The doctor had given the condition a name, *adipish* ... *adipoch*, something like that. But there was no translation for it in Lao. The doctor had remarked how uncommon it was, but that submerging the body in damp earth in such cold conditions had changed the chemistry of the fat and turned it into a thick soapy substance that maintained the shape of the original body. According to the doctor, Lit was very lucky to see such a sight in his lifetime.

Lit didn't feel at all lucky. He just felt sick. The cheesy smell was crawling through the cloth that covered his lower face and he knew his stomach couldn't take what the doctor was about to do.

'I'm going in,' Siri said innocently. 'Hold on to your breakfast.'

He held a scalpel that glistened in the morning light.

Lit began to sway.

The night officer had woken the security chief at midnight to tell him the doctor had found the second Cuban. The message was that there was nothing to be done but guard the body until morning. Lit had arrived at six with two aides and was met in front of the concert cave by a smiling Siri. Without any attempt at disguising their respective disgust, the aides manhandled the body from its bath and onto a stretcher. They carried it through the long tunnel to where it now lay.

As they worked, Siri had updated comrade Lit on everything he'd learned since they'd last met. Lit applauded the coroner's skill in the art of detection and made copious notes in his book. But now, with the scalpel hovering above the abdomen of the cadaver, he volunteered to make himself scarce and return later when he was feeling better.

At that time, and no sooner, he would be happy to hear the results of the autopsy.

Obviously, a rickety table in an open-air kitchen and a cloud of curious flies was not the ideal setting for a post-mortem examination. But the relative wholeness of the body made everything just that little less unpleasant. The only sign of disfigurement was a twenty-centimetre incision at the top of the abdomen. The fact that it had been submerged in damp earth for all this time might have affected the wound's appearance, but it seemed to Siri that there was no scar tissue or tumour, suggesting that this surgery occurred after Isandro's death.

As they worked through the standard autopsy procedures, it was hard to believe this was a six-month-old corpse. Almost immediately, the reason for the hole in the abdomen became apparent. Someone had created the aperture in order to hack through the centimetre of tough diaphragm muscle and break into the heart cavity. Once there, they'd carefully cut loose and pilfered the heart. All of this had taken place after Isandro's death.

'Can I say "That's weird" yet?' Dtui asked.

'Go ahead,' Siri told her.

'That's definitely weird.'

'And do you know what else is odd?'

'Give me a clue.'

'Do you see any evidence of parallel scars on the chest?'

'You're right. Not one. That's weird too.'

And they were still left with the dilemma of finding out what actually did kill the Cuban. There were no other wounds, no internal traumas they could find, and, without a lab, they weren't in a position to analyse any of the stomach contents. Everything pointed to the big man dying peacefully irrespective of his sparkling good health.

Although the findings were able to tell them what didn't happen, rather than what did, they left Dr Siri and Dtui in a fascinating quandary. As they bagged their samples, they went over the scenario of that night. The Cubans are seen carrying a comatose, possibly dead, Vietnamese beauty to these caves. Isandro dies peacefully and is buried in a watery grave. Later that same night, Odon is killed in a horrific fashion. But their victim vanishes without trace, in some way escaping a second grave that may have been intended for her.

They put Isandro, in some semblance of order, into a body bag that the Security Division had left for them, and returned to the guesthouse to get themselves cleaned up. They were still confused, yet strangely invigorated by the mystery they had been presented with. It wasn't yet ten. Panoy kneeled with them at the coffee table, playing cards with her good hand. She'd worked her way into the hearts of the guesthouse staff, even that of the frightening manageress, who usually waited for Siri and Dtui to be away before coming to play with the girl.

The intake of misguided capitalist lackeys had dried up until after the concert. In two days the first delegates would be arriving in Vieng Xai. Those not invited to stay as honoured guests of the Lao politburo members in their own houses would be put up here in the guesthouse. Hopefully, Guesthouse Number Two, under construction at a frenzied pace at the far side of the town, would be ready to accept the overflow. But, until all this happened, the workers at Guesthouse Number One had nothing much to do other than fall in love with a four-year-old orphan.

Yet, despite their free time, the staff still didn't allow any flexibility when it came to a timetable. Siri and Dtui had left before breakfast time and still had two hours before they'd be allowed lunch. They sat on the veranda, drinking tea and nibbling sunflower seeds, watching Panoy talking happily to the two-dimensional royal family. Fortunately, Lit turned up at ten thirty with two slabs of peanut brittle that the three of them devoured with relish. Putting considerable effort into making eye contact with his intended, Lit announced his findings in the task Siri had entrusted to him earlier.

Before giving up his information, he wanted to firmly establish that what he was about to tell them was absolutely confidential as it concerned a mission that was still classified. This information could go no further than the veranda upon which they sat. It was, he informed them, a national security issue. Siri reminded him that nobody at the table, including Panoy, was likely to be passing anything on to the Americans, so he should get on with it.

'Very well,' Lit began. 'The unit, and it was only a unit, that was stationed at the Xam Neua intersection that night, was a guerilla outfit whose mission was to conduct clandestine operations inside Hmong-occupied territory. It was set up shortly after the ambush of Colonel Ha Hung's men, two months earlier. A number of its members had been in Ha Hung's battalion and most had been involved in the earlier search for their commander's kidnapped daughter.'

He told them that the unit had since been disbanded and the men dispatched to other sections, but he proudly produced a carbon copy of the names of its original members. He handed it to Siri who ran his finger down the list. Although he doubted a list of the names of Vietnamese soldiers would have much meaning to him, one name leapt from the paper. Siri took a pencil from his top pocket and made a circle around it. He smiled at Dtui and Lit, but didn't bother to tell them why.

'Are you free, comrade Lit?' Siri asked.

'Dr Siri, in two days, I have to ensure the safety of sixty foreign dignitaries, almost our entire cabinet and forty-odd generals. Before then, I have to solve a murder mystery to the satisfaction of the President. If you could do anything to make that possible, I would gladly not sleep for the next seventy-two hours.'

'Good. Then, let's go for a drive.'

As Lit drove and Dtui sat silent in the back seat, Siri described, perhaps in too great a detail, the findings of the autopsy. The young man nodded at the right times, but Siri could see that he was out of his depth. He was doing a job he saw as temporary, but knew he had to do it to the best of his ability in order to leave it. Thus he was willing to afford Siri every strand of cooperation he had to offer. Often, Lit looked in his rear-view mirror, not to check whether they were being followed, but in order to establish the day's first eye contact with Dtui. In spite of the width of his mirror and Dtui's breadth, she always managed to be somehow just outside the frame. In fact, the journey almost ended in disaster at one point. Lit, with his eyes on the mirror, failed to notice that the road led directly into the river. Siri had woken from his catnap just in time to yell a warning.

It was a journey that Siri knew well. When they turned off at the appropriate kilometre marker, the same ragamuffin Lao guard was there beneath his hay shelter. They didn't even stop to be lied to by him. The poor man slowly got his hunting rifle from his shoulder and eventually manoeuvred it into a firing position, but by then the jeep was long gone. Not a problem, as he didn't actually have any bullets.

Ten minutes later, Siri, Lit and Dtui were sitting around a table in a tent that contained nothing else. Siri had pulled his old friend Captain Vo to one side to explain the situation. This was no longer just an informal chat. Events had reached an official level which involved military protocol and records and witnesses. So, while the Vietnamese were setting up all the official rigmarole, Siri had nothing to do but sit between Dtui and Lit like an Italian grandmother at a date. Dtui was grateful, Lit annoyed.

The silence was relieved by a serious procession of men in dress uniform who filled up all but one of the remaining seats around the table. It occurred to Siri that this was probably not the most convivial atmosphere to induce a career soldier to admit to premeditated murder. In his head, he went through a number of strategies to elicit a confession, but even as Sergeant Major Giap walked escorted into the tent, saluted, and sat in the last seat, Siri still hadn't the vaguest idea of how he could get the man to talk. As it turned out, he had nothing to worry about. Captain Vo took the lead.

'Sergeant Major Giap ... ?'

'Yes, sir?'

'In January of this year, you were a member of a unit of Viet Minh troops stationed thirty kilometres from Xam Neua.'

Giap looked around at the faces of the strangers and realised the army expected him to say what he knew, secret operation or not. 'That's right, sir.'

'One night,' Vo continued, 'a tradesman working in Vieng Xai came to your camp and reported he'd seen the two missing Cubans. Is that correct?'

Siri supposed that if the sergeant major had said no at this point, the matter might have been dropped. But once again the old soldier looked around at the expressionless faces of his accusers and seemed to know instinctively that these were all questions to which there were already answers.

'Yes.'

The captain looked harshly into his eyes. Siri saw that this was no longer the laughing man with whom he'd played chess deep in nameless jungles. Captain Vo had hardened into a leader who demanded unswerving loyalty and total honesty from the men under him.

'When Dr Siri was here before,' he continued, 'you apparently found it unnecessary to mention this rather important fact. Could you explain to us why that was?'

'He didn't ask, sir.'

The captain quickly assembled a smile that held back a lot of damage. 'He's asking now, Sergeant Major.'

There was no halfway for the old soldier; be silent and get shot, lie and get shot, spill the beans and get court-martialled and then get shot. It wasn't a great choice. This was the Vietnamese army. There was nowhere to appeal. If you screwed up, justice was swift.

'We got picked individually by our lieutenant,' he began. As he spoke, one of the uniformed officers recorded his words in shorthand. 'He rushed round and only selected those of us who'd served directly under the colonel. Some of us had been involved in the search for the daughter. He gave us the choice to join in or not. Of course, we all did.

There were seven of us, I suppose eight if you included the old Hmong scout. It all had to be discreet – no guns. We had no jurisdiction to do what we planned to do. We made a vow not to talk to anyone about it, whatever happened.

'We got moving as quick as we could. We weren't sure how long the Cubans were going to be around. We went in the one truck, parked a kilometre from the cave and ran in.'

'What did you take as weapons?' the captain asked.

'We all had knives. A couple of the men had crossbows for long distance.'

Siri mentally slapped himself for his narrow thinking. Of course there was no bullet in Odon's wound. It hadn't been caused by a gun at all. If he'd been hit by a crossbow bolt, the attacker could have pulled it out. The wound would have been identical to that of a bullet. He looked at Dtui to see if she'd worked it out also, then realised she was sitting in ignorance listening to a language she'd never had cause to learn.

Giap continued. 'We went into the military caves from both ends. The lead man in each team had a lamp with a red filter. The team that entered through the auditorium saw it first. After all the searching we'd been doing, it was heartbreaking. I can't begin to tell you how mad we were at that sight. She was dead, sir.'

'Miss Hong Lan?' Siri asked, although he felt like an outsider at a military tribunal.

'Not just dead, Doctor. Gutted. She was lying there in a wet grave with her insides hanging out. Stabbed by the look of it. But you'd have to stick in the knife and move it around to get the size of wound she had on her. It was sick, really sick. It had to be the damned Cubans that did it.'

'You only saw the one body?' Siri asked.

'One was enough.'

'Sergeant Major, this is important.' Siri knew he was hijacking the inquiry but there were a number of questions that had to be asked in a hurry. 'Where exactly was the body?'

'In a grave. There was that little stream running through the cave and the hole was just beside it.'

'But there was only the one grave.'

'Yes, sir.'

'And was it completely uncovered?'

'Not exactly, Doctor. Her legs were covered in sand and there was a little spade there, like we'd disturbed the Cubans before they could finish the job.'

'And the water had washed the blood from the body?'

'That's right.'

'Was there any blood anywhere else? Any suggestion there'd been a fight of some kind?'

'Didn't notice any. But don't forget we were using torches with red filters.'

'What happened next?' the captain asked.

'We went looking for the bastards. We didn't think it was just that they should get away with it. We figured if they'd heard us coming and run off, they couldn't be far away. The Hmong scout picked up a track outside the concert cave, running feet.'

'Just the one track?'

'Yes, sir. We figured the Cubans had escaped in different directions. We searched, I don't know how long, an hour? Two? Then we found one of them up there in front of the President's old cave. He was singing, sir. I swear he was singing. He was wearing just this pair of old football shorts and dancing and goddamned singing. Sir, people like that don't deserve a fair trial. We got him with a crossbow, but it didn't finish him off. He was still staggering around. We were on him, all of us. I tell you, he was strong, strong as an ox. We hadn't planned on the concrete thing.'

'But you had planned to kill him,' the captain said.

'Not really, sir.'

'You took knives and crossbows.'

'Just for self-defence, sir.'

'I don't believe you. Go on.'

'Sir. Well, the concrete was there and it was still wet. When we pushed him under he sort of came out of a trance and realised what was happening. He fought like a tiger, scratching, kicking. Then it went quiet. The archer pulled out his bolt, we smoothed the concrete, and got the hell out before anyone could come up there and see what all the singing and screaming was about.'

The men around the table sighed visibly when he stopped talking.

'Sergeant Major,' the captain asked, 'did you find the second man?'

'No, sir. We went back the next night but there was no trace.'

'And, what did you do with the girl?'

'We filled in the grave, took her out to the truck, and brought her back to the camp. The lieutenant got in touch with the mother in Hanoi and explained what had happened. We thought she'd travel back or ask for her daughter's body to be shipped over there for a funeral, but she didn't. She just told us to give the girl a decent burial and send her a lock of her hair.'

'Where did you bury her?' Siri asked.

Thangon was a small enough village for everyone to know everyone else and their business. Even the people on the ferry had recognised young Geung. He'd been a celebrity after all, one of the town crazies for eighteen years of his life. Mr Watajak hadn't exactly been delighted to see his son, but he put on a show for all the neighbours. Geung's father was alone now and getting old. His wife had left her drunken husband long ago. All the kids had grown up and gone to the city. Apart from his monthly trips to Vientiane to steal money from his offspring, he just stayed in or around his little hut. This was the same hovel in which Geung had been born and had lived before his move to Mahosot.

When Geung had emerged from his exhausted sleep that first morning, and seen everything as he remembered it, it was as if all the other stuff – Vientiane, the morgue, Dr Siri, Dtui, the trip to Luang Prabang – had all been part of the coma. None of the dream had really happened and he was still a teenager in Thangon. He called to his brothers and sisters, called to his mother, but only his father came. Except his father was much older than he should have been – and the house was dusty and empty.

The neighbours came by regularly to bring food and drink and put balm on Geung's dry skin. He remembered their faces. He remembered the old midwife, who had been old when she birthed Geung and was still old today. She used a syringe to drain the fluid from Geung's ears, a duty she'd performed regularly while he was growing up and, as ever, hers was the first voice to enter his head when his hearing returned.

'It's lovely to see you back, young Geung.'

Hearing brought him back to reality. He could make out questions now from the curious visitors, and answer them. In a place with no electricity and no other entertainment, people came by to listen to his memories of the hospital, Dr Siri's morgue and the cases they'd worked on. Of course, his version was simplified and left out some rather vital details, but for the simple people of Thangon that was probably not a bad thing.

There was no way he could know what was slowly happening there in his old home. His father, the wise seer, in order to feather his own financial nest, had turned out children with the same regularity as a factory producing meatballs: 'How clever he is, that Watajak', the people of Thangon had said, 'seven kids and he'll never have to work again.' And here he was today sitting in the shadows like a fool. Who respected him now? Who listened to him? He watched as people came to hear the wise words of his son. The moron had become a genius.

17

AUTOPSY OF THE PINK ORCHID

The people from Vientiane had already arrived in Vieng Xai to set up for the concert. The following day, the flight from Hanoi would bring the entertainers. There'd be a day for rehearsals, then, on the Sunday morning, the delegates and Party chiefs would start to arrive. Comrade Khong was therefore most insistent that Dr Siri should move the body out of the concert hall kitchen immediately.

Comrade Khong was a severe man with a large chest and menacing eyes. No earthquake, no invasion, and certainly no autopsy would stand in the way of his carefully charted preparations for the Friendship and Cooperation Concert. The housekeepers were equally indignant about the slices of dismembered mummy littering the President's meeting room. They too had to go. So it was, absolutely barred from Guesthouse Number One, which was undergoing a top-to-bottom spring clean, that the two Cubans were returned to the scene of the first act – the Kilometre 8 Hospital.

Lit had spent the night writing and copying his detailed report. It lacked only one final paragraph outlining the findings of this last autopsy, that of Hong Lan, the Pink Orchid. Now he sat on the bench in front of the same middle-school classroom where Siri had spent his night with the buffaloes. None of the patients in the other buildings who looked out at him through their windows could work out why he was wearing a gas mask.

If they'd sat beside him they would have known. Inside the classroom, sweating and confused, Siri and Dtui sat either side of the skeleton that had once been a beautiful Vietnamese girl. They wore three surgical masks apiece over their mouths and noses. The middle mask had been liberally spread with aromatic Tiger Balm. But nothing could possibly take away the awful smell that permeated the room and everything in it. They'd laughed at comrade Lit when he arrived in his mask. They told him their noses were used to the smell of death. But, if the glass hadn't been so restrictive, they would both now be wearing the extra two he'd brought along for them. In all their time in the morgue, they'd never smelled anything like this.

One mummy, one body preserved by adipocere but now reacting to the air, and one more, interred in a plastic body bag and subjected to the natural ravages of bacteria, all rotted at their own pace, each with its own unique scent of death. The combination was overwhelming, but the doctor wanted all three together to make comparisons and provide inspiration. During the autopsy of Hong Lan, they found their first similarity. Just as in the case of Isandro, what traces remained of the diaphragm suggested that it had been punctured. The body bag had slowed the process of decomposition sufficiently to leave a number of clues that might otherwise have been erased by vermin. Although there were no organs left within the carcass, score marks on the inside of the ribcage suggested there had been some amateur surgery conducted from the inside.

Those two points combined indicated the possibility that Hong Lan's heart had also been removed.

The tendons and ligaments had so far resisted the decomposition, and the uterus was still partly intact.

'My goodness, take a look at this,' Siri said to Dtui.

'What is that?'

'Why don't you tell me?'

'Well, they look like fibroids, but she was only, what, eighteen?'

'Unusual, isn't it. I wonder whether this is the reason for her hospitalisation.'

'I thought fibroids were benign.'

'Not always. And don't forget there may have been cysts as well. There wouldn't be any trace by now if there had been.'

'Is there some way we can find out?'

Siri cleared an area behind the cervix to get a better look at the spinal column. 'Oh, my.'

'What?'

'Can you see?'

'What is that? What's happened to her spine?'

'It's been eaten, Dtui. The cancer spread from her uterus and infected her bone marrow. It started to destroy her spine. She must have been in terrible pain at the end.'

'Could it have killed her?'

'If it didn't, there's no doubt it soon would have.'

'So what does this all mean?'

Siri pulled down his masks, more in need of air than protection from the smell. He gasped in a few deep breaths and swallowed back the nausea in his throat.

'It means she was in great distress for the last few months of her life. We can only hope her jailers were giving her painkillers.' The memory of the dried opium in the President's cave came to his mind.

'Surely they couldn't have been so heartless ...'

'You know? I think ...' He was too slow to choke back the second arrival of bile and Dtui watched with amusement as he turned away from the table and vomited. She'd outlasted the great surgeon.

Half an hour later they were giving Lit their findings. They'd walked away from the room and were sitting in the shadow of the hospital mountain karst but the smell was still in their noses. They admitted they couldn't prove the cancer had killed Hong Lan. In order to get to her diaphragm, an attacker would first have to puncture the abdomen. That could have caused enough bleeding to kill the girl, but there was no evidence to prove or disprove such a thing. And, as with Isandro, they could find no other obvious cause of death. Comrade Lit was happy to write in the final paragraph of his report that there had been 'evidence of foul play in both instances'. He closed with, 'the hearts of both bodies had been removed, and given that there was only one other suspect present, it has to be assumed that Odon was responsible for these two deaths'.

As his major crime, the body found in the concrete path, had been solved, he was more than pleased to leave the other two cases pending. He was sure his superiors wouldn't expect him to interview a dead suspect. He knew the army would have to decide for itself how to punish Giap and the other members of the lynch party. Given the ugliness of the crime they were avenging, he guessed it would take the form of a rebuke and a demotion rather than a firing squad. But it was no longer his concern. He was off the hook.

Before he left to file the report, he announced to Dtui that he would be back later to complete the 'unification arrangements'. This she took to mean the wedding, and wasn't at all surprised that he was able to make an engagement sound like a merger. She walked with Siri along the skirt of the mountain and breathed in the scents of the wild tiny bladderwort that grew in abundance there. They'd become accustomed now to keeping to well-worn tracks. She doubted she'd have the courage to stroll over unmarked fields or through virgin forest ever again.

Both she and her boss were troubled and neither had spoken since they'd parted company from Lit. The man had been so elated. It was as if one more barrier had been lifted between him and his next promotion. Siri noticed her glum look.

'Are you thinking about what to say to comrade Lit?'

'No. Not really. That can take care of itself.'

'Then what is it?'

She stopped walking and put her hands on her hips. 'I've got a bad feeling about this case.'

'Me too.'

'All right. You go first. What's worrying you?'

'Probably all the things that are worrying you. Let's go over it.' They went to a shaded boulder and sat side by side. 'I know it looks like we've reached the end of the story, but I keep thinking we've missed an essential part of the plot.'

'That's exactly it. I'm having a lot of those women's intuition twinges. The mother worries me. You know? They still hadn't found her daughter but she waltzes back to

Vietnam as if it didn't matter. Then when they did find the body she couldn't even be bothered to come back for the funeral. Her only daughter. That doesn't sound like a very warm mother–daughter relationship to me.'

'Perhaps she was unbalanced by the death of her husband.'

'So, you'd hold on even tighter to the relationship that remained. No. Something happened between them. I'm sure of it. Are you still hosting Isandro?'

It was a surprise question. Siri had forgotten all about the wayward spirit. 'I don't think so. I don't know. I haven't felt anything since we found the body. I haven't shimmied once in the past twenty-four hours. It was never really a possession, more like a presence – an influence. And that's another thing that didn't ever sit right. If Odon and Isandro were as evil as everyone's painting them, I wonder why I didn't feel that? Why didn't I ever sense their power? I don't know. I wonder …'

'What?'

'I wonder if we're not seeing what we've been told to see.'

'What should we do?'

'We could go back to Vientiane, tell everyone Inspector Maigret and his faithful lieutenant have solved yet another dastardly crime, and know deep down that we haven't …'

'I like the second alternative.'

'I thought you might.'

One of the few Lao involved in the shady dealings of the Cubans was Mr Sounsak, the young doctor who had purportedly aborted the monkey's foetus from the Vietnamese maid. Although Mr Sounsak had since been transferred to a hospital in Savanaketh province, Miss Bong, the lady he'd been dating at the time, was still living in the village at Kilometre 8. This gossip had been provided enthusiastically by the kitchen staff at the guesthouse.

Siri and Dtui had put together a hypothesis – an alternative scenario for the mysterious events in Huaphan the previous year. Working along this shadow plotline, they were going back over events, reexamining issues that didn't fit their new story. Miss Bong was a sturdy, sunburned woman with a back already crooked from a lifetime of stooping in paddy fields. It was there they found her planting young rice shoots, too busy apparently to stop her work to talk. This was obviously a subject she wasn't particularly happy to discuss.

Dtui wasn't too happy either. 'Is this field safe to be walking around in?' she asked.

'No safer than any other, auntie,' the girl told her. Dtui was prematurely exploded by the reply. Her pieces flew in a million directions. 'Auntie?' The woman was a good ten years older than herself. Had she aged that much over the past week? But once she'd recollected her parts into a semblance of decorum, she noticed neither Siri nor the woman had spotted her detonation. It was a wound she'd have to bear alone.

'Couldn't you stop for a moment and talk to us?' Siri was saying. 'I'm getting a stiff neck.'

'We have to get these in before the big rains come,' she said. 'Can't be wasting my time with idle chat.' It was clear she hoped her rudeness would make the city folk leave her alone.

'All right.' Siri sat on the bank of the field. 'Then tell us about comrade Sounsak.'

'Nothing to tell.'

'You were going out with him when …'

'We were engaged,' she interrupted.

'Sorry. You were engaged to comrade Sounsak at the time he had a strange and rather disheartening experience at the hospital.'

'Yeah? What was that then?'

'Something involving the foetus of a monkey?'

She looked at Siri the way you would a lizard attempting to open a can of corned beef. 'Eh?'

'He didn't tell you about it?'

'We didn't talk a lot about monkeys.'

'About a pregnant Vietnamese woman who produced a stillborn ape? He didn't mention that to you?'

The woman looked at Dtui. 'Is your grandad all right?'

Dtui sighed then spoke slowly to her because she obviously wasn't very bright. 'There was a Vietnamese housekeeper,' she said. 'She used to cook for the engineers working on the hospital here.' The woman began to positively punch the poor little shoots into the mud. 'Did you know her?'

Siri saw that the woman's body answered yes. 'What can you tell us about her?'

Comrade Sounsak's ex-fiancée stopped her work and lifted her head to the intruders. 'What can I tell you? What can I not tell you? I can tell you she was a whore, and a gobbler-upper of other women's men, and a devil. Is that enough for you?'

Siri cast a look at Dtui that suggested the next question would be better coming from her. She picked up on it.

'What did the bitch do to you, sweetie?' she asked.

Miss Bong turned her back on Siri and directed her

venomous eyes at Dtui. 'She preyed on them – men who were in happy loving relationships. She flashed her well-used Vietnamese titties at them and swished her squashy hips and lured our men away.'

'The whore,' Dtui agreed. 'And your man … ?'

'Was swept away like the rest of 'em. And when she fell pregnant, what fool was it dumb enough to front up and take responsibility for being the father? She was the inkwell on the paymaster's desk. Every man in the village had dipped his pen there at the end of the month, but my stupid Sounsak was the only one to own up.'

'And?'

'And she had it. He even birthed it himself.'

'And it survived?' Siri asked.

'I wish it hadn't.'

'What happened to them?'

'Ran off that same night. Acting like they were in love or something. Never saw him again.' Her eyes were starting to dampen.

'That's terrible,' Siri nodded, although his expression was one of fascination. 'Did you ever hear anything about the woman and the two black Cubans?'

'Oh, yes. She had a special grievance against those two.'

'She didn't like blacks?'

'She would have done, given a chance. They were the only two with enough sense to leave the devil alone. She tried all her tricks, but she couldn't get those two boys into her bed. We heard her boasting that it wouldn't be long before she got that big one between her legs. Then when her sexy wiggles didn't work on him she tried the little one, but he wasn't having none of her either. So she went around telling everyone they was – you know – together.'

'That's the kind of thing she was saying?' Siri asked.

'She was the sort that couldn't believe a man could resist her if he was a real man.'

As they drove back to the guesthouse, Dtui looked at her boss. He had a glazed look on his face that she'd seen a few times before. 'So, do we now have a complete understanding of what happened?' she asked.

'We're getting there, dear nurse.'

'She could have been lying.'

'Possible.'

'Or her fiancé didn't tell her what really happened up there. He could have been trying to protect her.'

'That's possible too. But there's one more possibility that I want to ride with.'

'Good, I'll eventually work it all out too once I get over the trauma of suddenly becoming middle-aged. What's next?'

'Sleep. We should turn in for the night. I have several phone calls to make to Vientiane, then I'm hoping for a dream or two. I'm sure your fiancé has given up waiting for us tonight. In the morning we'll go for a little drive. If everything works out the way I hope, everything should make itself crystal clear before the end of the day. I think we could even stick around for the concert the following evening without feeling too guilty about leaving our Mr Geung alone in the morgue all this time. I bet the poor chap's bored out of his mind.'

'Hello?'

'Hello?'

'Civilai?'

'Yes. Who's that?'

'The Empress Dowager of China.'

'Siri? Is that you? Awful line. God, you sound like you're standing in a tub of lard.'

'Yes. It's my new hobby. Have you missed me?'

'Have you gone somewhere?'

'I'm in Huaphan.'

'Really? I'm off there myself, for the concert.'

'I hope they're not letting you sing.'

'No, I'll just be doing my exotic dance. You know, the one with the feathers?'

'I'll make sure not to eat anything greasy before it starts. Look, I need a favour.'

'You surprise me.'

'Do you have anyone there who can speak Spanish?'

'Yes. Why?'

'What time is it in Cuba?'

The crow and the sparrow lay in the paddy mud barely breathing. Their eyes were glazed. Two men knelt over them: the teacher and the acolyte. Behind them stood an elderly couple, darker than the night around them. The woman put her hand on the young man's shoulder and told him to go ahead. The teacher nodded and the dark-skinned novice took up the birds gently in his hands and held them together as if in a prayer. He pressed his palms together, softly at first, then, as the birds became one, he clasped his fingers shut, and squeezed till a slither of smoke escaped from his grasp and wafted upward. He opened his palms and the birds, and the old couple, and the teacher were gone. But the novice remained. He smiled at the observer of this dream and slowly, without the aid of language, set about explaining to Siri what he had just witnessed. Before the morning sun rose, the old doctor understood everything.

18

FRIENDSHIP, COOPERATION AND DENGUE FEVER

Mr Watajak had once been an early riser. Out there in the boondocks the sun dictated when to sleep and when to rise. But farmers had even more sensitive clocks in their brains that told them when the dawn sun was rising over the South China Sea, an hour before it reached Laos. So, when it finally clambered over the horizon, the farmers were already out tending their crops. But rice whisky can rust the cogs of those old brain clocks something horrible. When Mr Watajak awoke in a sweat this morning, the sun was already baking the east wall of his old hut. He was alone. The solitude threw him into a drunk's 'what happened?' panic.

He'd been getting used to having the moron there, attracting neighbours, being smart, getting better, making him laugh. In truth, old Mr Watajak had got quite fond of the boy. He even considered keeping him there. He was a strong kid. He might even be able to bring some of the paddies back to life if the rains ever came. He might even make some money from the people putting in fish farms. There was a lot of potential, yet now the bamboo hut was empty but for himself. He was so mad about it all he had a drink. And, after the first couple of swigs, the brew reminded him how lonely he was. He was going to miss the little moron.

They'd told him. They'd all told him. The neighbours and the travellers and the kids out at the temple school. He'd kept asking because he wanted an answer that wasn't 'thirty kilometres'. Thirty kilometres didn't work for him. He wanted something like 'a long time', or 'several more nights of getting bitten by mosquitoes', or 'longer than it takes for a body to rot'. By now, Mr Geung could tell them the names of every town he'd passed through, probably could remember the names of everyone who'd been kind to him on the way and their kids. But he still couldn't get his head around thirty kilometres and what that meant as far as when he'd be at the morgue to see how much trouble had happened there.

They'd told him it didn't matter. They could wave down a truck driver, get him on a bus. When he was ready to go to Vientiane, arranging him a ride would be easier than getting wet in a river. But, for some reason, nobody was really surprised when they went to see young Geung at his house that morning. It was the day of the big treaty signing with the Vietnamese and the government had called a two-day holiday. The father couldn't tell them where his genius son had gone, and by the looks of him he was too drunk to care.

Geung had started off early. The sun was behind his left shoulder and he stuck to the edge of the road. Walking was the only sure thing. Every time he'd found himself in a vehicle it had taken him in the wrong direction. Things had always turned out badly. No more cars or trucks for Mr Geung. No, sir. He was ready for this last test. His shoulder wasn't worrying him any more. His blisters were dry and painless and his muscles were rested. His sunburn was healed and he could hear again.

He felt bad that he'd had to stay so long in Thangon. That old man, his father, made him feel sad, but he wasn't sure why. Some voice in his head had told him he ought to stay. It wasn't the voice that reminded him constantly of his promise and his obligations. The past few days had been confusing for Geung. He didn't know which voice to listen to, then Dtui came back. He was glad to see her. She sorted it all out for him.

She reminded him of this thing called 'love'. It was something she liked to talk about a lot. She told him that even though there were times it didn't seem possible – times when you'd much sooner find fault and hate – these were the times you most needed to love. She told him his father deserved it. He didn't have to earn it. He was family, and there was a rule that family got a share of love from each other just by being born of the same blood. Geung wondered when he'd be getting his. But perhaps it was something you only got back if you gave it out. His father had nothing. Even Geung could tell that. A little something would probably do him good. That's why, on the night before Geung restarted his long march, he'd kissed his drunken father on the forehead and told him he loved him.

The confused man had pushed his moron son away in disgust and wiped the gesture from his skin as if it were a slithering insect. He told his son things that could have hurt, but didn't. Geung said how proud he was to have a smart father who came by every month to tell him news and see how he was. As he turned in for the night, he could see the old man doing a lot of thinking about things. He might have even cried a little, but rice whisky does that to a man too.

Geung walked with confidence now, certain it wouldn't be too long before he saw something familiar. He hoped the feeling of nausea that rose in his throat would pass, but it didn't. The headache stayed with him too. It had been five days since the dengue mosquito had chosen him, and this would be the day when the fever arrived. Already the virus had been replicated in his blood and his gums were beginning to swell.

In Vientiane, a fountain pen, shaken once to unclog the ink, was scratching the names of all the delegates on the Treaty of Friendship and Cooperation. It officially tied the Lao to twenty-five more years of bullying. Even before that ink had dried on the parchment, all those in attendance would be loaded into air force transporters and helicopters and carried off to Huaphan. They'd be wined and dined and treated royally (although that adverb would never be mentioned). At 7PM they would decide which grey safari shirt to wear, have a final cocktail, and walk to the concert cave to watch a spectacular display of Vietnamese talent.

Of these events, Mr Geung knew nothing. All he was sure of was that the morgue hadn't been swept for ... goodness knows how many days. The cockroaches would have colonised the examination room. There was probably a mountain of dead bodies piled in front of the door, and all because Mr Geung had broken his promise to his friends. Unacceptable. Totally unacceptable. He deserved whatever punishment he got. He fell to his knees and threw up into the slender panic grass beside the road.

19

WHEN EVERYTHING YOU THINK
YOU KNOW IS WRONG

It was the day of the concert. Although they could have gone in for the kill on concert-eve, Siri and Dtui decided that one more day of interviews and field work would leave no doubt in their minds. There was also an important phone call from Vientiane expected. The guesthouse landlady was devastated that these medical people were still there, still occupying two valuable rooms. Thank goodness the 'evidence' had been removed or she'd have to explain that to comrade Khong from Vientiane, too.

On the afternoon of concert-eve, Dtui had taken Panoy back to her village. These were the days before the exodus to the big cities when 'neighbour' still meant more than just 'the person next door'. Panoy's mother lived opposite a woman who had been widowed in the same conflict that had claimed Panoy's father. She took the little girl from Dtui as if there were no question as to where she would grow up, who would care for her. Just like that, the village had painlessly filled the gap in Panoy's life like white blood corpuscles healing a wound and leaving no scar. There had been no debate, no discussion.

Dtui was breathless with admiration for these people. Her own mother had been one of their kind. Dtui was born in such a village but had no recollections of it. This was Laos. These were Lao people. Her people: kind, selfless, and honest. Ninety per cent of Lao tilled the soil and cared for each other just like this. Dtui sat under an awning in the central square of this thirty-hut village, and saw what her country could so easily become if it were left to society to manage itself.

The village children were already playing gently with Panoy, naturally recognising her frailty. People nodded and laughed about simple things. They brought sweets and drinks for the nice nurse who'd rescued this child of the village from the edge of death. Everybody was busy, but at the same time, relaxed. They all had time to talk with Dtui, and if they had no questions to ask they would just sit with her and put their hands on hers.

And while she sat there, she noticed something else. As in every other village, the livestock, the babies and the dogs all shared the same dust. The chickens pecked away all day at ants that barely carried a calorie between a thousand of them. Toddlers built up immunity from disease by growing up with dirt, but it was one little boy's playmate that caused Dtui to take a second look. It was an odd creature like nothing she'd seen before. From a distance, it looked like a small black pig. But there was something different about it. Where it should have had trotters, it had paws. Its tail was short and curly but it wagged from side to side. Whereas you'd expect it to snort and oink, this animal yapped at the little boy and was apparently enjoying their game.

It would have been quite simple to ask someone. She could have gone closer to confirm that this piglet had mud on its feet and a heavy cold, but instead she decided it was time to go. Even though she was in an animistic village in what was now officially an agnostic country, she had a few words with the Lord Buddha before she left. She promised never again to joke about the laws of nature. The lesson had been learned. 'Sorry, eh?'

She kissed Panoy on the cheek, knowing the girl would never remember her if they met again. She thanked everyone, although none of them was sure what they were being thanked for, and walked out of the village. Her mothering instincts had swollen in her chest, and at that moment, she'd reached a point where nothing seemed more important than marriage and a family of her own.

In comrade Lit's mind, there was only one reason why Dr Siri and Nurse Dtui would still be in Vieng Xai. The Cuban case was closed and yet they were still there. The security arrangements for the concert had kept him busy since filing his report. He'd stopped by at the guesthouse the previous day but nobody had seen hide nor hair of the two. He'd called again in the evening but they still hadn't returned. His mind should have been focused on today's big event, but he couldn't get Nurse Dtui out of his head.

Lit had come to the conclusion that Dr Siri had agreed to act as her witness when she accepted his offer of marriage. Siri had phoned and asked him to pick them up in his jeep. He dropped off his deputy to oversee the final arrangements at the concert cave and drove to the guest-house, his heart flapping like the frantic wings of a butterfly. When he saw his betrothed on the front steps, the early morning sun bringing out the natural rouge of her cheeks, he could hardly breathe. What a fine choice he'd made.

But when Siri and Nurse Dtui got into his jeep, there was no talk of wedding arrangements. Siri asked him to drive them to Xam Neau. It was terribly inconvenient under the circumstances, but the doctor assured him this was a most serious matter that couldn't be avoided. His passengers refused to tell him the purpose of their journey. Left to his own imagination and the silence, Lit conjured up a trip to the central market to buy good northern silk for her wedding gown, even a visit to a fortune-teller to decide on an auspicious day for the ceremony. Perhaps this was how it was done. He'd never married before so he could hardly know. But he was too pleased with himself to spoil the day by complaining.

In fact, he didn't become anxious at all until the doctor directed him into the makeshift hospital compound and asked him to park in front of the director's office.

'What are we doing here, Doctor?' he asked.

'We've come to visit Dr Santiago.'

Lit was enraged by this announcement. 'We've what? Why didn't you tell me this was your plan?'

'Would you have come if I had?'

'I ... I have no business here.'

'No? What about the business of revenge?'

'I have no idea what you're talking about.'

'Yes you do. You've been petrified of Dr Santiago for too long, comrade Lit. It's time to stand up to him.'

'You're wrong.'

'Am I? Then would you like to tell us what happened to that finger of yours?'

'I don't ...' He looked at Dtui in the rear mirror. What effect would all this have on her? Would she lose respect for him? Nothing showed on her face. Siri climbed down from the jeep and pointed to the key in the ignition. The confidence on the doctor's face buoyed Lit somewhat. It made him momentarily believe there was a possibility for him to get out from beneath the shadow of the damned Cuban. He turned off the engine and stepped down from the jeep.

Santiago didn't look up from his papers when the three uninvited and apparently unwelcome visitors entered his room, but he smiled and said something to Dtui.

'He says he's been expecting you for some time,' Dtui told Siri. She stood to one side. Her role throughout this interview would merely be that of interpreter. She would translate Siri's questions as best she could and try to catch the Cuban's answers. She wouldn't become involved in any conflict that might arise. This was what they'd agreed.

Santiago looked at Lit as he entered the office, his eyes sparkling with mischief. Again he spoke.

'Dr Santiago thinks it's very brave of you to get so close to him again. He asks whether your magician friend, that's you, Doc, has given you the confidence to come here after all this time. He says Dr Siri won't be able to help you.'

Siri noticed a pallor wash through Lit's face and immediately began to understand the hold Santiago had over people.

'In that case, perhaps, before he dispatches us all to Hell,' Siri smiled, 'he'll allow me to run through my theory. Tell him he's free to correct any mistakes I make.'

'He wants to know if this is really necessary,' Dtui said.

'Perhaps the doctor would allow me just a few moments of indulgence,' Siri began. 'Comrade Lit, as you've learned from painful experience, Dr Santiago is much more than just a brilliant surgeon. He is also a very senior practitioner of Endoke. It would appear to many people that he is very competent at performing this dark art. In fact, if you check the records, you'll find that his transfer to this god-forsaken communist outpost had nothing to do with his medical skills, great though they might be. It was his last chance – the only work he could get. They kicked him out of his own country because he was a menace. Isn't that right, Doctor?'

Dtui tried her best to keep up. She told Siri the Cuban didn't want to interrupt his story.

'Oh, yes. I think he knows we're getting to the interesting part.' Siri leaned back in his seat and looked into the mocking eyes of his old friend. 'Because, you see, comrade Lit, when Odon and Isandro arrived in this country, they had no knowledge whatsoever of the spirit world. They were hardworking, studious boys who just wanted to come to a struggling Third World country and share their skills. They learned our language and took pains to understand our culture. The reason they were popular wasn't because they cast spells to make people like them. They were popular because they were truly nice boys.

'One of those boys, Isandro, met a patient at the hospital, the beautiful daughter of a Vietnamese colonel. Her name was Hong Lan, and in the two months she remained convalescing at Kilometre 8, the two of them fell deeply in love. There was nothing improper about their relationship. The girl was ill and he was her nurse. They talked and got to know one another, and whatever chemical it is that makes a relationship fizz and bubble, that's what happened to Hong Lan and Isandro.

'The girl had many suitors but had met nobody like this boy. He was handsome and intelligent and very kind. She was so confident that this was the man she wanted to spend her life with she even told her mother. That, as it turned out, was the biggest mistake she could have made. A foreigner, and a black foreigner at that, whatever could she have been thinking? Her mother was devastated, her father incensed. Word could never get out of their daughter's insanity. They transferred the girl to another hospital, but the humiliation wouldn't go away. The blacks had to go. Our friend Dr Santiago was entrusted with that duty.'

When this translation arrived at the Cuban, he twirled his hand arrogantly in the air like a musketeer. Siri smiled, shook his head, and continued.

'Fortunately for him, the doctor had experienced his own small disaster around the same time. Some children playing in the tunnels, ones they'd been specifically forbidden from entering, came across a peculiar altar. They went and told their parents, who reported the matter to the authorities.

'This, comrade Lit, was the altar I told you about at the Sheraton de Laos. It had certainly been the scene of small sacrifices and black spell making. It was Dr Santiago's personal temple, the shrine in which he practised his magic – where he put together his evil potions and curses. Dr Santiago doesn't wear his amulets to protect himself from other exponents. He is a devotee. They are his chain of office. The altar had nothing to do with the interns, but by accusing them of using black magic, showing people the evidence, making up stories of their curses, he was able to turn people against them. The Vietnamese were only too happy to accept the idea that Isandro had charmed their daughter with his spells.

'To the boys, Santiago was a sympathetic countryman, a kindly old uncle. He told them he believed they were innocent of the accusations, but public opinion had left him no choice but to have them return to Cuba. It was all very neat. The colonel came one day with soldiers to arrest them and transport them by force to Hanoi. Up to that point, everything had gone very well for everyone except the boys. They could have left Vietnam then and that would have been the end of it. Only Isandro's love for Hong Lan and Odon's friendship to Isandro were stronger than their will to survive.

'They escaped before they could be put on a plane and somehow worked their way back to Huaphan. It must have been a journey riddled with difficulties, fraught with danger. No help from anyone – soldiers everywhere who would certainly have mistaken them for American servicemen. But they beat the odds. When they got back, they hid where they knew they'd least be expected to, in the old cave of the President. And they brought Lan to stay with them. It was no kidnap. Once she got word from Isandro that he'd returned, the girl had happily conspired with them to arrange her own rescue.

'Isandro and Hong Lan knew by then that her cancer was incurable, that she had no more than two months to live. She didn't want to spend the last of her days with a mother who taunted her daily – reminded her how she'd dirtied her family name. No, Hong Lan wanted to be with the man she'd fallen in love with. She wanted the last weeks of her life to be the happiest.'

Dtui's translation flagged as she fought back the tears. Santiago sneered and offered her a tissue.

'Apart from foraging for food,' Siri continued, 'hunting game, keeping his lover free from pain, Isandro was also gathering his thoughts. There must have been many conversations, the three of them holed up in the cave with nothing much else to do. They knew the altar at the Sheraton had to belong to someone. There weren't that many Cubans to choose from. Perhaps they heard from Hong Lan that it was Santiago who had made the accusation to her father about the boys. Or perhaps they remembered the story about a pretty young nurse – the one we saw briefly when we first came here. She was a good girl by all accounts, with a fiancé back in her home village. Nobody could understand why she was so eager to fall into the old doctor's bed.'

Santiago laughed when he heard the translation and asked why Siri should be so jealous. Was it so inconceivable the old Cuban was irresistible to young girls?

Siri ignored the comment. 'Perhaps they remembered the Cuban bookkeeper who had suffered from an infection of the throat. How they'd questioned the need for a tracheotomy for such a small ailment, then recalled that this meant he had been forced to return to Havana before completing a full audit of the doctor's books.'

Unseen behind his desk, Santiago had worked open a drawer. At the front was a small wooden box with a colourful Hunan Tea emblem on its top. But the grey powder it contained had taken many months to blend and infuse with its magic.

'Or perhaps they'd heard of your own unfortunate run-in with the doctor, comrade Lit,' Siri continued.

'I don't think …' the security head mumbled nervously.

'Come, comrade,' Siri told him. 'You have nothing to fear here today. Trust me.'

Lit did in fact draw confidence from Siri's words. He was angered by the constant grin the old Cuban wore on his face. He sighed and told a story he'd avoided relating to anybody.

'We'd had one of our many disagreements,' Lit began. 'They'd told me Dr Santiago was to be the overall supervisor of the project, but the Vietnamese soldiers were annoyed because he knew nothing about engineering. Some of the decisions he made they considered to be downright dangerous. I remember …'

'Go on.'

'I remember pointing my finger into his face and telling him he was wrong about some important issue. He stared at me and told me that was the last time I'd ever use this finger. He said something about me underestimating his ability. I laughed at him and left, but when I woke the next morning, this finger was already bloodless. In a few days it had begun to wither. I know he did it. I don't know how, but from that day on I stayed clear of him. I too have heard stories of his wizardry.'

'Well, now you know,' Siri said. 'And so did Isandro. I imagine he was quite upset when he realised the doctor had set them up and caused them all this hardship.'

'So, if you're saying the two boys had no connection to this black magic circle, why did Odon have the scratches on his chest?' Lit asked.

'Yes, I admit it took me a while to work that one out. It especially threw me that Odon had the marks and Isandro didn't. Then I got to wondering what benefit the boys could gain from their knowledge of Santiago's little hobby. If, for example, they threatened to expose him, write to the project directors in Havana and tell them what their resident representative was getting up to out here, what did Santiago have to offer them in return? And that's how we come to the deaths. They all knew Hong Lan would soon be dead. But Isandro couldn't bear the thought of losing her. They discussed the possibility of their souls being reunited for eternity. Odon told Isandro of a ceremony he'd heard about, an old Palo practice where an elderly couple in a town near his own had taken poison. A shaman had been recruited to unite their souls in death.'

Santiago asked Dtui how her doctor could know such a thing.

'I spent a very pleasant time with Odon last evening,' Siri smiled. 'You'd be surprised what information two men without a common language can share with the aid of a little mime and a pointed stick, tell him.'

Siri laughed and Dtui enjoyed translating the words. The coroner continued, 'The Cubans decided if Santiago here was such a great high priest, he would know of the ceremony and be able to perform it. This he would agree to do in return for their silence. For some reason, Santiago refused to perform it himself. He did, however, agree to teach Odon. The scratches were a part of the trappings, I imagine. My technical knowledge is lacking from here on. I wonder if the good doctor would be kind enough to talk us through the ceremony so we may better understand what happened that night.'

Santiago was taken by surprise. He'd been busy manoeuvring open the lid from the tea box without being noticed. But he agreed to pass on the secrets of the ceremony. Siri was curious as to why he would give up such presumably classified information so readily. But he went into great detail and seemed inordinately proud to be passing on his knowledge. It appeared that for the rites to work, the hearts of the lovers must still be fresh. Santiago suggested that it would be best of all if they were still beating when they were removed, but conceded that this is often a little too gory for most people. The important thing was for the bodies to stay in perfect condition for as long as possible after the deaths.

'Hence the watery grave,' Siri added. 'Why?'

Santiago told Dtui that the couple would appear together in eternity the way they looked when the transfer was complete. He insisted that even the undead had a sense of the aesthetic and would prefer their loved ones to be relatively free of rotting flesh. For three nights before the ceremony, the priest mixes a special concoction, a paste. Only the very best priests know the ingredients and the incantations used to mix them. The Cuban began to lead Dtui through a complicated description of the components. He boasted of his own skill, told her how many years of his life he had dedicated to the science of the macabre. He was, he told her, one of the greatest exponents of the dark arts.

Siri interrupted this tirade. 'Dtui, thank the doctor for his commercial. But perhaps he wouldn't mind getting back to the night in question.'

Santiago laughed again.

'What's so funny?' Lit asked Dtui.

She seemed to squirm a little before she answered. 'He said he can tell us everything we want to know, because ...'

'Because, what?'

'Because the three of us will remember nothing of this meeting. He says when the sun comes up tomorrow, we won't even know who we are.' Dtui and Lit seemed to pale at this announcement. Only Siri saw a funny side to it.

'I look forward to that,' he said impatiently. 'But Civilai and I have done that trick no end of times with a bottle of rice whisky. It isn't so hard. Now, the ceremony?'

Santiago told the doctor that he had a good deal of bravado for a man soon to meet a horrible end. He admired him for this and agreed to describe the rites in detail. The priest, he said, removes the hearts from the lovers. These he cuts into very small pieces on the altar and mixes with the blessed paste in a mortar. Over and over he chants the incantation, over and over till he falls into a deep trance. He knows nothing beyond the actions he is to perform. On the altar, the same altar where he has cut the hearts, he models the paste into the shape of a bird. It is a bird with the wings flying. There's no need for the priest to be a great artist. Just the crude simple shape of a bird is enough. This figure must then be concealed. Nobody must see it or touch it in order for the bird to develop its own life and symbolically fly to eternity. Then the lovers would be together for ever.

'And how long does this process take?' Siri asked.

Santiago thought for a second. It was hard to say. Weeks? Months? Sometimes years. Sometimes not at all. It depended on the will of the lovers. Then, all of a sudden, Santiago sighed and removed his glasses. It was as if he had decided he'd said enough. His whole demeanour changed. He removed the tea box from his drawer and placed it on the table in front of him. His voice became gruff and his eyes bloodshot as he growled at his guests.

A tremor entered Dtui's voice. 'He … he says he's enjoyed talking with us but now it's time for us to go.' She abandoned her role of translator. 'Doc, I don't like the look of this. I don't think we should let him …'

But before she could complete her warning, Santiago had taken the box in his left hand and scythed it through the air in an arc. The powder it contained blew in a cloud around the three guests. They could smell the ashes of long-dead beasts and the stink of putrid spices. They could hear the loud angry mantra spat repeatedly from between the Cuban's nicotine-stained teeth. Although their eyes were stinging from the dust, they could see Santiago back against the wall with his arms raised to an unseen god.

Dtui was expecting some manifestation, blisters, horns sprouting, a feeling of uncontrolled evil rising inside her, but all she could manage was a sneeze. Lit sneezed also. Siri walked out of the cloud of powder with his hand over his mouth and nose and stood staring at the Cuban, now prone on the floor behind his desk.

'You can tell him to stop all this rot. It didn't work,' Siri said.

'But, why didn't it?' Lit asked, taking his gun from his belt and pointing it at the confused Cuban.

'Because it never does,' Siri told him. 'Our Dr Santiago here is a phony – a charlatan. He's only the great high priest of Endoke in his own mind. He couldn't conjure up a bubble in a bottle of Lao beer.'

'But that isn't possible. You said he was thrown out of Cuba because …'

'Because he was a nuisance, not because he could actually perform any of the magic he professed to know. They thought he was a nutcase. His experiments got in the way of his medicine. Nobody was going to hire a surgeon, no matter how talented he might be, if he believes the dark spirits are guiding his hand on the scalpel. Dtui, do you want to get him up off the floor before his joints freeze up?'

Dtui helped the old doctor back into his seat, still mumbling an ancient curse – still not believing his victims were conscious and coherent.

'I'm not saying he didn't study all the dark arts,' Siri continued. 'I'm sure he did. I'm sure he's a veritable authority on all the rites and rituals of Santeria and the Palo Mayombe. But, the fact is, any old José can't just declare himself to be a grand magician any more than I could announce to the world that I'm Mr Universe. You have to have something special. You have to be touched by the spirits. Our Santiago here, despite his enthusiasm, I'm sorry to say, doesn't have it.'

Deprived of a translation, the Cuban sat at his desk with a curious look on his face. Lit stood shaking his head. 'But he did … he must have. What about this?' He held up his finger that drooped sadly like a fractured stick insect. Siri walked to the towering refrigerator in the corner of the office and opened the door to reveal thousands of trays of neat Petri dishes.

'Comrade Lit, if a man has no natural ability to perform miracles, and most men don't, they resort to trickery, to conjuration. Once we established that our friend here was a fraud, it was just a question of going through the tricks to explain them. Some he just made up. Others had more earthly explanations. Take his supposed love potion, for example. We met the young nurse who had been charmed into his bed. But it wasn't a spell that got her there. He'd caught her stealing medicines to send back to her village. Her body was payment for him keeping his mouth shut. Simple blackmail.

'In fact, many of his other miracles could be explained scientifically. Among other things, he is quite a brilliant chemist. Look at all this. I've been trying to work out how he killed your finger. As you were all billeted in the same caves, I have to assume he infected you with some virus. He has a vast collection of cultures. It wouldn't have been that difficult to creep to your bunk at night and touch you with some contaminated sample he'd been working on. Perhaps we can get that information out of him when he comes out of his shock.'

Comrade Lit was crestfallen. Could he really have been duped like a simple villager?

'Every odd event that happened here,' he said, 'I marked down to Santiago and the supernatural. I was too afraid of the reaction from my superiors to report any of it. In fact, I was too afraid of him. Do you not suppose he might have had something to do with Colonel Ha's death during the ambush? That was inexplicable.'

'Once a popular myth begins, it takes on a life of its own,' Siri said. 'The colonel was so distraught by the news of his daughter's condition, he'd become more and more dependent on opium to pull him through. I'm afraid the ambush came at a time when he was too consumed with smoke and his own grief to appreciate the reality of the situation. This we found out from his batman. The colonel wasn't fit for duty. He shouldn't have been on that patrol. But it had nothing to do with witchcraft. He'd spent the previous night smoking and the drug had unsettled his mind.'

'So, the last hope of Isandro and Odon was a mirage. They'd been fooled too.'

'Yes, and no. The reason our friend here refused to perform the ceremony was certainly because he knew he didn't have the ability to produce the result they all hoped for. By handing over the responsibility to Odon, he also removed the pressure from himself. You see? Dr Santiago believes wholeheartedly in his magic. It must be terribly frustrating for him to be such a failure at practising it. But I sense, and perhaps he did too, that Odon had some innate ability. By preparing Odon to perform the rite, I imagine the doctor could vicariously experience success.'

'Are you saying that Odon was a shaman?'

'No, he wasn't. I'm saying he was probably able to channel. Perhaps he was more open, more committed than Santiago. He believed all the mumbo jumbo would work, that his friend and his friend's lover truly had a chance to be together into eternity. I'm saying that enthusiasm made him a very appealing vessel for the spirits.'

'You think he might have been successful?'

Siri's thoughts returned to his first visit to the President's cave, to the wardrobe and the shadow of the mysterious bat. 'It isn't impossible,' he said. 'He might actually have hit on the right formula for once.'

'Should I tell him his magic worked, then?' Dtui asked.

'Goodness me, no. We don't want him believing he actually possesses the ability to send people off into eternity. He'd be putting us all on the bus to gaga land. The less enthusiasm he has, the better. I get the feeling Dr Santiago will be recalled from his post. Civilai tells me the embassy was very interested to hear about his background. I think he may be going home soon.'

Dtui looked down at the old Cuban, still vainly searching for an appropriate spell to dispatch his guests to the middle earth. 'Okay, perhaps one last question,' she said. 'If the ceremony was successful like you say, and Isandro and Hong Lan are now sitting under a bo tree in heaven somewhere sharing a bottle of fizzy nirvanan nectar, why is Odon's spirit so restless?'

'Ah, yes. Good question,' Siri agreed. 'Originally I thought his spirit just wanted a hunky, physically perfect body in which to dance the nights away. That's why he chose me. Then I started to wonder what could have happened to make him so unsettled. I found the answer when I met the Hmong scout: the one who led the raid that night. He's an interesting old character. He's quite eccentric. In fact, he wears the nails on his little fingers long and varnished. It's some traditional thing.'

'The nail in the mummy's tomb.'

'Right. But I didn't pursue that. He told me about that night. He seems to remember that when the labourer arrived to report his sighting of the Cubans, the raiding party had already been selected and was in a state of preparation.'

'What? How?' Lit asked.

It was Dtui who answered his question. 'They'd been tipped off by somebody else.'

'And I think we can guess who,' Siri added. 'Santiago wanted the ceremony to go ahead. He was curious. But he was also afraid that Odon might continue to blackmail him when it was all over. Or maybe he was more afraid word would get out that the doctor was a fraud. I doubt Santiago expected the Vietnamese soldiers would kill him. Perhaps he didn't care, but once the young fellow was out of the way, they would have found enough circumstantial evidence to suggest Odon was the Palo priest.'

'So Odon's spirit knows that and he wants revenge,' Dtui said.

'Which leaves only one thing to do,' Siri decided. He went to the desk and smiled at Dr Santiago. The Cuban seemed to have recovered from his shock and was again looking more confident. 'Could you tell the good doctor that we know everything. I can't pretend to like what he's been doing, but I still have great respect for him as a surgeon. I'm sorry he won't be able to practise his profession any more after this, but I wish him good luck in the future.'

While Dtui translated, Siri offered his hand to the Cuban and gave him a warm smile. Santiago slapped his palm into Siri's and returned the smile. He seemed surprised at the strength with which Siri grasped, more like the coupling device on a railway carriage than a handshake. And then he seemed to understand.

The Cuban screamed and tried in vain to remove his hand from Siri's. Whatever force it was that transferred between them passed swiftly like a worm down a hungry chick's gullet. Dtui watched Dr Santiago squirm and shift on his seat. His posture improved and his demeanour seemed to change. By the time Siri pulled his hand away, a different person seemed to be seated at the desk.

Comrade Lit noticed the change also. 'Dr Siri, can I ask what just happened then?'

Given everything the security chief had just heard, Siri decided there was nothing to be gained now in keeping secrets. 'Comrade Lit, for the past week, I have been hosting the spirit of Odon. He first came to me at Santiago's altar. At the time I thought he was trying to abuse Nurse Dtui here, but, as it turns out, his aggression was directed towards Santiago. I should have realised that earlier.'

'That no self-respecting spirit would want to abuse sweet little me?' she asked. She had abandoned all attempts at translation. She felt no obligation to be polite to the old Cuban now.

'That there was no logical reason for it,' Siri said. 'Spirits are predictably logical. Odon just wanted to clear their names. To point us in the right direction. Now, he's steering the man who caused his death.'

'So what should I do now?' Lit asked.

'Oh, I think the doctor will be quite cooperative. He may even confess to a thing or two. You should offer him temporary accommodation in your nice security complex for the night, perhaps have a little chat with him tomorrow with the Cuban delegation. I think they'll be surprised to hear what he has to say. I imagine they'll want to contact the families of Isandro and Odon and see what they want done with the bodies. I'm sure our politburo would gladly ship them home.'

'Shouldn't Hong Lan be buried with them?' Dtui asked.

'Oh, I don't see why,' Siri replied. 'They're just bodies. Their souls are already together.'

20

THE PLIMSOLL PIROUETTES

The concert was scheduled to begin at six thirty. It was almost eight and Dr Siri still sat beside an empty chair fifty metres from an empty stage. The first twenty-six rows had just started to fill with the backs of famous Lao heads and heads that were probably famous in other communist countries. The politburo members were there with their wives, including Civilai and his lovely spouse, Mrs Nong. There was a cordon of uniformed troops seated between the VIPs and the common people at the back. As they had no official invitations, Siri and Dtui were in the poor seats.

People were being shown to their places by ushers who had once been senior military officers under the royalist regime. They had undergone almost two years of re-education and were considered to be trusties. They wore borrowed shirts and ties and expressions of defeat. Today's assignment was barely a humiliation compared to some of their experiences out in the jungle. Many of them didn't know that their king and queen had joined them in their exile, and most couldn't care less.

Fashionably late, the president and prime minister, and the heads of the Vietnamese delegation arrived to thunderous applause from the audience. They turned and returned the applause before sinking into the sofas and armchairs that formed the front row. As was the case in any event, large or small, in the People's Democratic Republic of Laos, proceedings couldn't begin without an insufferably long speech mentioning everybody involved in the revolution and their grandfathers. Dtui turned up towards the end of it.

'I thought you weren't coming,' Siri said, not trying to keep his voice down, as most people in the commoner's section were chatting and having a good time. Socialist microphones had an extra notch to cope with Lao audiences.

'I was busy having two traumatic events,' she told him.

'You saw Lit?'

'That was the first. It wasn't exactly like breaking his heart. More like disturbing his life schedule. You know what I mean? In fact, I get the feeling our little show this morning might have already put a few doubts in the comrade's mind about my suitability.'

'He knows you weren't involved in any of the shenanigans.'

'Yes, but he must have noticed I wasn't particularly surprised by any of it, either. I didn't scream or fall about convulsing in panic. Perhaps that's what he expects from a woman. He still seemed a little shell-shocked by the whole affair. He didn't exactly beg me to reconsider.'

'Just as well. You'd already made your decision.'

'Yeah. But it would have been nice to have had a suitor for a couple of months. Maybe taken him to a dance or two and shown him around to the girls. I could have introduced him to Ma.'

A scythe of accidental static from the speaker cut through the audience. The people hushed guiltily.

'And you spoke to her?' Siri whispered.

'Yeah. That was the second trauma.'

'Goodness me. Why?'

'She read me a letter.'

'Bad news?'

'I'm not sure.'

'But it traumatised you?'

'It shocked me out of my bloomers.'

'Are you going to tell me what it said?'

A procession of musicians in pink and yellow filed down into the orchestra pit with their instruments. It seemed a terrible shame that such pretty costumes should vanish from sight so soon. The sound of music rose from the pit almost immediately and the elaborate speaker system sent it rolling around the dome of the roof. The chamber vibrated. The natural acoustics alone would have filled the cave with a much friendlier sound. Siri felt Dtui's warm breath as she shouted into his ear.

'It was from the examination board.'

'What did they say?'

'I have to be ready to leave for the USSR in December.'

'You passed?' The overture came to a sudden halt just as Siri whooped with joy into the silence. Some of the senior cadres looked over their shoulders in disappointment, but the commoners laughed and put their hands together for the unseen musicians. Siri felt no embarrassment whatsoever. He was so delighted he would happily have run up onto the stage to make the announcement. He kissed Dtui on the cheek and held onto her hand throughout the concert. His smile didn't once leave his face.

The proceedings went on into the night. Beautiful Vietnamese ballerinas in army uniforms pirouetted in plimsolls. Acrobats did unthinkable things with chairs. A girl balanced upside down on a donkey that ran in circles on the stage and pissed on the electric wiring which smoked briefly. A small choir of angels in red scarves and berets sang party songs, the ballerinas returned for a rousing dance with rifles, a North Vietnamese pop star sang a romantic ballad that brought tears to the old men's eyes.

And, the final performance of the night was a Lao *ramwong* dance that snaked down from the stage and collected members of the audience. Civilai was one of the first out of his seat. He waved when he caught sight of Siri who hoped his friend had left his feathers in Vientiane. Those behind the army cordon were not allowed to join the main snake so they merely stood where they were and danced on the spot. Dtui and Siri faced one another, bobbed to the music and ran their hands through the air like mismatched reflections in a mirror.

Behind her head, in the shadows of the side caves, in the nooks and crevices, Siri could see the departed. They waited patiently for their turn. Once the old men had gone back to their houses, there was to be an official shindig for the young and the young at heart. As a special dispensation for the exceptional event of the day, they'd be able to dance till the early hours. Although the party-goers would suspect nothing, Siri knew the spirits wouldn't want to miss anything as fantastic as a chance to strut their stuff with the living.

Civilai had no place in his heart for modern music, so he'd flown back directly after the show with the other party-poopers. There was room on the helicopter, so he'd wangled spots for Siri and Dtui. The journey was made all the more pleasant for Civilai by having Siri yelling the events of the previous ten days in his ear above the chop of the rotors. With his own life having become so predictable and pointless, it was a tonic to have Siri's marvellous stories to keep him enthused.

'How come the Vietnamese didn't find Isandro when they discovered the body of the girl?' Civilai asked, never letting Siri get away with any gaps in his logic.

'I have to assume Odon buried his friend first and disguised the grave so it wouldn't be discovered before the process was complete. He was just about to do the same to Hong Lan when he was disturbed by the arrival of the soldiers.'

'You don't want to make this a police matter? You have enough evidence against the Vietnamese militia and the guide?'

'I get the feeling the army will be taking care of this in its own way.'

'As they seem to take care of everything else.' Civilai almost had all the facts straight in his mind. Only one question remained and he knew the reply would be conjecture. 'Any idea how the couple died?'

'The bodies were too far gone to tell. The girl may have died from her disease. If she was still alive, I imagine the lovers drank some poison together once they got to the cave. It was a love pact, after all.'

'And you honestly believe the hocus pocus worked and the lovers' souls were reunited in the afterlife?'

Siri thought again to the locked cupboard and the escape of the unseen creature. 'I can't be sure. But I'd like to think so.'

'After all these years, you're still a romantic.'

'When you get to our age, old brother, you start to wish you gave more time to romance when you still had the chance.'

'You're right.' Civilai leaned across to Mrs Nong and whispered something in his wife's ear. Whatever it was, it caused her eyebrows to rise and a blush to fill her cheeks. She looked out of the far window and smiled uncontrollably.

'I hope you didn't just make a promise an old fellow like you won't be able to keep,' Siri said.

Dtui and the doctor had arrived in their crowded suburban shelter for the homeless at 3AM. The mongrel bitch was still asleep on her nest and a company of geckos were gathered around the porch lamp like three-dimensional wallpaper. The human guests were sleeping. Siri did a quick headcount and found he'd inherited one new housemate since they'd been away. Apart from Monoluk, Dtui's mother, there was Mr Inthanet from Luang Prabang, Mrs Fah, whose husband had passed away, and her two children. And now there was a monk of all things, asleep on Siri's hammock in the backyard. None of these people stirred.

Siri and Dtui ate and slept a little, but by six they were both as wide awake as the early cockerels on the roof. By then they had to face the inquisition from their housemates. 'Who died? How? Who did it?' Obviously the dull radio dramas weren't stimulating enough for them. The doctor did as good a job as he could of summarising their adventures in the north-east, but was glad when the time came for them to leave for work. Halfway into the city he realised he'd forgotten to ask about the monk, or perhaps he hadn't been ready to get the reply, 'What monk?'

He and Nurse Dtui arrived at the hospital at their usual time. It was Monday morning and their experience in the north-east felt like a different time in an entirely different country. Siri parked his motorcycle in his regular spot and Dtui unlocked the morgue doors. There was a stale smell inside rather than the familiar stench of bleach and disinfectant. They assumed this was the smell of a morgue unused for ten days. But it was clean and everything was in its place, just as they'd left it.

They opened the windows to allow the hot air inside to change places with the hotter air outside. They sat at their respective desks ready to collate their fragmented recollections of the Huaphan case. It was likely to take them the better part of a day to put it into a form that even Judge Haeng would be able to make head or tail of. It was twenty minutes after eight o'clock when Mr Geung staggered in through the doorway like a drunkard. He hadn't even stopped to take off his boots. Siri and Dtui looked up to see him silhouetted there, swaying. The only thing keeping him up appeared to be the uneven smile on his face.

'Hello, Geung, honey,' Dtui said. 'What in blazes has happened to you?' She stood up and began to walk towards him.

Before sinking to his knees and crashing onto the concrete floor, Geung heard the doctor's voice. It was such a wonderful sound – a sound he'd been afraid he'd never hear again. He'd imagined this meeting as he staggered painfully through the outer suburbs and across the city – as he fell into and out of trances beside the busy streets. He'd dreamed of seeing the faces of his workmates and here he was, the morgue and his promise intact. He couldn't have been happier. This too was his destiny.

'Mr Geung,' the doctor had said, looking at his watch. 'You're late.'

BEWARE THE SNOWY-HAIRED
AVENGER

As head of the National Department of Justice, Judge Haeng could, technically, have found a lot of things to keep him busy every day of the week. Yet, by hanging on to senior staff who knew the workings of the department far better than he, and by not initiating any new projects, he managed to have a lot of large gaps in his daily schedule. These he filled with visits to his family fish farm, afternoon trysts with colourful nightclub singers, and, his particular favourite, just kicking off his shoes and taking a nice long nap. If napping had been an event in the Asian Games, Haeng would certainly have been the Lao national champion. He had everything under control and was proving to everybody that he could capably fill the shoes of those corrupt royalist rogues he'd condemned so often at village seminars.

He became particularly upset, therefore, whenever the politburo gave him tasks that took away his three-hour lunches and 'just say I'm in court' afternoons. The signing of the Vietnamese agreement had turned his life into a hellish succession of meetings and formal dinners and interminable speeches, many his own. The Hanoi justice delegation had been particularly irksome. They'd insisted upon seeing the inner workings of the Lao legal system. Not only was that mechanism lacking oil, it was also missing a number of irreplaceable spare parts. He could hardly confess to this. So, Judge Haeng had set about orchestrating an elaborate deception.

He moved men from outlying police posts to fluff up the two stations visited by the Vietnamese, and stage-managed a fake trial for the central courthouse. He shifted four brand-new microfiche viewers from the old USAID compound and set them up at the criminal records department. As none of the Lao records were on fiche and nobody knew how to operate the equipment anyway, on the day of the delegation's visit, there was a sudden and mysterious power outage which meant the visitors had to leave without seeing the system in action. The judge was exhausted and thanked the heavens that the Vietnamese only had one more half-day before he could be rid of them.

One member of the group was a doctor, a coroner of all things, who had convinced his compatriots that a review of the justice system could not be complete without a visit to the morgue. Judge Haeng had argued against this with all his breath – the smell, the sight of blood, the heat – but they all seemed to be in agreement with the annoying little doctor. It occurred to Haeng that perhaps every country had the thorn of a national coroner in its side. But he had no choice. On the eve of the visit, following a farewell banquet at the old presidential palace, Haeng had his driver take him out to Dr Siri's house deep in the new suburbs behind the That Luang shrine. It would be his first visit to the place. It would also be the first time he'd seen Siri since his trip to the north-east, and since the removal of his moron from the morgue.

On the car journey over there he took a number of deep breaths and prepared retorts for the flak sure to come his way. Siri was insolent, but occasionally competent. The old man had done a reasonable job in Xam Neua. Haeng would begin by telling him so, get him in a good mood, tell him how satisfied the Party was with his work. He would not allow the doctor to bully him on this moron issue. He was, after all, the head of the Justice Department and Siri was just a worker. But still he felt his hands tremble as he walked through the tall front gate and into a well-tended yard. The front door was wide open and he could see Siri in the back kitchen. Haeng clenched his fists and called Siri's name, but was totally unprepared for what happened next. Siri raised his arm and smiled and trotted through to the front door. He was so polite, so friendly, that Haeng wondered whether he'd confused him with someone else. But Siri took the judge's arm and led him inside.

It was an awful place, a menagerie: old people, invalids, brats running amok. Siri had turned perfectly good government housing into a slum. There would be a report to the housing division about this, no question about that, but there was a more pressing issue. He hurriedly acknowledged the introductions and immediately dismissed the names of Siri's gang from his mind. As soon as he could, he herded Siri and Dtui onto the front step. He asked for assurance that they would be neatly turned out for tomorrow's visit, white coat for the doctor, crisp white uniform for the nurse. It was also vital that there be no what he referred to as 'patients'. Siri asked whether he meant 'dead bodies' and Haeng told him 'of course'. If there were any bodies in the freezer, Siri would have to get there early and clear them out.

Siri had been so bold as to ask where they should dump a body, were it to arrive before the delegation turned up, but Haeng didn't give a hoot what they did with it as long as the morgue was spotlessly clean and presentable. Siri and Dtui assured him there would be nothing dead to spoil the reputation of the national mortuary. They assured him it would be a day like no other. So it was that Haeng drove home that night with a lighter heart. The only possible flash flood to spoil an otherwise exemplary cruise of Justice Department efficiency had been diverted. And, miracle of miracles, there had been no mention of *that* matter. This Siri character was proving to be trainable after all. Haeng lay back in his seat and smiled for the first time all day.

The entourage of shiny black Zil limousines pulled up in front of the morgue at nine fifteen the following morning. The hospital director was there to meet the delegates. He had a speech written and planned to give each of them a wrist garland of orchids. But it was a stinking hot day and the cars had kicked up a mist of dust. The Vietnamese wanted nothing to do with the director's foolishness. They wanted merely to get the final pointless visit over with and head off to the airport. They'd all been in Laos far too long already. They pushed past the director and a chorus of applauding nurses and headed for the shade of the morgue entrance. The director recognised at least two senior Party members, a judge and two police generals as they shoved him out of the way. But his camera still hung by his side and he had no photographic evidence that his hospital had been honoured so.

The delegates were met in the vestibule by Dr Siri in a spotless white lab coat and, of all things, a shirt and tie. A stethoscope hung gleaming around his neck. He stood beside a beaming Judge Haeng and welcomed the Vietnamese in their own language. He had no need of an interpreter although this left Haeng at a slight disadvantage. Despite completing much of his undergraduate education in Hanoi, Haeng's Vietnamese was infected with a horrible Lao accent and his comprehension was lacking. The doctor said he regretted there were no bodies to show the guests but he invited everyone into the cutting room regardless. The throng shuffled forward to find Dtui in front of the large freezer door. She was immaculately groomed and dressed in her whitest uniform. She'd even gone so far as to attach a bright pink *champa* flower above her ear. She smiled sweetly and pulled open the freezer door like the hostess on a Thai television game show.

The visitors stared into an empty freezer in a bodyless morgue and wondered what they were doing there. Judge Haeng was glowing. It was as if he wanted to shout his delight, but somebody beat him to it. The deathly cry came from one side of the room, from behind the door that led to the samples store. That door suddenly flew open, catching a senior policeman a blow to his shoulder, and the most incredible sight presented itself. There was an audible intake of breath from every visitor. A dark-skinned man, perhaps of Indian origin, topless and unshaven, waded through the crowd of frightened onlookers to stand beside the judge. He wore only a very brief sarong and in his open palm he carried what appeared to be a human brain. It dribbled fluid onto the spotlessly clean concrete floor. He appeared to be laughing but no sound came out of him.

Comrade Nguyen, the Vietnamese coroner, was the first to speak. 'Judge Haeng,' he said indignantly. 'What's the meaning of this?'

It was clear from Haeng's expression that he'd suddenly recognised the half-naked man. Wasn't this the nutcase who strolled aimlessly around the city begging for food scraps? Wasn't this the serial flasher who had been arrested repeatedly and spent several nights in jail? This was the man they called Crazy Rajhid. What was he doing here in the morgue? Haeng was so shocked he passed on the question in Vietnamese.

'Siri, what's the meaning of this?'

'Yes, gentlemen, I suppose I should explain,' Siri said. 'You'll have to forgive the appearance of our new morgue technician.'

'New morgue … ?' Haeng began in Lao. He felt an obligation to laugh, to pass on the impression that this was all a joke and he'd been party to it all along. Siri heaved himself up onto the cutting slab and began to address the audience.

'You see,' he began, 'Mr Rajhid here is the only person we could find who'd agree to work for the half-salary we are allocated for this position.' Rajhid had sunk to the floor and was moulding the brain like silly putty into the shape of a mushroom.

'I don't think …' Haeng began, still smiling but unable to phrase a Vietnamese sentence with sufficient aplomb to rescue himself.

Siri continued. 'We used to have a well-qualified, in fact, brilliant technician who was perfectly happy to work for a pittance. He had more experience than either myself or Nurse Dtui, here.'

'What happened to him?' Nguyen asked. All of the other delegates had shuffled forward, entranced by the first authentic show of their visit.

'Well, I'm sure he had a good reason, but Judge Hae ... I mean, the Justice Department, fired him.'

'I didn't actually fire h ...' Haeng tried again. His smile was wilting like a worm on a spit.

'Why?' Nguyen asked. 'Why fire a perfectly good technician?'

'Because ...' Siri paused for effect. 'Because he had Down's syndrome.'

There came a mumble from the group.

'You fired a man because he was a mongoloid?' the leader of the delegation asked with an expression of disbelief on his face. It was conceivable he would have done the same – probable that none of the assembled dignitaries would have hired one in the first place, but group dynamics work wonders for one's indignation.

'I ... I didn't fire him,' Haeng said. 'I reallocated him.'

'Why?' Nguyen asked. 'Wasn't he serving a valuable role for the socialist state? Wasn't he contributing to the community?'

'He certainly was,' Siri replied.

Rajhid had put the brain on his head and was now modelling it like a hat. One of the generals looked at him in disgust then turned to Siri. 'Can we talk to this mongoloid – see for ourselves?'

'I'm afraid you can't,' Siri told him. Both the doctor and Dtui lowered their heads. 'You see? He was shipped north under armed guard. He got all the way to Luang Prabang but such was his loyalty, such was his love for his job and his responsibilities here, that he turned back. He walked,

257

yes, comrades, he walked all the way back to this morgue. For ten days beneath the biting summer sun he marched' – a sob was heard from the direction of the freezer – 'five hundred punishing kilometres he walked. But, as you can imagine, the journey weakened him and on the way he contracted dengue fever. When he arrived here he was barely alive. He collapsed right there behind you.'

The crowd turned back as if expecting to see the body still there on the concrete. Siri took the opportunity to look up at Haeng, whose teeth were so tightly clenched they could easily have welded together. The delegation turned back to see the young nurse with tears rolling down her round cheeks.

'He's dead?' someone asked.

'He might as well be,' Siri replied. 'It's touch and go.' He could see the Vietnamese glares slicing through the judge who stood exposed and unarmed beside him. Siri expected one last defensive volley from him and he wasn't disappointed.

'We ... we're doing everything we can to keep him alive,' Haeng said, not terribly convincingly. He'd had no idea the moron had come back. 'If he makes it, naturally we'll be honouring him for his courage and dedication.'

'Let's hope you do,' said the senior cadre. 'This is exactly the type of spirit we want to see in a socialist state. It would be a marvellous incentive for normal people. If a mongoloid can show so much valour for the Party ...'

'Exactly,' someone agreed.

'A medal at least,' said Dr Nguyen.

'Walked all that way – marvellous,' said the policeman.

Soon the morgue was awash with enthusiasm and hope for this slightly defective but nonetheless courageous soldier of the revolution. Someone suggested they should visit the brave warrior, show their support, and they all trooped out of the morgue and across the hospital grounds to the intensive care unit. Crazy Rajhid joined the pilgrimage, so left in the cutting room were Dtui, Siri and his old friend Dr Nguyen.

'Well, I think that went quite well, don't you?' said the Vietnamese doctor.

'Thanks to you,' said Siri. 'I'm in your debt.'

'I'll think of something, don't worry. Maybe send me some of these pretty nurses.' He smiled at Dtui. 'Well, I think I should join my team, don't you?'

They laughed and shook hands and Nguyen walked jauntily out of the cutting room.

'Well,' said Dtui. 'I had no idea what you were all talking about but I can still see bits of Haeng's face littering the floor, so I know it worked.'

From the shadows of the vestibule came another figure. Haeng's chief clerk, Mrs Manivone, walked out into the fluorescent lighting slowly shaking her head. She'd watched the whole thing from the wings and knew her boss only too well.

'He'll never forgive you, you know?'

'I know,' Siri said, and smiled his most devilish smile.

'I'm serious. He can make life very difficult for you, Dr Siri.'

'You don't suppose he'd fire me and banish me to the countryside?'

'You'd like that, wouldn't you.'

Siri smiled again. Manivone started to laugh. She walked over to the coroner and sniffed at the air by his cheek. A Lao no-contact kiss. 'I suppose you know you're my hero,' she said.

Siri squeezed her hand, blushed a little, and walked out of the cutting room. Manivone put her arm around Dtui.

'How's Geung, really?'

'He'll live,' Dtui said. 'In fact, this morning he was looking a little too flushed. Dr Siri had me talcum powder him down.'

'You want to swap bosses?' Manivone asked.

'Not on your life, sister. Not on your life.'

Keep reading for an excerpt from

ANARCHY AND OLD DOGS

by Colin Cotterill

1

A NOTE TO A BLIND DENTIST

The post office box was eighteen across, twelve down, and it had a loop of wool wound around the door so Dr. Buagaew wouldn't miss it. He traced the keyhole with his left hand and inserted the key with his right. From inside the wooden chamber came the scent of bygone correspondence: of brown-paper parcels and glue, of old parchment and secrets. His hand fell upon a thin envelope. He knew it would be there and he knew what it contained because only one other person was aware of the post office box address.

He re-locked the door, folded the envelope, and, having put it in the inside pocket of his jacket, turned back in the direction of the exit. The Bureau de Poste was crowded. It always seemed to be so. He could hear the unruly scrum of ignorant villagers fighting their way to the counters. There were the sounds of pencils tapping urgent messages on postcards and the crinkle of the thirty-*kip* wrapping service. On the far side of the room, people shouted loudly into the long-distance telephones, sharing their most intimate stories with half of Vientiane.

It was all part of the hubbub of the city that Dr. Buagaew disliked so much. If it hadn't been for the letters he wouldn't have traveled there at all. It was his habit to get off the bus beside the morning market, cross over Khu

Vieng Avenue, collect his mail, and return on the same bus. He had no other business. In the capital of the People's Democratic Republic of Laos in August of 1977, traffic wasn't a fitting word to describe the infrequent passings of motor vehicles. Only those with familial or professional connections with the socialist government could afford to tantalise their tanks with petroleum. Two cars passing at the same time would be considered a traffic jam. Even midmorning, dogs stretched out on the warm asphalt and motorists had no qualms about going around them.

That might be the reason Dr. Buagaew had never considered the road to be a potential danger. It could explain why he didn't stop at the broken stone kerb or take a great deal of notice of the engine sound. Once his bamboo cane had negotiated the cracks and potholes of the pavement, all that remained was to find the wire-mesh fence on the far side and follow it to his bus stop. The onlookers later concurred. They'd never seen anyone hit by a truck before, and it was such an unlikely event a man would almost have to throw himself beneath the front wheels for it to happen. Even then, the vehicle would probably be traveling slowly enough to slam on the brakes and avoid any embarrassment.

It was therefore agreed the old blind man must have been in deep karmic debt to have stepped in front of the runaway logging truck. What were the odds? A large Chinese vehicle? A stuck accelerator? A young driver bailing out in panic some twenty yards earlier? The truck had careened past the post office and crushed Dr. Buagaew before slamming into the wooden public-address-system pole at the corner of Lan Xang Avenue. The latter stood defiantly for several seconds before swaying and crashing down onto the empty street.

This tragedy was a talking point that afternoon but very few tears were shed for the anonymous blind man. The locals didn't have room in their souls for someone else's misfortune. Vientiane had a certain mood about it these days. The government was starting to look like a depressingly unloved relative who'd come to visit for the weekend and stayed for two years. These were uncomfortable times in a country not unused to discomfort. The drought had wrung every last tear of moisture from the sad earth. The seasonal monsoons had held off, and a few brief mango flower showers were quickly sucked into the ground and forgotten. The World Bank was donating rice, but with few trucks and little petrol, most of it hadn't found its way beyond the cities.

It would be a good time, one would imagine, for a novice socialist government to ease up and give its downtrodden population a break from petty regulations. The Pathet Lao had come to power in 1975 and even the prime minister admitted they hadn't achieved too much since then. But the jungle-trained administration adopted a policy of disguising its lack of ability by baffling the populace with red tape. No fewer than six signatures were needed for permission to ride a bicycle from one prefecture to another. The death of livestock, even from natural causes, had to be accounted for in writing. And heaven help a family intent on adding an extension to its hovel. A small copse of trees' worth of paper and an entire octopus of ink would be used up by the ensuing paperwork.

Some fifty thousand former Royalist officials were now in re-education camps, and the positions they once occupied had been either left empty or filled with Party cadres unqualified for the work. They all did their best, but best doesn't always amount to competent.